THREE OF CUPS

A NOVEL **Kathy Wilson Florence**

Three of Cups is a work of fiction. While every effort has been made to keep accurate with dates and general details of historical events, other names, characters, businesses, places and incidents are either the products of the author's imagination or used in a fictitious manner. Any resemblance to actual persons, living or dead, or actual events is purely coincidental.

This book is dedicated to my female peeps.
Your energy, camaraderie and loyalty ignite my favorite
conversations, ideas and mischief.

Books by Kathy Wilson Florence

Three of Cups

Jaybird's Song

You've Got a Wedgie Cha Cha Cha
(non-fiction)

• • •

Praise for Jaybird's Song:

Florence's skillful portrayal of '60s Atlanta elevates this novel to striking historical fiction. An absorbing family saga provides a first-person account of Atlanta during the crucial civil rights era while also covering the early 21st century. —*Kirkus Reviews*

Impressively entertaining while at the same time thoughtful and thought-provoking, "Jaybird's Song" is a consistently absorbing read from beginning to end. Exceptional and with admirable attention to historical detail. — *Midwest Book Review*

"The maidens are barefoot and free, their robes flowing, and together they appear to be dancing. Fully engaged with life, two women raise their cups with their right hands and the other toasts with her left hand. The right hand is the hand of giving and the left hand receives, so their poses show they are able to both give and receive abundantly."

— Liz Dean, *The Ultimate Guide to Tarot*

"The Three of Cups indicates vitality and balance and the feminine principal in the sphere Binah. Perhaps indication of the relationship between three friends, or of the bond between three generations of women."

— Millie LaMurphy

"The three goddesses pictured on the Three of Cups tarot represent the virtues of Strength, Temperance and Justice and are pictured together raising their cups in a joint toast, connected almost to the point that they appear as one. The three can also symbolize the tree of life and refer to the three stages of femininity: maiden, mother and crone."

— Madam Sylvia

Three of Cups

Illustration: Sharon A. Moore

Part I

RACHEL: JULY 1998

As the elevator descended toward the lobby, Rachel's jaw was clenched and her eyes shut tight. She couldn't remember if she'd noticed anyone else when she'd entered the elevator cab on the 35th floor, and she couldn't remember if there had been any stops.

The bell rang, the door opened and Rachel held her breath, willing herself to slowly open her eyes.

She was alone.

Her mind registered the familiar marble-floored lobby and the bustling sounds of people outside as the elevator doors made a jump and began to close.

She flung her knockoff Yves Saint Laurent bag between the doors and drew in a deep breath once they'd reopened.

She'd quit.

She'd said her peace.

She hadn't cried.

Her voice hadn't quivered.

She knew her face was burning red but she didn't care.

She'd walked right out the door of the wildly successful internet firm that had been at the top of water cooler conversations since it had exploded with the dot-com surge seven months before.

She stepped onto the sleek marble lobby and willed herself to keep her eyes straight toward the heavy revolving doors fearing she would make eye contact with Audrey, the friendly concierge who had helped her so many times when Mitch had made a ridiculous, last-minute request of her.

I'll find a way to tell her goodbye. But not today.

She counted her steps—just three—as she pushed her hands across the cool metal bar and wheeled through the revolving door and into a thick wall of sun, humidity and street sounds. A muggy afternoon in late July on Peachtree Street in downtown Atlanta and an odd combination of smells—fresh pizza from one direction and sour smelling garbage from the other—brought her back to consciousness as she acknowledged the depth of what she'd just done with a string of deep breaths. She put her hands to her flushed cheeks.

"I don't have a job," she said to no one.

The sudden rise in temperature—or perhaps the garbage—made a queasy orbit around her stomach and into the back of her throat.

"I quit my job and don't have a new one to go to tomorrow," she muttered toward the back of a MARTA bus that sat at the corner.

The bus rolled backward a few inches and spit black soot toward Rachel's feet.

"I no longer have to answer to the requests of the idiot Mitch Logan," she responded.

She didn't realize how loud she'd said it until a woman in front of her with hair pinned into Princess Leia buns stopped and turned to look at her with furled brows, squinty eyes and a question mark across her snarled lips.

"Sorry," Rachel stammered. "A job thing," she added as a half-hearted means of explanation. She made a quick pivot onto Harris Street.

Turning the corner, she leaned against the yellow bricks of a coffee shop and looked at her watch while questions whirled through her head.

1:20. Should I call Mother and Dad and let them know I've quit my job? Should I drive to Oodles and Poppy's? What am I going to do tomorrow? What's my next step?

Lunch, she decided, and ducked into Fitz's Diner.

The lunch crowd had thinned as Rachel peered at a row of booths that had already been cleaned. On the other side of the room, booths were still piled with plates of half-eaten sandwiches and ketchup-filled plates.

"Sit wherever you'd like," she heard someone call. Rachel looked up and saw a friendly face peeking around one side of a double swing door in the kitchen. "I'll be right with you."

"Great. Thanks," Rachel called looking around for the restaurant's newspaper bins.

The *Atlanta Journal and Constitution* bin was empty but a discarded section of the newspaper was folded in half and lying atop a nearby table. She thumbed through to find the Sports and Lifestyle sections, but no classifieds or help wanted ads.

Tomorrow then.

She tucked the newspaper under her arm, grabbed a copy of *Creative Loafing* that was stacked neatly in a bin nearby and chose a seat by the window.

It had been seven months since Mitch Logan had hired her as a marketing assistant within five minutes of their first meeting at a coffee shop. He didn't even have an office then, but his goals were lofty and all indications pointed to success for Quince powered by the new opportunities of the burgeoning World Wide Web.

She began the week before Christmas of 1997 and by February the company was growing so rapidly Mitch had hired an outside marketing firm without even mentioning it to Rachel until a bill for the first retainer fee came across her desk and she asked him about it. Her job quickly morphed into full-time gopher for whatever outlandish need Mitch had and expected at a moment's notice, and most of her job entailed picking up the pieces for his haphazard mistakes.

While business doubled every month, Mitch was not handling the success well. His head looked like a pressure cooker ready to explode and more and more he aimed his wrath at Rachel. She had forwarded a fact sheet to *Business Week*—at his request—and his subsequent tantrum pushed Rachel over the edge. After being interviewed for a story on Quince and its rapid success, Mitch had put an outdated fact sheet on her desk with a note to fax to the writer. When the story was released, he blew up at Rachel for not catching his error. After checking her calendar and files, she pointed out that he had handed her the fact sheet with orders to fax as soon as possible on the same morning he'd sent her on a wild goose chase to find eight box seat tickets to that night's Braves vs. Philly game—complete with a stretch limousine from the office at 4 p.m. with a half-dozen bottles of Don Perignon on ice and two dozen hot Krispy Kreme doughnuts. Thanks to Audrey at the concierge desk who secured the tickets, she'd made it happen, but Mitch neglected to even thank her. The fax, however, he refused to forget.

Once it happened, Rachel realized she'd been waiting for a last straw. Mitch called at all hours with needs that couldn't wait. She hadn't been out with friends in months. She was working late every night. She'd barely even engaged in conversation with the roommate she'd found via a bulletin board posting in a coffee shop. Short of dinner at her grandparents' house most Sunday nights, she hadn't had a social life since she joined Quince.

And she was 26. Pretty, she knew, but she'd never spent anytime thinking about her looks or a boyfriend or her life's goals. Growing up as a military brat, her life had always been scripted for her, and she'd always assumed all those details would work themselves out as she worried about her career and having fun. It was turning 26 earlier that summer though, that made her realize: (1) She wasn't having fun, and (2) She was no closer to a boyfriend or the rest of her life than she was when she graduated from the University of Georgia four years before.

"A grilled cheese, please," Rachel said as the waitress placed a napkin, fork and knife at her table.

"Would you like tomato on that? We just got some nice red, juicy ones this morning at the farmer's market."

Rachel looked up and noticed the waitress' blonde curls tucked inside a hairnet and surrounded with a stretchy pink headband. Her nametag had a pressure-sensitive blue label maker tag with the name "Dawn.'" The "w" was barely visible.

"Yes, please. And a Coke and a side of fries."

"You got it, sweetie," Dawn said tucking the menu under her arm and greeting a police officer that entered the restaurant.

Rachel skimmed the Lifestyle section of the *AJC* and then picked up the *Creative Loafing*. The alternative newspaper had been around for years and she and friends in college had picked it up many times to laugh at the personal classified ads. One of their favorites: "KWNF— (Kinky White Nudist Female) seeks male or female to share sex, recipes and poetry."

"Hot enough for you out there?" asked Dawn as she placed the Coke in front of Rachel and pointed to the Coca-Cola glass filled with straws at the end of the table.

"Muggy too," Rachel replied, dabbing her nose and forehead with her napkin.

Rachel sipped her Coke as she perused the newspaper stories covering local concerts and art exhibits.

Dawn delivered the sandwich and fries. Rachel devoured every bite as she skimmed the newspaper stories. A few paragraphs in and she realized she wasn't reading at all, but instead thinking about Mitch Logan and wondering if he would call and try to get her to come back.

Should I have stuck it out at least until I had another job?

An ad for a fortuneteller caught her eye: "Don't know where to turn? Wondering what your future holds? Ask Madame Sylvia. Psychic. Numerologist. Astrologer. Palm Reader. Tarot Cards. Crystals."

Rachel knew the location. Madame Sylvia's studio at the corner of

Cone and Luckie Streets was just a few blocks away.

She studied Madame Sylvia's photograph in the black and white ad. A short, thin smile sat like a dash underneath an oversized nose. A line at the bottom of the ad determined her decision: Walk-ins Welcomed.

She checked her watch.

Why not?

"Great idea with the tomato," she said to Dawn as she paid her lunch bill and stepped back out into the thick heat toward Madame Sylvia's.

At 31 Cone Street, a metal chair with a pot of moisture-starved geraniums on its seat sat underneath a faded sign that hung catawampus on one nail from the building's stone façade. It read, "Readings $25. Cash and credit cards. No checks." A weather-worn door had long ago been painted violet with the words "Madame Sylvia" in ethereal-style lettering embellished with a star and a moon on either side. A hand-painted sign hung from the doorknob announced: "Fortune Teller Is In. Knock Loudly."

Rachel checked her watch once more. It wasn't even 3 o'clock. She would normally be at the office until at least 6 p.m. She knocked loudly at the door noting at least three layers of other colors peeking through the violet.

"Whoa!" a voice from inside sounded annoyed. "No need to knock down the door," she heard as the door opened toward the inside and a short, stout woman wearing an embroidered dress like the ones Rachel had seen in the straw markets in the Bahamas joined her on the stoop.

"Sorry," Rachel stammered. "The sign..."

"Well, how do you do, pretty lady? Don't mind me. I think I'd fallen asleep doing today's crossword and you must have startled me," she said showing a folded newspaper with only one vertical entry into the puzzle completed in red ballpoint. Her dash-style lips didn't curl toward a smile, but her eyes squinted friendly and bright.

"Are you Madame Sylvia?" Rachel asked the woman who had seen at least 30 years since the photograph in the ad had been made.

"In the flesh! And who might you be?" she said holding the door open with one hand and sweeping the other toward the darkened room. "Step inside. No air conditioning, but I have a fan blowing in here."

With the sun ricocheting off the hot pavement of the street and burning at her back, Rachel was anxious to get out of the heat, but the dark room offered only slight relief. It smelled of moldy bread and dust. A grey cat sat directly in front of a fan on the floor. Wrinkled sheets were messily tucked around the cushions of a chair and a sofa. A reading lamp offered the only other light in the room. A painting of Elvis on black velvet was hung high above the sofa.

"My name is Rachel. Rachel McCarthy. I saw your ad in the newspaper."

"Well, step this way, Rachel," Madame Sylvia said pointing toward a second room where a square table covered with deep purple satin was positioned with two chairs in the center of the room. Tiny purple lights hung from dozens of ten-penny nails and draped across the walls. She pointed to one of the folding chairs and Rachel sat.

"I've never done anything like this before," she said as she studied the ringlets that accented Madame Sylvia's grey hair that had been pulled haphazardly into a crocheted silver chignon.

"Ahh, a virgin!" Madame Sylvia said with an odd lilt that reminded Rachel of the cartoon villain Snidely Whiplash.

Her heart skipped a beat and her eyes darted for the door.

"Don't let me scare you, Rachel McCarthy," Madame Sylvia laughed.

Rachel lifted her eyes. She wondered if her heartbeats were visible through her blouse.

"I'm teasing you," Madame Sylvia added, her voice now calming and steady. "This will be fun and important. I sense that today has been a stressful day for you."

No more than five-feet tall, Madame Sylvia looked more harmless than mysterious. Rachel noticed a tear along the shoulder seam of her shapeless dress. Rachel relaxed and settled back into the idea of a psychic reading.

"So twenty-five dollars for a palm reading? I'm not sure what to expect from this..." Rachel tried to act businesslike before agreeing to the transaction.

"Twenty-five dollars," she answered. "But it's the tarots that have been speaking to me of late." Madame Sylvia took a glance at both of Rachel's palms and gently pushed them back toward her lap. "Let's see what the cards have to say, Rachel McCarthy."

She opened a small trunk that sat beside her feet and pulled out a black satin bundle. Inside was a set of tarot cards at least twice the size of playing cards and Rachel noted the intricate line drawings and brilliant colors on each.

Madam Sylvia shuffled the cards and then asked Rachel to cover the stack with both hands.

"Let's see what the tarot tells us about you, Rachel McCarthy."

She turned over the first card and placed it in the center of the table.

"Hmmmm," Madam Sylvia said and lifted her head with her chin pointing toward the card. She remained quiet.

Sitting across the table, Rachel searched Madam Sylvia's face, but received no clue. The card pictured a beautiful angel with wide wings. He was holding two chalices and standing in a river with beautiful flora lining the bank behind him. The word 'Temperance' was written in blockish letters across the bottom.

Nothing about the card looked alarming and she studied the angel's face at the top of the card. A round shape that reminded her of the sun sat on his forehead.

"The Temperance card is one of the four virtue cards from the major arcana sequence of the tarot," Madam Sylvia said. "Sagittarius the Archer."

Rachel studied the card. The Roman numeral XIV—14, she surmised—was printed at the top.

"The Temperance card indicates balance. Note how the Archangel Michael stands with one foot in the water and with one foot on a stone in the river. And note that water is flowing in both directions from the chalice he holds at his shoulder and the one he holds at his hip."

"Balance?" Rachel's voice was suddenly deeper than the last time she'd spoken. She sat up straighter and cleared her throat.

"Unfortunately, however, the card is reversed. It's upside down, facing you in this instance, but not in line with the reading of the tarot. Temperance Reversed indicates an imbalance with aspects of your life. Perhaps, a struggle between your career and your personal life or perhaps a change in one or the other?"

"Wow," Rachel said. She stopped, fearful to confirm Madam Sylvia's suggestion, but intrigued by the truth of her words.

She flipped the next card and placed it crossways over the first.

"The Five of Pentacles," Madam Sylvia said. Her brow furrowed as she looked at Rachel and cocked her head. "Are your finances a concern to you?"

Rachel's chest clamped with the question and her admission flowed without thought.

"Well, I quit my job today. And I don't have another one."

Madam Sylvia placed the next card at the top of the table and flipped it over.

"The Queen of Cups. You're intuitive. I recognized that in you right away. More, you are strong and sensitive. This card can also indicate that you have a strong female in your orbit. A best friend or mother, perhaps?"

Madam Sylvia noted the blank look on Rachel's face and offered, "A sister?"

My sister is in California. I rarely see her.

Rachel almost offered the information, but instead thought of her grandmother, Oodles. Again, she opted not to mention the name to Madam Sylvia, skeptical she'd already revealed too much and that she would find Madam Sylvia molding everything she'd say into the reading.

"Someone you treasure very much," Madam Sylvia continued.

Rachel had to admit that was a fit.

"My grandmother and I are very close."

"Indeed," said Madam Sylvia. "

Her mind raced as Madam Sylvia continued to turn over cards but the words and her explanations didn't register. Instead, she counted up her upcoming expenses for car note, rent and utilities and tried to estimate her checking and savings account balances.

"The Death Card," said Madam Sylvia and Rachel's attention returned.

Rachel peered at the image that faced Madam Sylvia: A knight in black armor on a white horse with the word "DEATH" in capital letters across the bottom. She raised her eyes to Madam Sylvia just as her mind registered that the knight had the face of a skeleton and took a second look.

"That can't be good," Rachel said.

"Actually, not true. A reminder of our own vulnerabilities and frailties, the Death card often indicates endings and new beginnings, perhaps the opportunity to let go of what you no longer need in your life or the entrance of something or someone very new."

Just as she finished her words, a wind chime hanging in the corner of the stagnant, breeze-free room tingled two quick notes.

"And that sound, Rachel McCarthy, indicates to me that this may be pointing toward a new relationship in your life."

Rachel frowned. "I haven't had a date in three months," she said.

"Maybe you haven't met this person yet," Madam Sylvia said brightly. "How do you feel about mustaches, by the way?"

"The Death Card is telling you I'm going to meet someone with a mustache that is going to bring a big change to my life?"

"Could be, Rachel McCarthy. The tarot is mysterious, but its clues are always there. It's up to you to be watching for the signs. The mustache part is my idea, however" Madam Sylvia laughed. "Just a feeling I have."

Each new card formed a circle around the original two. Madam Sylvia turned over a new card and placed it to the right of the center cards.

"The Three of Cups. Interesting," she said.

Madam Sylvia paused and closed her eyes before continuing.

"The three goddesses pictured on the Three of Cups represent the virtues of Strength, Temperance and Justice and are pictured together raising their cups in a joint toast, connected almost to the point that they appear as one. The three can also symbolize the tree of life and refer to the three stages of femininity: maiden, mother and crone. The number three is significant here, as is the element of water."

Rachel frowned and reached for the bag at her feet. Suddenly uncomfortable, she was willing to stretch this or that to look for a path in her life, but her skepticism had reached its limit. Even if she tried to place herself as one of the three water-bearing nymphs to guide her toward her next move, there was just no strong female connection to two others that made sense. Oodles, yes, but her mother and sister were both living across the country, she had no real best friend and she'd barely had the chance to get to know her roommate. She suddenly felt the need to get to her car, her apartment—away from the ethereal and back to her more pragmatic means for managing her life.

"Thank you, Madam Sylvia. This was fun." She pulled out her wallet and placed a twenty and a ten on the table. "I appreciate your time."

"Well, it's been a pleasure, Rachel McCarthy. Do you mind if I give you the change in quarters? I'll have to pull out my laundry money for the change."

"Sure, that's fine," said Rachel as she stood by the door and watched Madam Sylvia pulling scarfs and shoes and books from a large tote bag.

"I know it's here somewhere," she said, pulling out three cans of cat food and a flashlight as she continued to dig around the bottom of the tote.

"Actually, we're good. Please keep the change," Rachel said as she opened the screened door and hurried into the bright outdoors and onto Madame Sylvia's stoop. She felt like she'd been there for hours, but her watch confirmed it was barely past 4 o'clock.

Despite the annoyance of the oddly mixed messages, Rachel felt an affirmation and calm as she thought back to Madame Sylvia's words. She'd never been in a position to not know what was ahead for her. Her military upbringing had the U.S. government making decisions for her family as they relocated from one Army base to another. After high school, she'd received acceptance to both her first and second choices for college. She met her freshman year roommate two months before they moved into Brumby dormitory at the University of Georgia. Six months before graduation she had been offered an entry-level marketing position with Atlanta's most popular Top 40 radio station. After three years, she left that position on a Friday and started working for Mitch Logan the following Monday.

Madame Sylvia's predictions whirled through her head as she traversed the concrete stairwell and punched her key fob until she heard the familiar beep coming from her car in the International Avenue parking deck. Madame Sylvia had been matter-of-fact and confident with what lay ahead for Rachel McCarthy's life just minutes after meeting her.

It feels a lot more uncertain and complicated to me.

She started the car and headed home.

MANDY: FEBRUARY 1968

"Amanda, dear, I am calling to let you know that Rochester has six feet of snow and your father's gout is acting up. I'm afraid we won't be able to make it to the wedding."

"Oh, Mom. Really?" said Mandy, dropping to the chair in the Morningside rental she had shared with three others since she came to Atlanta. "I really want you to meet Adam. He finishes up at Fort Benning soon and there is a good chance he'll leave for Vietnam even before the baby is born. Do you think you could come down before he leaves? Or at least when the baby comes in May?"

"I'd love to, darling, and I hope it will work out. Meanwhile, I understand your brother will be there to represent the family?"

"Scott called last week. He says he'll be here, but you know Scott. I guess we won't know until we see what way the wind is blowing on Saturday."

"Send pictures when you can but try to send some of just your faces. I haven't told anyone here about your condition."

"My condition. Right." Mandy placed a hand on her growing belly and rolled her eyes as her mother moved on.

"I'm putting a check in the mail though. Tuck it away for something special for you. Will you and Adam be taking a honeymoon?"

"A honeymoon doesn't fit into the military's plans right now, Mom. We'll have Sunday and Monday though before he has to report back."

"Well, that's lovely then, Amanda. How do you plan to wear your hair? You know I've always thought your bone structure would be perfect for a tight, low bun. Something similar to Grace Kelly's? She does a lovely French twist as well. Would you like me to send you some pictures? *McCall's* did a wonderful spread on her. I still have the issue."

"No thanks, Mom. Please tell Daddy I'll miss him too."

Mandy hung up the phone. She had already told Adam not to expect anyone from her family to attend the wedding. Scott would want to be there and would try, but her brother was easily distracted. She'd made up her mind that if he called the day before and couldn't make it, she would move on without hurt feelings.

Her mother's news was disappointing, but not surprising. Charles and Eve Everly had been supportive parents, but always at a distance. She knew they loved her, but neither showed a lot of outward affection. They were providers, but they provided what she requested and rarely offered parental advice or visible love. She was committed to being a different kind of parent for their baby.

Adopted separately when the Everlys were both close to forty, Mandy and her brother Scott had been extremely close growing up in northwest Georgia. Their father an accountant and their mother a speech therapist, both placed high priority on their careers. Their modest home was filled with antiques and "priceless" finds from their travels before adopting their children. The Everly siblings' play was limited to their bedrooms, the backyard and their neighborhood and completely restricted from the museum-like living and dining rooms.

Thanks to their neighbor, Miss Maisy, it all worked out fine. Never married, Miss Maisy was a retired nurse, a great cook and a fantastic joke teller. She moved into the Everlys' spare bedroom for Charles and Eve's annual trips to Palm Springs, anniversary weekends when they'd check into an Atlanta hotel, and anytime Mandy or Scott were sick and out of school so that Charles and Eve wouldn't miss work. The siblings adored Miss Maisy and when she died of an aneurysm on the morning of Mandy's high school graduation, both Scott and Mandy were so upset that they refused to attend the commencement ceremony.

After Miss Maisy died and Mandy entered college, both siblings embraced free-love and hippie ideals for a while. Scott's senior year grades plummeted and he was suspended for a week for marijuana found in his locker, though he never owned up to it being his. He started college a few times but was more strongly committed to living on his own and making his own money and was happy to travel from job to job and city to city to do it. Mandy, on the other hand, was anxious to settle down, start a family and be an attentive, loving parent.

When her father was offered a job with an accounting firm in Rochester, New York, during Mandy's junior year of college, Eve and Charles Everly took off with little concern of how their children would fend without them. By then Scott had enough money saved from construction work. Mandy was working part time while in school. Neither followed them there or even visited.

Mandy gathered paper cups, beer bottles and several burnt incense sticks from the counter and dropped them in the trash. It was rare for her to be alone in the three-bedroom apartment. Roommates tended to move in and out. She was often not even aware who was living there or who was crashing on the sofa. She'd been the only consistent one there since leasing the apartment. She was growing tired of hounding strangers for their share of the rent and even more tired of chasing people out of her own room. She'd installed a lock after coming home one afternoon and finding a naked man and woman she'd never seen before smoking a joint on her unmade bed.

She couldn't wait to marry Adam and move into the military housing where they could set up house and a nursery for their baby. She was eager to be an adult, make a home and leave behind the free-love hippie mentality she'd been surrounded by for so long.

Adam's draft into the Army happened soon after they found out they were pregnant. The arbitrary and random draft selection had zapped every man she knew, with exception of her brother, who could have used the discipline and direction most of all.

Mandy had completed almost three years of college and hoped she could pick up a few more semesters during Adam's service. Adam had completed a few semesters but stopped to work full time, so he wasn't able to show college enrollment as a means of avoiding the draft. When he returned, their plan was for Mandy to get a part-time job so that Adam could get back into college at least part time, and they would trade off college enrollment until they were both able to complete their degrees. Adam had interests in engineering; Mandy was getting close to the nursing degree she'd need before starting clinicals.

Walking into her room, she picked up the photograph of the two of them at a concert the summer before. They traveled with friends in a Volkswagen van all the way to Monterey, California, to see Jefferson Airplane in concert with The Who, Grateful Dead and more, then hitchhiked all the way back to Atlanta.

They were both barefoot. Adam's dirty blond hair had been down to his shoulders at the time. He wore a tie-died t-shirt and cut-off jeans. Her thick, chestnut-colored hair was down to her waist and was crowned with a headband made from daisies, dandelions and ribbon. Her skirt and long, off-the shoulder top looked heavy for the outdoor concert in June.

She liked the way they looked together though: Her head cradling just inside his broad neck, his arm wrapped around her bare shoulder.

She ran her fingers through her long hair as she studied the photograph. It was their beginning, but it wasn't where they were going. Adam was more mature than any other man she'd been with before and she couldn't wait for their wedding in just four days and the arrival of their baby in just four months.

She walked into the kitchen and pulled a pair of scissors from the drawer and picked up an empty cardboard box she found next to the trashcan. Then she walked into the hall bath that the three bedrooms shared and shut the door.

Thirty minutes later, the door opened and Mandy emerged walking tall with a short pixie haircut. She carried the box out to the back porch, dropped it into the metal can and placed the scissors back into the kitchen drawer. Then she walked into her bedroom and locked the door to try on her wedding dress and veil.

GINGER: AUGUST 1971

A honeysuckle vine covered a neglected picket fence along the outside of the laundromat and its fragrance offered a welcome respite to the muggy August air.

Ginger dropped the wicker basket to the steamy asphalt, wiped her eyes with her left hand and her forehead with the right. She flung the tears from her fingers and then studied the sweat that glistened across the palm of her hand. It was riddled with tiny black gnats, now suffocated in her sweat. She dried her hand on the back of her shorts and with a deep breath, picked up the basket filled with her dirty clothes.

Just an hour south from Ginger's Atlanta home, Columbus, Georgia, sits squarely along the "gnat line" that separates the Piedmont from the Coastal Plain. The topography shift runs through the center of the state and across the Deep South and is easily identified by the zillions of pesky bugs that call it home.

It had been less than a week since Pete's platoon deployed to Vietnam and she'd cried every day since. She had moved to Fort Benning to be with her new husband and to settle into the Army base apartment. They spent three weeks together and aside from the looming departure he spent his days preparing for, the time together had been perfect. She sewed floral curtains to hang on either side of the small base apartment living room windows. She tried her hand at cooking. And she prepared romantic evenings with candlelight, dance music on Pete's stereo turntable, and a rotation of sexy nightwear she'd received from a shower given by a long-time family friend that lived next door to her childhood home.

She'd met one couple, Wendy and Mike and their new baby Jennifer from next door, but had barely left the apartment since Pete left, and knew no one else in Columbus.

Inside the laundromat, large metal fans blew the stale air. It wasn't a lot cooler, but the bugs seemed to avoid the fans so Ginger selected a washer and dryer near the back and in the path of the oscillating breeze and started a load of whites and a load of colors.

She wondered if she'd fallen asleep, lulled by the white noise of the fans and machines, when she was startled alert by whistling.

Ginger recognized the tune immediately: "Red, Red, Robin" was a long-time favorite.

Growing up, as soon as she and her brother and Mother and Daddy had finished their dinner plates and Mother had given the signal that they may all get up from the table, she'd run to her father with the same request every night: "Whistle me some songs, Daddy."

And every night Mother would say, "Scrape and rinse your plate first, Ginger. Put the milk and butter in the fridge. And Carlton, you're in charge of taking out the trash."

"Yes, ma'am," the Hill siblings would say in unison as they went about their familiar chores.

And every night when she finished, Daddy would pull her up on his lap and whistle a handful of her favorite songs until she would guess the name, sing along for awhile, then stop him mid-melody with a plea for another.

They had more than thirty favorites that Daddy could whistle and Ginger could identify, but "Red, Red, Robin," was among the repertoire every night. And when she'd had enough, he'd lift her back to the floor. To finish the routine, they'd form little 'O's with their fingers and thumb and hold them up to their eyes, put their faces almost nose to nose and say, "See ya in the funny papers!" Then they'd point at one another before she'd run outside or into the next room to play.

This time though, the whistler was a woman. A woman whose hair was closer to pink than it was auburn or blonde. A woman whose black peasant-style skirt with brightly colored crewel embellishments was oddly set off by a pair of dingy crew socks worn with yellow Dr. Scholl's exercise sandals.

Ginger wondered how the woman could keep her feet from slipping off the shoes as she watched her push a squeaky grocery cart from the Big Star filled with her dirty laundry. Without missing a note, she dumped her clothes into a washing machine on the same row of the laundromat where Ginger sat on a pistachio green bench with her clothes squishing and spinning in the machines closest to her.

The woman completed a second round of the chorus, parked her shopping cart between two machines and walked toward Ginger.

"Toodle oooh! I don't believe I've made your acquaintance!" she said as she stomped awkwardly in the wooden sandals.

"Oh, hi," said Ginger as she stood. Her legs were sweaty and they made a slurping sound as she lifted from the plastic seat. "I'm Ginger. Ginger McCarthy."

"Well, nice to meet you Ginger McCarthy. I'm Millie LaMurphy. And Ginger, by the way, is a perfect name for a woman with such beautiful red hair."

"Oh thanks," said Ginger, reaching for the end of the long braid that hung over her shoulder. "You too."

"It's a wonderful strawberry blonde just like mine."

Ginger nodded, though the color of strawberry ice cream came to mind as she looked at Millie's curls. She guessed her to be in her early fifties. Her eyes were rimmed in electric blue eyeliner, but her smile was even more illuminating, and much more natural. So far, she shared few interests with the people she'd met and was excited at the hint of a new friend.

"Your husband stationed here?" Millie asked.

"Well, just me for the next eleven months or so," said Ginger. Without thinking, her hand dropped to her stomach. "My husband is in

Vietnam. At Camp Eagle Army Base. Until August next year."

"I bet you're missing him then."

Ginger noted a grease stain on Millie's trendy but too-tight "wet-look" blouse as the image of Pete wearing his olive-drab cap and uniform filled her head. Just six days earlier, he had departed for the plane headed for Vietnam. She saw him bend and peek from the front window of the plane hoping to catch her eye for one last look, but apparently the glare kept him from seeing her and her exaggerated waves.

"I'm missing him terribly," said Ginger. "He was here for three weeks and we moved into military housing. We've been married for eight months, but until this last leave, I'd been living at home with my parents in Atlanta."

"Well, welcome to Columbus," Millie said spreading her arms as if to showcase the laundromat's features. "I reckon you'll need some friends if you're going to be here until August. I know every single person in this Georgia town."

"I'd love to meet some friends," she said hopefully.

The washing machine on the left—the one filled with Ginger's whites—made a buzzing sound just as the laundromat door flew open and hit against its opposite wall with a bang followed by the tinny sound of metal against cinder block. Both Millie and Ginger turned to see a tall and handsome, dark-haired man enter.

He made his way toward the front two dryers, long-since quiet and cooled from their earlier cycles, and smiled at the ladies. They watched as he pulled all the items from two dryers and dropped them into a wicker basket, picked it up under one arm and turned to leave.

Ginger noted his broad shoulders and clear blue eyes.

He paused briefly at the end of the aisle, then made a deliberate turn toward them, smiled and tipped an imaginery hat. "Good day, ladies! Enjoy your afternoon."

Ginger wondered if she'd seen him wink as they watched him walk confidently out the door. "So, who's that then?" she asked.

"I have no idea," said Millie.

RACHEL: JULY 1998

Since she'd left her job on Wednesday, Rachel slept late on Thursday, filled a note pad with a list of to-dos and job ideas, added Quince to her resume and had twenty copies printed at Kinko's, called her parents in New Mexico and her sister Roxanne in California, had dinner with roommate Cameron for the first time ever, read the classified ads from top to bottom, vacuumed and washed her car, and called Audrey, the office building concierge, to let her know what had happened.

"Oh my God!" Audrey exclaimed. "I just saw Mitch Logan whirling through the lobby! He was red as a beet and he looked like his head was going to fly off his body. I'm glad you're away from him, Rachel. He's a madman and it's just a matter of time before he implodes."

She hadn't looked back with regret at all, despite the fact she wasn't sure how she was going to pursue the final check she was owed. She was already feeling relief from being away from Quince and Mitch Logan, but decided it wise to not concern herself with her checking account balance for a few more days.

"I can put a good word in for you at several companies here in the building," Audrey added.

"Thanks, Aud, but I'd just as soon not see Mitch for a while and working in the same building could get a little awkward. Can you meet for lunch later this week?"

They settled on a date, and satisfied with all she'd accomplished, Rachel picked the phone back up and punched in the number for Oodles and Poppy. Sunday night was a standing date at her grandparents' house, but Rachel phoned to see if she could come over early and stay the weekend.

While she'd moved around to eight different schools in twelve years, from military base to military base, she'd spent weeks in the summer with her grandparents at their Tudor-style home in Atlanta for as long as she could remember. Oodles and Poppy lived in Garden Hills, a community of 80-year-old bungalows not far from Peachtree Street in Buckhead, just a few miles from downtown. There was a community pool and a playground nearby and Rachel considered some of the friends she'd met there some of her most consistent friends.

"The Hills of Garden Hills," Poppy had painted on a sign that hung from S-hooks beneath their mailbox.

Van Hill and his wife Margaret had purchased their home in 1945 and raised their two children—Rachel's mother and her Uncle Carlton—there. As the oldest grandchild, it was Rachel who penned them with the names Oodles and Poppy— "Oodles" because it was one of Oodles' favorite words, as in, "I've got oodles of food in the fridge if you're hungry"—and Poppy, just because it suited him.

Poppy was a whistler and a singer and unless he was fast asleep, he was likely doing one or the other.

Both retired school teachers, Oodles and Poppy had become honorary grandparents for most all of the kids in the neighborhood. Oodles loved to bake and all the kids knew she'd have an oatmeal cookie or a cinnamon roll to offer them any time they'd stop by. Poppy would play games and kickball or monkey-in-the-middle with the neighborhood kids in the park and would whistle songs for them in a game where they would see how quickly they could name the song.

Their house sat high on its lot, and from the driveway you could see the tops of the condominiums and office skyscrapers that had been added to the Buckhead skyline during the previous decades. The eight-foot iron door opened to a patterned combination of walnut hardwoods and slate tile that led to a country kitchen with a pine table that could seat twelve.

Rachel's own parents were living in White Sands, New Mexico, just settling in after three years in Puerto Rico at Fort Buchanan. Her dad served in Vietnam and then signed on as career Army when he returned in 1972 and was now a Colonel with just another five years before he could retire. His military career had moved the family from New Jersey to Texas, Hawaii, Germany, Japan, Virginia and California while she was young. None of the children went with them to Puerto Rico. Rachel had finished her senior year at the University of Georgia and was working at the radio station. Her sister Roxanne had stayed in California and lived with a friend for her last year of high school and then enrolled in San Diego State. Her brother P.J. left college mid-way through to play guitar and travel with a rock-and-roll band across the northwest.

Some summers she shared time at Oodles and Poppy's with P.J. and Roxanne, but almost every year she'd been able to stay for at least a week without her younger brother and sister.

Rachel dialed the familiar number and cradled the phone's handset between her shoulder and her ear as she gathered her thick auburn locks into a lumpy ponytail.

"I couldn't think of anything I'd enjoy more, 'Chel, honey," said Oodles. "Poppy and I would love to have you here for the weekend. What would you like for dinner? Lasagna, pork chops or fried chicken?"

Rachel smiled. Oodles' longtime nickname for her—'Chel, honey'— had always felt like a warm blanket. "Fried chicken sounds awesome, Oodles."

"Fried chicken, it is."

"Yeehaw, doggies!" Rachel heard Poppy yell in the background. "Will you bake some of those biscuits, too? Maybe a little milk gravy for the top?"

Rachel smiled. "I'll be there in the morning, Oodles. I love you."

"I love you too, sweetie. Poppy's really excited that you picked fried chicken, by the way. He's dancing a jig!"

Rachel laughed, hung up the phone and picked up the classifieds.

Madame Sylvia's tarot reading said the number three was significant.

Rachel pondered what that meant: The third day from the reading? The third job she pursued? Three interviews until she received an offer? Three weeks? Three months?

Oh Lord, this kind of craziness really will make me nuts. Maybe I just need to get some irons in the fire and find a job.

After reviewing the jobs she'd found listed in the *Atlanta Journal and Constitution* classifieds, she prepared cover letters and typed envelopes for three positions and made plans to buy stamps and drop them in the mail on the way to Oodles and Poppy's house the next morning—the third day if you started with the day she'd quit.

MANDY: MAY 1970

The toothpick came out clean and Mandy pulled the yellow sheet cake from the oven and placed it on a loomed potholder atop the Formica counter. She had to move the canister set to the high chair to make room for the mixer and now had to shove the mixer into the corner to make room for the cake.

Someday, when Adam gets home, we'll buy our own house with lots of counter space and a big window over the kitchen sink where I can look out at green grass, a swing set and a picket fence.

She'd already packed the stroller with party hats, a pitcher of strawberry Kool-Aid, paper cups and plates, napkins, forks and the camera her parents had sent when William was born. She looked at the clock on the wall and hoped she had time to frost the cake before William woke from his morning nap.

This would be the second time she and her two-year-old son had spent his birthday alone together and she was grateful to know that the cake and an afternoon at the Army base playground would be enough to make him happy. William's only friends were the toddler children of the women she sat with at the park several times a week. The women were the closest she'd found to friends since moving to Fort Benning Air Force Base two years before.

The cliques on base were maddening. The Army's hierarchy extended to the wives and even to their children. "What is your husband's rank?" was always the first question asked in conversation, and friendships were made—or squelched without a chance—depending on the distance between.

Mandy found a group of women whose husbands were sergeants and staff sergeants like Adam. They had become friendly acquaintances and shared parenting stories around the picnic table on the hill near the monkey bars, and though none seemed to have time or interest in getting together outside of the playground, she looked forward to the park as much as William did.

She filled out invitations for the May 4, two o'clock party and handed them out at the playground the week before.

The last time she'd seen her husband, Mandy had been seven months pregnant. It was in the middle of the night that they'd kissed goodbye, he hugged her swollen belly and lingered on the folds of her maternity dress with a long kiss before he headed for the plane that would take him and the other soldiers from the 58th Infantry Platoon to South Vietnam. The Army had made it a practice of transporting troops in the middle of the night to avoid the war protesters that amassed at the base and the airports and streets. Scads of anti-war protests were filling the cities, but small groups wearing peace sign shirts, holding picket signs and shouting 'End the war'- and 'Stop the draft'-type sentiments were rampant around the base and at public gatherings all around the country.

While anti-draft and anti-war postures were spreading like Napalm wildfires across Vietnam, the number of men drafted each year had escalated to the hundreds of thousands. Though all men between 18 and 25 were required to register and report when their names were called, many were finding means to dodge the draft and avoid military service all together. Others were registering as conscientious objectors and accepting civilian service or avoiding frontline fighting by refusing to join on grounds of religious or philosophical objections to war. In an effort to make the system more equitable for all, a lottery system had been established the December before to determine the chances of being drafted using birthdates and initials for designating those to be called.

Meanwhile, casualties numbered nearly fifty-thousand since the war had begun more than a decade before. Though the majority of soldiers taken as prisoners were from the U.S. Air Force, two-thirds of those killed had been soldiers from the Army.

Mandy spread butter cream frosting and brightly colored sprinkles over the cake, sealed tin foil over the nine-by-twelve-inch pan and taped two birthday candles to the top. She dropped a silver Zippo lighter into the pocket of her sleeveless shift and walked to the second bedroom of their family housing apartment to check on her son.

William was sitting up, rolling the train back and forth on the Busy Box strapped to the spokes of his crib. He looked up with a drooly smile when she entered the room.

"Are you ready for a party, Mr. Birthday Boy?"

He stood and stretched his arms, and Mandy lifted him to the changing table.

William had been slow to talk but was making progress. "Birthday cake" sounded more like "burday cade" as he repeated the words while Mandy changed him into a fresh pair of shorts and a plaid shirt.

"William's birthday party," she enunciated slowly.

"Wuz burday pah," he repeated.

Mandy stopped in the bathroom to put on some frosted pink lipstick and added a pair of large gold hoop earrings. She ran her fingers through her short pixie hair and then strapped William into the stroller that was loaded and ready for them at the unit's front door. Balancing the cake on the stroller's canvas top, they headed to the park.

Lois was already there with infant twin daughters asleep in a double pram. William spotted her three-year-old son David on the slide and ran to join him. Mandy's favorite of the women at the park, Lois had covered the picnic table where the group always gathered with a gingham tablecloth and a couple of stuffed animals for decoration. Lois had a sister that lived just one town away, so between the sister, her three children and her husband overseas, she had little time for

Mandy and William outside of their park visits, so Mandy was particularly happy to see her and grateful for her help.

The other ladies arrived with their children, diaper bags and birthday gifts in tow and gathered around the table while the toddlers ran to the park's slides, swings, monkey bars, sandbox and merry-go-round. Donna, the group's youngest member at just 19, handed each mom a cold bottled Coke from a paper bag and the ladies sat at the picnic table and chatted while their kids played.

Just a small grassy area with a handful of picnic tables, an outbuilding with restrooms and the simple playground equipment, Fort Benning's park was nothing special, but it served the purpose for the gathering and the camaraderie between moms and children. Its grassy knoll, surrounded by dozens of azalea bushes blooming in pinks, reds and whites, overlooked the main entrance road and the building that housed the Army base's top officers and the Post Commander's office.

"That's the third officer vehicle I've seen arrive in the last few minutes," Lois said as she looked toward the parking lot. "And each time a warrant officer has met them at the car before they entered the building."

The ladies all followed Lois' eyes and watched as three men got out of an officer's jeep, spoke briefly with a uniformed enlistee and entered the building.

The entrance road and Command Post parking lot were quiet again when David ran to his mother with tears running down his face. "Joannie won't share the slide," he cried.

"Maybe it's time for cake," Mandy said, then turned toward the swings. "William, kids, come on over."

"Joannie, come here," Donna yelled. "Everyone come on. It's time for birthday cake."

Mandy uncovered the cake, placed it at the center of the table and pushed the two birthday candles into the middle, while Lois wiped all the kids' hands and faces with a washcloth she had in her diaper bag. Kim passed out the party hats, Donna set the table with plates, napkins and forks, and Cheryl poured cups of Kool-Aid.

Mandy lit the two candles and the small crowd sang and smiled at William as he fussed and tugged at the elastic on his hat. As soon as he heard the "dear William" part, he smiled and stood on the bench, knowing it was time to blow out his candles. It took three blows, but the candles stopped flickering. Mandy pulled the pan to the side of the table and stood behind William so that he could hold the knife handle with her while she cut square-shaped pieces for all the guests. Once they were all served, Mandy pulled out her camera and took pictures of William and each child eating their cake and then stepped higher on the knoll to capture the entire party.

"There's another one," Lois said, looking back at the parking lot. Mandy followed Lois' eyes and then noted a group of four men talking together outside a side door to their right.

"Seems like something is going on," Cheryl said.

The ladies took another look at the group of men talking in the distance and at the parking lot, but soon pulled their attention back to the children.

"My present first!" David cried.

Mandy passed William his gifts one by one. He opened books, a toy truck, a Mickey Mouse Club album and a tub of Tinker Toys.

Two women walking their bicycles with two children came into the park from the other direction.

"Do you know if something is going on?" Lois called to them. "We've seen a lot of cars and officers."

One of the women separated from the others and walked toward the party before speaking.

"There has been another protest and they think some students have been killed," she said. "It's at a college in Ohio."

"Students?" said Donna. "How can that be?"

Without word and a bit of guilt, Mandy knew she shared relief with the other women that the news wasn't from Vietnam. The women gathered their children and helped Mandy pack her stroller with the gifts and the pan of leftover cake as they muttered questions among themselves.

"Why don't we go back by the commissary," Lois suggested. "There are some televisions in the common area. Maybe we can find out there."

Cheryl and Mandy agreed, while the other two said their goodbyes and promised to catch up later.

The commissary was abuzz when they walked through the door and the televisions were surrounded by people watching a special news report describing a barbaric scene at Kent State University in the small town of Kent, Ohio. The newscasters were careful not to offer any theories or reports of confirmed deaths, stressing that the scene was chaotic and that confirmation of details would be coming. Students involved in a campus protest march that had started days before had been asked to disperse and had not complied.

"We can confirm," said the newscaster, "that shots were fired by members of the Ohio National Guard into the crowd. Students from the crowd are feared dead."

Concerned and anxious to keep their children away from the imminent panic, Mandy, Cheryl and Lois corralled their children and strollers through the building and out into the fading afternoon sun.

That night, Mandy avoided the television news until she fed and bathed William and he was asleep in his crib.

"There remain many unanswered questions," the correspondent said as photographs of the massacre flashed across her black and white television. "We can confirm, however, that four unarmed Kent State University students have been killed in the open fire during the mid-day protest. As many as ten more have been injured."

She pushed the silver button and the television went black again.

God, when will this war ever end?

GINGER: SEPTEMBER 1971

Ginger could see the reflection from the silver trailer's aluminum façade gleaming from behind the trees, but she drove her white Vega hatchback back and forth three times before getting the nerve to pull down the gravel driveway.

She slowed the car as a chicken clucked across the gravel in front of her tires. A hound dog lying in the shade of a pecan tree lifted its head just long enough to catch Ginger's eye and then lay back down to continue its nap.

She could see no movement inside the trailer and was beginning to wonder if she should just turn around and go home when she heard, "Toodle oooh, Ginger McCarthy! Over here!" coming from behind the right side of the car.

Millie's face popped through the open window on the passenger's side. Today's eyeliner was lilac.

"I was just picking some flowers and some mint for your visit," she said.

She held up her hands and proudly displayed a bunch of green sprigs in one hand and a bouquet of yellow dandelions in the other.

"So park your car and come on in! Let's get our friendship started. Time's awastin', as they say!"

Millie stepped around the car and moved toward the trailer. Ginger watched her pluck a small sprig from the bunch of mint and carefully place it in front of the hound dog's nose as it slept. She turned around and smiled at Ginger as she reached the top of the three-step wooden platform that led to the trailer's front door.

Ginger turned off the car and grabbed her purse from the front seat as she said a little pep talk-prayer under her breath and opened the door.

"That's Maximilian," Millie said as Ginger walked toward the trailer with an exaggerated arc to avoid the sleeping dog. "Friendly as they come!"

A rip in the screen of the metal front door looked like it had been patched with a messy line of X's sewn with pink embroidery thread. Millie held the door wide as Ginger walked in.

Christmas lights zigzagged the ceiling of the trailer through the two rooms that served as kitchen and living room. Filtered light twinkled from the lace curtains that hung against the windows of the backside of the trailer and scattered polka dots of golden light across a soiled sofa of plaid tweed and a floral Queen Anne chair. A round table next to the window in the tiny kitchen was centered with a beautiful Irish lace doily.

"Let me put these flowers in water and I'll put on some tea," Millie said as she pulled out one of the three metal folding chairs that circled the table. "Have a seat."

"I baked some banana bread," Ginger said presenting a small package from her purse. She'd carefully wrapped four large slices in waxed paper and tied a blue ribbon crosswise across the stack with a bow on the top. "I hope you like it."

"Well, I swanee," Millie sang as she centered a small vase of dandelions on the doily, "banana bread is my favorite!"

"Have you lived here long, Millie?" Ginger asked.

"Oh, a little over four years, I suppose. Maximilian and I are quite happy here," she said. "I style hair here too, by the way. Have a nice group of ladies that come in for a set and comb-out once a week or so."

Ginger looked around the small trailer as she heard the whistle of the teakettle. She assumed the two doors at the rear led to a bedroom and bathroom, but there was little room for more.

Millie placed a cup of steaming tea in front of Ginger and one for herself on the opposite side and sat down.

"Mint in your tea?" she asked.

"Just a little sugar, if you don't mind," Ginger replied.

They chatted about the hot, sticky dog days of summer and the laundromat and Maximilian. Millie pulled the teapot from the two-burner stove and said, "How about a little banana bread with this next cup?"

She blew a piece of fuzz off the top of the stack of two plates as she placed them on the table and untied the blue ribbon and opened the waxed paper that held the banana bread.

"So, tell me about your husband. What's his name?"

"Pete," Ginger said. "Peter James McCarthy, but everyone calls him Pete. We met in Atlanta. Where I'm from."

"Big town, Atlanta," said Millie.

The comment felt surprising to Ginger, as Columbus was just a little more than an hour south of Atlanta near the Alabama line. As lonely as she'd been, it was the first time she felt far from home.

"Mmm. Yes," she said. "Pete's from Indiana. We met while he was in basic training for the Army. We married last November, but so far we've barely been in the same town more than a couple of weeks."

A cuckoo clock on the trailer's wall popped open with a brightly colored bird and three loud cuckoos.

"Time to feed the fish!" said Millie as she hopped to her feet and ceremoniously sashayed across the room to a fish tank that sat on a wooden plank atop two upright cinder blocks. She was still wearing the yellow Dr. Scholl's sandals, but this time with no socks. Her toenails were badly chipped with the remains of a neon orange polish. She sprinkled two fingerfuls of something from a wooden bowl into the tank and sat back down and picked up another piece of banana bread.

The trailer's light darkened as a cloud moved across the sun.

"Maybe it's time I be going," said Ginger, wiping her own fingers across the folds of her cotton skirt.

"What do you mean? We are just getting to know one another, Ginger McCarthy! Please stay and let's continue our chat."

"Well, a few more minutes maybe," said Ginger acknowledging to herself she had nowhere else to go or anything else to do. "Have you always lived in Columbus?"

"Born and raised," Millie said proudly. "But I traveled for years in between before settling back here."

"Do you have a family?" Ginger asked and immediately wondered if she shouldn't have.

"You mean other than Maximilian?" Millie said smiling.

Ginger could tell that Millie sensed her regret with the question as she quickly continued to assure her that she'd done no harm.

"Well, I never knew my mother and my dad passed when I was 19. But I have a son. Haven't seen him in many years but I hope to soon."

Ginger noted the first sign of sadness she'd seen cross Millie's face. "And Mr. LaMurphy? Your husband?"

"Oscar Swift was technically never my husband. He traveled with the circus and we met in Anniston in 1955. We never married, partly because Oscar didn't have a birth certificate and that was a requirement for the few places we'd checked, but he called me his wife and I called him my husband. We were very happy for many years. And since we are speaking technically," she continued, "LaMurphy's not technically my name either. It's Millicent Lavonne Murphy. I smush it all together and call myself Millie LaMurphy. I think it has a nice ring to it."

"I think so too," Ginger laughed noticing for the first time a little plastic bee Millie had clipped among her pinkish curls. She worked carefully trying to form her next question, but she didn't need to as Millie quickly offered more.

"Oscar had a lion act and I was selling tickets at the circus entrance. We traveled across the country in a train. After six months, he made me part of his act. I loved that but went back to ticket sales when I got pregnant with our son."

Ginger noted Millie's perfectly aligned teeth and rosebud-shaped lips. If her eyes weren't so heavily decorated, it would be easier to notice her mouth—definitely Millie's best feature. She was gaining confidence that having Millie as a friend would make Columbus, Georgia, a lot more fun while she waited for Pete's return.

"But, where is your son?"

"He's with his dad in the circus. He's eleven. Probably starting pubation about now," she said and paused. "But I haven't heard from them for almost five years."

"Pubation?"

"You know how kids go through that time before they start to become teenagers," Millie said. "He lived with me until he was six while Oscar continued traveling. He'd send money to us every month. But the circus came to Columbus back in the summer of '65. Oscar took O'Ray with him when the circus moved on. I got a few letters from him the first year, but I haven't heard anything since."

Ginger's mind was reeling to determine if "pubation" was really an acceptable vocabulary replacement of "puberty," until the sadness of Millie's story set in and she moved on.

"Oh, Millie, I'm sorry," she said. "And his name is O'Ray?"

"Oscar Ray Swift, Jr.," Millie said with a sad smile. "We called him O'Ray for short. He's the spittin' image of his daddy."

"Can you contact the circus management to learn anything?"

"I send a lot of letters but they all go unanswered. I'm hoping they'll bring the circus close enough for me to travel to the show soon so I can see for myself."

"Gosh Millie. I can't imagine..." said Ginger. "I wish I could think of a way to help."

"You can! Be my friend while you're here. I know everyone in town and we can make this town a lot more fun for you," Millie chirped. "You think you'll be here until August, you say?"

"That's what we know for now. Pete's been in central Vietnam for five months. He got really lucky to get a two-week leave home, but I likely won't see him again for another ten months or more."

"Well, let's start by getting together and filling some of your time," said Millie. You're welcome any time for tea. There's a community garden not far from here. I can get you set up with a little plot and we can garden together," she said. "I have autumn squash coming up soon and you can help me tend it this fall. Plus, we have an old theater in town that's just been gussied up. We can go see a play!"

Ginger struggled for an opportunity to respond to Millie's rushed spill of ideas while at the same time she imagined the letter she'd pen to Pete to tell him about her new friend.

"I'll introduce you to everyone!" Millie continued. "Oh, and the Muscogee County Fair starts this week. Let's go on Saturday!"

Two days later, Ginger sat at the picnic table just inside the base's entrance finishing a letter she had started to Pete while she waited for Millie. It was a hot Saturday and the Georgia sun beat down on Ginger's shoulders. The pine trees surrounding the small green did little to shade the table. She had already added a P.S. and a P.S.S. to her letter, but thought of one more thing she wanted to tell him when she saw Millie's black truck pull up toward the front gate and stop.

She was due for her period any day, but opted not to mention it and wait for at least one more letter before writing anything that might get his hopes up unnecessarily. If she were pregnant, she would deliver while he was gone, but if all went as planned, he'd be back in the states before the baby was more than two or three months old.

She tucked the five pages of her best stationery and envelope inside the paperback she'd been using to bear down and dropped it inside her purse. As always, when she wanted to tell Pete something faster than she could in her twice-a-week letters, she would picture a blue balloon filled with her thoughts flying out of her head, circling the earth and melting into the top of Pete's head on the other side of the world.

We'll be back from the fair in time for me to finish this letter and get it in the afternoon mail.

She knew mail call for the military troops was also inconsistent. Pete told her that he'd often get no letters from her for several weeks and then might get three or four on the same day. She'd started putting the date she mailed the letter on the back flap so that he could read the letters in order if that happened. Even so, she felt she needed to send him that instant message via blue balloon so he'd know she was keeping her promise of mailing a letter every Wednesday and every Saturday.

Ginger waved at the guard on duty as she exited through the pedestrian gate and heard Millie calling for her.

"Toodle oooh, Ginger McCarthy!" sang Millie from behind the truck's oversized steering wheel and through the passenger's window. "My, you look extra pretty today."

Ginger smiled as she flipped the folds of her red gingham sundress and opened the door of the big truck. Maximilian was spread across the passenger's seat.

"Scoot this way Maxie Pie," said Millie patting and pulling on the dog's fleshy skin. "Give Ginger McCarthy some room so we can get to the fair."

After some prodding, Maximilian moved toward the center so that Ginger was able to squeeze to the side and close the truck's door.

"Will Maximilian walk through the fair with us?" asked Ginger as they parked the truck among the other trucks and small tractors in a field covered with hay.

"Oh, heavens no! Max is much too lazy. He'll nap here along side the truck while we visit."

She pulled a metal bowl and a thermos of water from behind her seat and placed it front of the already napping dog. Then she pulled a pouch of aluminum foil from her bag and dropped four lemon slices into the water.

"I like to stimulate the old dog somehow," she said. "He barely moves all day, so at least I can keep him on his toes with something to smell while he sleeps!"

Ginger smiled and shook her head as she followed Millie toward the fair.

The smells of the carnival food, the livestock exhibits and the crowds of people mixed with the thick, dank air around the fair. A heavy rain earlier in the week had caked mud in spots, now cracked and dry but emitting another earthy odor into the mix.

Ginger pulled strips of cotton candy and let them melt into her mouth as Millie dipped a corndog into a cup of mustard and they surveyed the fair.

A man in an Uncle Sam costume and a woman dressed as Martha Washington stood on a small stage and waved to passersby from a voter registration booth. A sign bordered with red and blue stars read: The 26th Amendment Approved! Voting age now 18. Register here!

In the livestock barn, a barker wearing a straw hat and red suspenders shouted through a high-pitched megaphone at Ginger and Millie inviting them to have their photo made with a two-headed calf. They declined and moved on to the flower-arranging tent.

"We had three sets of conjugated twins in the circus when I was there," Millie said.

"Conjugated?"

"You know, Siamese twins? We had three sets."

Ginger debated the difference between conjugated and conjoined in her head, but decided to let it pass.

"I wrote Pete about meeting you," said Ginger as she waved to a clown on stilts that sprinkled glitter on them both as he walked by. "I told him about Maximilian and the community garden and the fair."

"I'm glad," said Millie. "We are going to have a lot of fun while you wait for him to come home." She stopped walking and shouted, "Look! A photo booth!" Ginger followed her eyes through the crowd. "Let's have our picture made and you can send a copy to Pete in one of your letters."

They hurried to the photo booth and sat side-by-side on the small bench. Ginger pulled the curtain shut as Millie dropped a quarter into the machine and the camera snapped its first shot with Ginger squinting and pursing her lips as she read the directions above the screen.

"Oops!" they giggled and quickly smiled at their reflections in the glass as the camera clicked away. Millie took a big bite from her corndog making Ginger laugh as the last click of the camera caught the scene and then turned the photo booth dark.

Millie pulled one arm around Ginger's shoulder and plucked the remaining pull of spun sugar from Ginger's cotton candy as the unlikely pair admired their four-photo strip in black and white.

"This is fun, Millie," Ginger said looking at her new friend. "I'm so glad I met you."

"Me too, Ginger McCarthy!" Millie said and as they strolled toward the truck hand in hand.

Maximilian was yawning by the truck when they returned. Millie pulled a small piece of her corndog from her pocket and knelt down to present the treat to the unimpressed hound dog.

Inside the truck, she pulled a pair of scissors from the console and cut the tiny photos. "One pic for Pete. One for you. One for me, and one for Maximilian!"

Rachel: August 1998

Rachel flipped through the sealed envelopes holding the resumes and letters she had neatly prepared on watermarked paper.

"Next in line, honey."

The postal clerk's deep southern accent jarred her back to her Saturday morning errands and Rachel stepped toward the counter.

"I'd like to mail these please, but also buy some more first-class stamps," she said to the woman behind the counter.

"A book then?"

"How many stamps are in a book?"

"Twenty."

"Yes. One book, please."

"You got it, honey. That will be $6.40. You can put the stamps on yourself and drop your letters in the box by the door."

Rachel thumbed through her wallet and thought about her upcoming rent as she paid for the stamps. She had noticed a temporary farmer's market set up just a block from the post office and wanted to stop and pick up some tomatoes and flowers and fresh fruit on her way to Oodles and Poppy's house.

Maybe I'll skip the fruit, she thought.

She'd passed on a shower and make-up that morning and instead had pulled on a pair of white shorts and an Atlanta Braves' t-shirt and pulled her auburn hair into a low ponytail. She had packed an overnight bag and put it on the back seat of the car.

As she approached the glass door to leave, she saw a broad-shouldered man pushing against it with his backside and she stepped back to wait. She could see he was tall and blond and she felt a bit ashamed and pathetic when Madame Sylvia's prediction of meeting a man with a mustache ran through her head. He was wearing a faded t-shirt and cutoff blue jeans. As he rounded the door, the profile of an attractive blond guy—her age or a little older, maybe thirty—came into view. She noted his tan legs and dime store flip-flops. Rachel watched him squeeze and balance twelve square cardboard boxes—four across and three up—in between his tan hands.

No wedding ring.

He cleared the door and turned face-to-face with Rachel. His face had a little Saturday morning stubble, but no mustache.

His white teeth flashed an impish smile as he raised one eyebrow and looked squarely at her.

She smiled and just as quickly dropped her head in an unconvincing attempt to look as if she hadn't even noticed him.

His arms tensed against the sleeves of his t-shirt as he squeezed the identical boxes. Rachel sensed from his careful movements that it wasn't weight, but rather the absence of weight that made his balancing task a challenge.

She waited as he pivoted toward the service counter. When their eyes met again, Rachel made an exaggerated glance toward the twelve boxes and then back at him.

"Juggler?" she teased.

He smiled and offered a fabulous smile and a half laugh. "Only with fire. And the U.S. Post Office frowns on open flames inside their offices. Something about a lot of paper."

"Let me guess then…" suddenly wishing she'd bothered with the shower and makeup. "Bagels. You bought a dozen bagels and you're mailing one each to twelve friends?"

"Good guess," he said. "But bagels come in a baker's dozen, so no.'"

"Unless," she began, "you had the bonus bagel for breakfast, then my guess could be right."

"Nope. Oatmeal. And you're 'O' for two.'"

"Next in line," a shrill voice interrupted.

"Whoops, that's you," Rachel said reaching toward the door. "I guess I'll never get to find out!"

As she hurried through the door and into the morning humidity she heard him call after her, "But you were getting warmer!"

Rachel hurried to her car, closed the door and screamed into her palms. She peered toward the post office, but the sun's glare deflected all images from the interior.

She put her keys in the ignition but couldn't bring herself to start the car as she kept her eyes on the front door. Glancing around the parking lot, she realized she'd parked her white Ford Escort in the shade of the parking lot's only tree. She quickly opened he door and ducked behind the steering wheel.

Maybe if I scrunch low in the seat, I can see him come out without him seeing me.

In the same instant, she saw a flash of blue behind the glass and the tall, blond come through the door. Rachel slouched low in her seat with her eyes steady. Pulling sunglasses from his shorts' pocket he stood by the door and looked through the parking lot. Her eyes focused on the front of his t-shirt as her mind worked to comprehend what she was seeing. An illustration of a mustache covered the entire front chest of his shirt. She watched him take another look through the parking lot and then turn and walk directly in front of her car without noticing her inside. She sat up as he passed to read the back of his shirt. In faded black block letters, the shirt read, "Sigma Chi Mustache and Cigars/Chi Omega Pearls and White Gloves Mixer 1986."

MANDY: APRIL 1972

Almost four, William wanted to stay up later and later, and Mandy realized extending his bedtime helped her pass the evening time too. But after a long day at the park, William was exhausted. She put him to bed just after dinner.

She pulled the bottle of Wild Turkey from the cabinet above the cooktop that she'd bought when Adam was home and poured the bottle's last shot over ice. She filled the glass with ginger ale and sat at the kitchen table to start her project.

She measured and lined the photos across the sides of the cigar box and drew a pencil mark to show where she'd need to cut each one to perfectly fit around the box's four sides. Earlier in the day, she had made a selection of her favorite photographs to use for the top. They were already cropped and stacked in order of how she would glue, then decoupage them onto the lid of the box.

The box was to be a birthday gift for Adam—a place for him to hold his pocketknife, Chapstick, wallet and other incidentals. She'd seen a similar one at her friend's apartment made with photos from magazines, but the one she would make for Adam would be completely covered with photos of their family.

She'd taken thirty-two photos to the drug store for extra prints. They were mostly of William, but others were she and William, Adam and William, she and Adam and two of her all alone. In the center, and larger than all the other photos, she would place the family photo they'd made when Adam had been home almost a year earlier for a three-week leave that began just a few days before William's third birthday. It was the only time Adam had seen their son and the three weeks together were as glorious and perfect as they were short and bittersweet.

Just as she'd hoped, Adam was impressed, in love, enthralled and enamored with their son from the second he'd met him. William favored Adam in terms of his build and his smile, but he definitely had Mandy's brown eyes. His hair looked like it might stay curly. He could have gotten that gene from either of them, though William's, so far, was much curlier than either of theirs. She'd spent weeks prior to Adam's leave talking with William about his dad and studying photos. They'd spent days shopping for the things she knew he loved—pistachio ice cream, blackberry jelly, plain white bread with no seeds or flour on the top, Cheerios—and she'd quizzed William on things he could know about his dad even before he met him for the first time. Though William had been slow to talk, he'd made a lot of progress after his second birthday. Adam, though, was amazed at every word that came out of his mouth and was convinced he was the smartest boy that had ever walked the earth.

The latest itinerary called for Adam's unit to return to the United States by June. He'd have several weeks of follow-up once he was back, and by mid July they would be ready to start their plans and begin living as the family she'd been dreaming of. Adam would find a job and hopefully be able to enroll in Georgia Tech within a year. Once William started school, they planned for Mandy to take classes to finish up her nursing degree. She ran through the months in her head for the millionth time—the rest of April, thirty-one days in May, and part of June.

About sixty more days and this will all be over.

When it was time for glue, she started with the family photo. It had been taken at Six Flags over Georgia where they had gone on the last weekend that Adam was home. William was on Adam's shoulders and Adam had pulled Mandy in front of him after they'd handed the camera to a park employee. He had one hand lying loosely around her neck and the other in the air holding William's back while his mouth was buried in the top of Mandy's hair and he kissed her head. His bulging arm muscle reaching around their son, his aviator glasses and the silhouette of his strong legs behind her much smaller ones, stirred her every time she looked at it. William had an oversized lollipop in one hand and the park's schematic map in the other and both were raised high in the air. She was wearing a pair of short white shorts, a red halter top, platform sandals and big gold hoop earrings.

It's not a bad picture of me either.

She'd already framed several copies of the photo and had sent one to Adam soon after he'd returned to Vietnam. She'd also sent one to her parents in New York and his parents in Atlanta and kept one for their home, but she couldn't resist using it as the focus of the decoupaged box too.

Around it, she glued photos of William the day she'd brought him home to their family housing apartment, his first birthday when she'd taken him to Adam's parents' home in Atlanta, and his second birthday which they'd celebrated at the park on base. She added photos of his first Halloween costume, one sitting in his high chair covered with spaghetti sauce and one of him hugging a goat at a petting zoo that they'd stumbled across at a shopping center one day.

Around those, she added the photo of her and Adam at a concert in California before they married and before she'd cut her hair, a photo of their wedding and a photo of her and William at the community garden in Columbus. He was asleep on her lap.

Once finished with the top, she glued more photos around the sides. These, she organized chronologically by date.

Outside of the Fort Benning Army base, much of the world was continuing to protest and spread rage about the country's involvement in Vietnam, but for Mandy, her husband's role in it all was down to few more than sixty days. She studied the photos. Satisfied with the design, she rummaged unsuccessfully through the kitchen drawer for something to pry off the lid of the varnish.

It was dark when she heard a distinct and deliberate knock at the door.

No one ever knocks at my door. Only my brother shows up unannounced and he couldn't do that at base housing without going through the guard gate.

She listened for William stirring, but heard nothing so she walked toward the door and peeked through the peephole.

Two uniformed men stood on the stoop.

She opened the door slowly.

"Mrs. Rooks?"

"Yes."

"Mrs. Rooks, I'm Sergeant Smithstone, and this is Lieutenant Johns with Fort Benning's internal communications office."

"Yes. Is everything okay?"

"Could we come in for a moment, Mrs. Rooks?"

She opened the door and they stepped into the tiny living room.

"Could we sit down?" Smithstone asked.

"I think I'd prefer to stand."

"Mrs. Rooks, I need to let you know that there has been a capture of three of the Army's soldiers from Lieutenant Rooks' company," he said.

"Oh my God," she said. Mandy dropped into the closest chair wrapped her hand around her neck, then buried her face in her hands.

"Our confirmed reports tell us that Lieutenant Rooks is one of those men. He is being held captive by the North Vietnamese and is currently at Hoa Lo in Hanoi."

"Is he hurt?"

"We have no report that he's been hurt, Mrs. Rooks, However, the capture is of great concern. The colonel has requested a meeting in the morning at oh-nine hundred with you and the Army's communication's officers so that you can be brought up to date on all the information available and we can discuss plans and procedures for you and your family from this point."

Images and sounds flashed through Mandy's mind. *Cold metal slamming doors. The slap of flesh across cold, dirty concrete. The acrid smell of urine, vomit, spoiled food.*

She shuddered.

"Mrs. Rooks?"

She looked up at him and realized she hadn't invited them to sit.

"Yes. I'm sorry. Would you like to have a seat?"

"No thank you, ma'am. Unless, you'd like us to stay until you are able to compose yourself." When she didn't respond, he continued. "Any additional details are under investigation and the colonel has asked us to assure you that you will learn everything that has confirmed at tomorrow's meeting. Mrs. Rooks, do you have family or a friend close by?"

"My son," she answered quickly, then slowly she continued, "and, yes, I have a friend. I will be there at nine o'clock."

He handed her a folded memo with details of the meeting.

"There is a number here if you need anything before tomorrow at oh-nine hundred."

She nodded, closed the door and peered through the peephole to watch them walk back down the sidewalk to a jeep parked at the rear of the parking lot. She went back to the kitchen for the glass of bourbon and brought it back to the chair. Her head filled with weight, but she was too afraid to cry. When she finished the bourbon, she opened the breadbox that she'd never kept bread, but had become a catchall for seldom-used things that she didn't want to throw away. She found the lighter and a half pack of cigarettes and with shaking arms, lit one.

When she'd figured out what to do, she lifted the phone again, dialed her best friend, and took a deep drag on the stale cigarette as she waited for her to pick up.

She's more than seven months pregnant, but I know she'll do this for me.

Weeks earlier in preparation, her friend had made arrangements for a sitter to stay with William when she delivered so that Mandy could be at the hospital when the baby came.

Mandy exhaled into the receiver as she heard her friend answer, then, "Ginger, something has happened and I really need you. Can you come over?"

"Of course I will. Are you okay? Are you smoking?"

"Yes. And, sorry. I'll tell you everything when you get here. But can you make plans to stay the night and then stay with William for a few hours in the morning?"

"Mandy, what happened? You're scaring me."

"Can you come, Ginger?"

"Of course, I'm on my way."

GINGER: SEPTEMBER 1971

"I'm so glad you met a friend and got to go to the fair," Pete wrote. "Millie looks and sounds like a lot of fun."

Ginger pulled a bottle of Coke from the commissary's Coke machine and snapped off the cap with the bottle opener attached to the machine. She settled into her favorite chair with Pete's letter.

Though dated consistently, his letters arrived more and more sporadically—sometimes two in one day—and Ginger could hear the concealed detail as he tried to sound up-beat about the barracks, the guys he had become friends with and the work they had been assigned to do. He described an upcoming election for a new president in South Vietnam as light-heartedly as if he were helping with an election of a high school student council, and Ginger was annoyed to believe he would really think he was fooling her.

The evening news had stories every night about new conflicts, additional U.S. troops moving into the war-torn country, street massacres and more. Every night she stood just inches from their black and white portable television with the eleven-inch screen studying the faces shadowed beneath the bubbled helmets searching for his face. She preferred learning the details of the war from conversations and listening to the back-and-forth discussions. When she could, she positioned herself in front of the console color television in the general-purpose room at Fort Benning's commissary for a clearer picture and where she knew others would be watching and sharing their thoughts.

She liked the busyness of the commissary and spent days hanging out there to write her letters or to read a book and to avoid the emptiness of their small apartment on base. There was a soft Naugahyde chair tucked in the corner of the general-purpose room that kept her out of view of the crowds where she especially loved to write.

As she settled into it, she made the decision she'd been circling around for two days:

I won't mention the period. It was lighter than usual, but I know I'm not pregnant, so I need to quit daydreaming that it might be true. No need to mention it to Pete now. August is a long, long time—and a lot of letters—away.

She began:

September 15, 1971

My darling Pete,

I am so proud of your bravery and I know you will stay safe for me and for our future children. I also know that Vietnam is a lot scarier than you let on in your letters. You don't have to sugarcoat all that for me. I hear talk among the other women and staff here and their stories are very specific about the horrors of the war there. I appreciate you trying to protect me from all that, but please don't. I want you to be able to share your true feelings with me. It's the kind of honesty we will need once we finally get to be together again.

I miss you so much, but thankfully Millie has been keeping me busy. A few days after the fair we spent some time tilling her vegetable plot at the community garden. In a few weeks, she should have squash and pumpkins and some kind of fancy lettuce ready. She's a lot of fun and possibly completely crazy, but I really like spending time with her. I don't really even know how old she is, but I'd guess a little younger than our mothers.

She was lonely and homesick in Columbus, but determined to

avoid traveling back and forth to Atlanta. She felt obligated and determined to do her duty of holding down her husband's home while he did his duty to the country.

I need to stay strong for him so he can stay strong for me. He doesn't need to be worrying about me.

She thought about how proud Pete was of the curtains she'd sewn for their apartment and how she'd tickled his butt as he stood on the stepladder to hang them. He'd told her the beef stroganoff she'd made was the best he'd ever eaten, though she knew the gravy was too thick and lumpy. She was determined to be a supportive military wife—someone he would fight to stay alive for and couldn't wait to come home to.

She went back to the letter.

It's still really hot and humid here. I'll be ready for some true fall days. I'm just seeing a few signs of the leaves turning color this week. I wish you were here to see how pretty some of these trees are.

Do you remember Mother's next-door neighbors, Sarah and Roy Thompson? Mother called me last night and said that Sarah has a niece that needs "a get-away," and wondered if she could come stay a few days with me on base. Her name is Lorna, and I have no idea why she needs such a getaway, but Millie has been nursing a bad cold, so she's been laying low and it will be fun to have someone new to talk to. I told Mother that she could come this weekend. We'll see. At least she's close to my age. Mother thinks she's 23 or 24.

I'm sending you a brochure for Disney World I picked up at the Big Star. It opened a few months ago in Orlando, Florida, and I'm thinking it could be a great place for our honeymoon when we finally get one.

I cannot wait to see you. And hug you. And kiss you. And more …

Write when you can.

All my love,
Your loving wife Ginger

Ginger folded the letter without rereading it, filled out the address she'd memorized and pulled a flower power sticker from a sheet of stickers she'd received with her purchase of gas at the Johnny Reb convenience store and pasted it to the back of the envelope underneath the date. The Army's mail service carried all mail to the troops with just a single U.S. stamp, so she licked the back of an eight-cent stamp with a photo of former President Dwight David Eisenhower, placed it in the corner and headed toward the commissary's post office.

Afterwards, she stopped to pick up a few items for her overnight visit from Sarah's niece Lorna. The Dr. Scholl's exercise sandals Mother had sent clopped rhythmically across the Formica floor as she exited with her groceries and walked outside to the briskest day she'd seen since moving to Columbus, Georgia.

Lorna was leaning against a car in front of Ginger's apartment when she returned. She didn't offer to hold the bag of groceries while Ginger fumbled for the key, but rather tapped her foot and rolled her fingers across the front door as if she were bored.

"My Aunt Sarah says you're kind of lonely here," Lorna said smacking a wad of orange-scented gum that Ginger could smell from across the kitchen table as they talked inside.

"A little, but I'm finding plenty to do while I wait for Pete," Ginger said. "I've put in applications at a local dress shop and also at the library, so I hope I'll have a full-time job soon. Or at least three or four days a week." She paused, "Is that why your Aunt Sarah wanted you to come here? Because she thought I needed company?"

Ginger grew more annoyed at the thought of entertaining Lorna for an entire weekend, especially if it was designed under false pretense. Lonely or not, she could find her own opportunities for fun, and it for darn sure wouldn't involved this gum-smacker with a pink cowl neck sweater, green skirt and bright pink go-go boots and a polka dot neck scarf.

"She thought I could use a 'get away,'" Lorna said rolling her eyes. "I've been living at home and I haven't been getting along with my old man. Or my mother for that matter."

"And you graduated from Duke. Are you working in Atlanta?"

"I've been working banquets on the catering team at the Hyatt Regency but they're only scheduling me one or two nights a week. The old man and old lady are getting tired of me sleeping late and not 'contributing to society,'" she said with another eye roll. "The hotel has two banquet rooms closed for renovations, so I'm not on the schedule at all this week."

"And your mother and Sarah..."

"Sisters. Twin sisters, in fact. So, what's fun to do in this town?" she asked looking down her nose as she surveyed the apartment.

Lorna's quick change of subject threw Ginger off for a few seconds, but she was prepared with ideas: "Well, if you like to read, we could go to an exhibit about Carson McCullers that's not far away. She's from Columbus, you know. Did you read, *The Heart is a Lonely Hunter?*"

Lorna dropped her face and stared at Ginger with heavy eyelids that nearly covered her pupils.

"Seriously? That sounds like the snore of the century. Don't you have any place around here to dance, or to drink and dance, or to drink and dance and flirt with men?"

"I don't know," Ginger stammered. "I haven't been inclined to go anywhere like that without Pete."

"I didn't come here to look at pictures of someone who wrote a book," Lorna laughed. "Put on something cute and let's go out."

Ginger dropped her eyes to her t-shirt and patched jeans. It was too late in the season for her gingham sundress. She didn't have a cowl neck sweater or anything pink for that matter, which she realized she was happy about.

She moved into the bedroom and stared into the closet. As she reached for her denim swing-line dress a terrible thought occurred to her: *What if I am pregnant? I can't go out like this if I'm carrying our child. What would Pete think of me going out with Lorna, anyway?*

She cupped her breasts to feel for swelling.

None.

I've definitely lost weight since Pete left for Vietnam.

She touched her stomach and felt nothing but ribs she hadn't remembered feeling for a while.

Who am I kidding? I'm not pregnant and I've known it all along.

She pulled the dress over her head and added a string of big white ceramic beads around her neck and a pair of navy platform shoes. She re-parted her strawberry blond hair and clipped each side with small barrettes.

And Pete's not the jealous type. If he were here, he'd definitely tell me to go out and have fun.

"Even though I don't think Pete would like Lorna any more than I do," she said under her breath as she walked out of the bedroom. Lorna was looking through a box of personal photos and quickly slammed the box lid as she heard Ginger enter.

"Better," she said with still-snarled lips. The wad of orange gum dropped from her upper teeth to the bottom as her eyes followed Ginger's outfit from the denim dress to the platforms. "Let's go have some fun."

RACHEL: AUGUST 1998

Oodles' fried chicken had been a favorite of Rachel and her siblings since they were little. And they always wanted it served Poppy's way—with white milk gravy on the side. As usual, her grandmother had added a side of snap beans and a plate of sliced tomatoes.

P.J. and Roxanne had spent almost as much time with Oodles and Poppy as Rachel had when they were young, but since the rest of the family had moved out west, she considered herself fortunate and grateful to have her grandparents all to herself.

Dessert was Oodles' famous peach cobbler and they all retired to the back porch after they'd finished.

Rachel waited until she and Oodles were settled into the porch swing and Poppy was in his favorite recliner before she told them about leaving Quince.

"You didn't give any notice with your boss, Rachel?" Poppy asked. "I'd be concerned how that would look for your references."

"I didn't, Poppy, but I just couldn't. I'd had all I could take of Mitch Logan, and it was becoming very clear to me that I had gone as far as I could with that job."

"It's one of those dot-com things that I don't really understand," offered Oodles. "But I hear that's a big thing. Maybe there will be another company that's similar that you could work for."

"Atlanta has a lot of new companies like Quince," Rachel said. "And I've already sent resumes to three jobs advertised in the paper this morning."

Poppy surprised her with his next comment. "Or maybe you'll want to look in an entirely different direction, Rachel. You're young and now is the time to make a change if you want to."

She debated telling them about the visit to see Madam Sylvia and her prediction of meeting a man with a mustache, but the idea was interrupted by their neighbor, Sarah, who had walked right in the front door when no one answered and poked her head out the back door and onto the porch where Rachel and her grandparents sat.

"I figured I'd find you two out here," Sarah said. "Hi Rachel, honey. So glad to see you, too."

Sarah and Roy Thompson had been next-door neighbors of the Hills since they moved there more than fifty years before. They'd never had children and when Roy passed away the summer before, Sarah had invited her niece, Lorna, to move in for a while. Lorna was nearly fifty, never married, and had been in and out of toxic relationships, as well as every imaginable life diversion including EST meditation, Amway, and most significantly, a strong affinity for scotch.

"Come on out and join us, Sarah," said Oodles pointing to the rocking chair next to Poppy. "Can I get you a glass of sweet tea?"

"No thanks, Margaret, honey. I just finished a plate of meatloaf but wanted to stop by and see if I could ask a big favor."

"Sure, anything for our favorite neighbor, Sarah. What do you need?"

"Well, I told you that Lorna has gotten active over at the Methodist church, right? She's helping out with the youth group and they are holding a bake sale tomorrow night after their Sunday night meeting. Lorna forgot to mention it to me until this afternoon, but she's hoping for some help. I thought if you were doing any baking, you might package up a few items for their sale."

"Oh gracious," said Oodles. "I made a peach cobbler, but after we cut into it, I'm afraid there's nothing left that would be nice for a bake sale. Van had a double helping."

Poppy rubbed his stomach and smiled.

"Rachel is spending the night tonight, though, so maybe we can whip something up for you tomorrow afternoon after church."

"That would be so nice. Just drop it by tomorrow if you get the chance to bake. Lorna would appreciate it so much."

Rachel and Poppy met eyes and shared a simultaneous eye roll without moving their eyes at all.

"Can I get you some cobbler, Sarah?"

"No thank you, Margaret. I'm just stuffed after my meatloaf."

"How about a bowl to take home?" Oodles asked.

"Well that sounds mighty nice then," Sarah said following Oodles back into the kitchen.

MANDY: JUNE 1972

As the war raged, Mandy stood in front of the television for the six o'clock news every night. She read every report she could find and knew that relatively few soldiers from the Army had been taken as prisoners. Hoa Lo Prison, called the Hanoi Hilton by both the soldiers there and the news reporters, had prisoners from the Navy and the Marines, but it was mostly filled with airmen—and primarily officers —from the U.S. Air Force.

While stationed at Long Binh Post near Saigon, Adam and two others had been captured by the Viet Cong—communist supporters who fought against the United States and the South Vietnamese. They had been traveling on a standard mission to deliver supplies to Bearcat Army Base to the south. According to the official documents Mandy had received from the U.S. Army four weeks after the capture, a fourth infantry officer —Lieutenant Roger R. Meehan—had been killed while he sat inside a jeep. The other three, including Mandy's husband, had been ambushed a block away and taken to Hoa Lo Prison in Hanoi.

She did receive occasional reports, but the details rarely changed and she knew that updates of the prisoners were limited mostly to secret codes that they were able to share with the outside. She'd reread all of his letters since he'd been deployed to Vietnam many times and noted his mention of a friend named Roger. The documents gave the address of his widow Susan Meehan in Pennsylvania, whom Mandy had written a letter of condolence.

In what had become a constant habit, Mandy rubbed her fingers across the engraved letters of her silver P.O.W. bracelet bearing her husband's name and date of capture:

LT. ADAM J. ROOKS

USA 4-7-72

Most everyone she knew wore a bracelet honoring a prisoner of war—either someone they knew directly or indirectly or a name received randomly. Bracelets were available through the government and order forms were easily found in the back of magazines and newspapers. They cost just a few dollars each, and whether they knew the prisoner personally or not, wearers made the pledge to keep the bracelet on until the prisoner—or their remains—had been returned to the United States. Mandy's parents and her brother, Adam's parents and his two sisters all wore a bracelet with his name and date of capture. She'd ordered one for their young son but was keeping it in her jewelry box until he was older.

The summer sun was bright and she could see only the shadow of the mail carrier as he waved to her from inside his truck before moving to the next house on Sycamore Street. Mandy carefully placed her iced tea onto the grass beside her and waved back as she kept watch over her four-year-old son skating on the sidewalk across the street.

Adam had been overseas when William was born and spent only three short weeks with him since. The last time, fortunately, was over William's third birthday and they both talked of that time often.

A puffy cloud moved in front of the sun and offered noticeable relief from the August heat.

"You're doing great, William!" she called as she stood and headed for the mailbox. "They may be calling you to join the Olympics before long."

She opened the mailbox. The crash and scream from behind her didn't register as she studied the envelope's red and blue diagonal striped border sitting atop the stack of mail.

"Mommmmmaaaaaaahhh!"

She heard it this time and snapped her head toward the street.

William lay on his stomach, his head turned toward her in horror as he screamed her name again.

She ran to him.

The metal top clamp of his right skate had become detached from his red sneaker and the skate was wrung around his ankle and lay awkwardly across the curb. His hand and elbow were bloodied and his face was red and scared.

"Oh buddy, I'm so sorry," she said lifting her son and kissing his head. "Let's take a look at you."

William's wails quieted to a loud whimper and his tears turned to thick streams as they raced down his shuddering cheeks and he struggled to steady his breath.

"You are a brave soldier," Mandy said as she examined his scraped knees, chin, elbow and palm and then unbuckled the skates from his feet.

William looked at his palm and then wiped his face with the back of both hands.

"Do we... have to... have... Bactine?" he asked between sobs.

Mandy smiled. "Let's get you cleaned up and filled with a cup of milk and maybe a cookie or two," she said. "We'll make a plan to get you better and back on those skates after that."

She turned and carried him and the skates back toward their rented house. Her heart skipped a beat as she opened the squeaky screened door. The sound reminded her the mailbox and what she's seen inside.

Please be from you, Adam.

Once inside, she willed her attention toward her son as she gently dabbed his scrapes with peroxide-soaked cotton balls.

Within a month of Adam's capture, she and William relocated from Fort Benning in Columbus to Atlanta. The Army had offered to move them closer to family and away from the base and military life. Her own parents were in upstate New York, but she opted to move to Atlanta where Adam's mother and father lived just a few miles away in Avondale so they could share time with William. The little two-bed-room cottage was not far from Adam's high school and it made her feel closer to him. Her own parents called every Sunday afternoon, when the long-distance rates were lowest, but hadn't yet found the op-portunity to visit since she'd moved from Columbus. Her only sibling, Scott, was single and often in and out of the Atlanta area following construction work.

"Daddy would be so proud of you William. You are a very brave boy."

She looked deep into his eyes and wondered how much longer she could keep him connected to the father he had shared so little with. She saw him drop his eyes and look at her bracelet.

"But I think Daddy and Dr. Shuler would both agree that these injuries will need a little Bactine to get you back to 'strong boy-who's-almost-ready-to-learn-to-ride-a-bike.'"

William's lips turned up with a slight hint of a smile but Mandy saw it quiver. He dropped his eyes again and hesitated before making a slight nod.

"That's my big boy," Mandy said. "Let's get these bandaged up and I have an idea for a special treat."

After settling him with a pillow and his favorite blanket on the liv-ing room couch, Mandy set up a metal TV tray with a glass of milk in William's favorite Flintstone's glass and two cookies. She headed toward their black and white console television set.

"It's time for Romper Room." she said.

William kicked his legs up and down on top of the tweed sofa cush-ion and smiled a milk-mustache-over-baby-teeth smile.

"Yippee," he said.

Mandy looked through the living room's big picture window and toward the mailbox.

"Just going to get the mail, sweet pea. I'll be right back."

GINGER: SEPTEMBER 1971

Ginger's head pounded. She opened her eyes, but only the left one actually opened. The right one was smashed against something, as was her nose.

She lifted her head just barely and her half-mast eyes worked to focus on yellow and white gingham as she breathed a smell that was also unfamiliar.

She pulled back further and stared at yellow and white gingham sheets and a pillow with a matching case.

Where in the hell am I?

She looked around. A window that filled only the top third of the wall to the left looked somehow familiar, but it was covered with starched white eyelet curtains that she'd never seen. She recognized a Pink Floyd poster with a blue and red poppy border.

My brother had that poster in his room when he was in college. Carlton loved Pink Floyd.

A pink vinyl chair underneath, modern-styled on three thin, chrome legs, wasn't familiar at all but the linoleum tile floor beneath it was similar to the floor in her own base apartment.

Where am I, and what in the hell am I doing here?

She looked to the right and saw another gingham pillow wrinkled against the blond wood headboard of the bed. A half-sheet of steno paper sat atop it.

Ginger looked around the rest of the unfamiliar room before reaching for the note.

"Good morning. Gone for donuts," the note read.

She struggled to remember the last thing she could.

There was a bar... There were Harvey Wallbangers...

Gone for donuts?

A bar. Harvey Wallbangers. There were two, maybe three men...

Lorna!

Lorna! She'd gone to a bar with Lorna. She'd danced. She'd even smoked a cigarette or two.

Ugh. That's what smells so bad.

She swallowed and gagged slightly at the bile that passed her taste buds then sat up abruptly and looked to confirm what her mind had already been hinting at.

She was naked.

She saw her purse was peeking from underneath her dress that had been tossed haphazardly on the floor. On top of the dress was her bra. Her panties, she suspected, were what she was feeling wringing her left ankle.

So who the hell is bringing donuts?

Before she'd even finished the question in her mind, a noise, something like a "Barrooommmmmm, barroooommmmm" hit her eardrums as the door swung open and a toe-headed toddler came crawling into the room pushing a toy truck across the linoleum floor.

She yanked the covers to her neck as the boy walked over to the bed and looked at her quizzically.

"Wez Unca Scott?" He couldn't have been more than two.

Uncle Scott? There was a Scott. I kind of remember there was a Scott.

"Um, he left to get donuts," Ginger said, fingering her wedding ring under the covers. "Who are you?"

"Willyum," he said matter-of-factly. "Who are you?"

Mercifully or otherwise, she didn't have to answer because a woman came into the doorway.

"William, leave Uncle Scott alone and let him sleep...."

She stopped abruptly as her face clearly registered the room's scene. "William, scoot on back to the kitchen and I'll get you some milk. Go now and I'll be right there," she said. "And don't forget your truck."

"Bye, bye," the boy said to Ginger as he rounded the bed and headed out the door.

Ginger saw the woman looking at her bra laying across the pile of clothes and then to her.

"I'm Mandy Rooks. And I'm guessing you're a friend of my brother?"

"Yeah, kind of," Ginger managed.

Mandy Rooks was about her same age. Her dark pixie-cut hair was pulled back with a rolled-up pink bandanna. She had huge dark brown eyes that even without makeup were surrounded by thick lashes. She was naturally pretty, a fact her oversized t-shirt and jeans didn't hide at all. Given any other circumstance, she looked like someone Ginger would love to be friends with. Pete kept entering her mind, but she gritted her teeth to keep the thoughts away until she could figure out what she'd done and where she was.

"I really should be going..." Ginger said, realizing after she said it that leaving would be difficult considering she didn't know where she was or how she'd gotten there.

They heard commotion from the kitchen and William's voice, "Donuts!" he screamed with delight, followed by giggles and wrestling noises from the boy and his uncle.

"I'll leave you to figure that out, but please be fully dressed before my son sees you again."

Ginger's conscience erupted with another explosion of shame as she considered various lies and means of escape, none of which came to her. Her father's most vehement lesson to his kids: "Own your mistakes and learn from them" passed through her head.

"Mandy," Ginger called as she heard Mandy closing the door.

Mandy stopped, turned toward her and waited.

Ginger steadied her eyes for the first time. "My name is Ginger Mc-

Carthy. I am not really sure what I've gotten myself into here, but I have a husband stationed in Vietnam that I love very much and I have to admit I don't even know where I am. Whatever I've done here, it's completely out of character and I'm horrified with embarrassment. I can only imagine what you think of me and my bra strewn across your floor, but Mandy, I could really use a friend."

Mandy looked at Ginger and then at the wall above her for a long time, her face unreadable.

"Tell you what. I'll leave you alone for a minute to gather your things and I'll keep the boys at bay. When you're ready, I'll leave William with Scott and I'll drive you home or to your car or wherever you need to be." She hesitated a moment, then added, "My husband is stationed in Vietnam too, and to be honest, I could use a friend too."

All at once, Mandy's kind words and lack of obvious judgment collided with the gravity of the situation. Tears filled Ginger's eyes as thoughts of Pete filled her mind.

"Thank you," she mouthed as she watched Mandy pull a folded towel and washcloth from the closet and place it on the pink chair and pull the door shut and walk out.

Ginger peeked under the sheet and cringed when she saw her panties wadded at the bottom of the bed. She pulled them on under the covers before she dared to expose her bare breasts to the unfamiliar room. Then, after planning each move in advance, she leapt from the bed, grabbed and pulled on her bra and snapped the back before she'd even taken a breath. She pulled her dress over her head, slid her feet into her shoes and surveyed the contents of her purse and wallet.

All looked normal.

Head still pounding, she picked up the towel and washcloth when a wave of nausea sent her to the pink vinyl chair. She feared she couldn't find a bathroom close enough to avoid encountering others. Before she had the chance to try, she heard a knock on the door.

"Come in," she said quietly, hopeful that Mandy would point her to a nearby bathroom.

The door opened slowly and a disheveled and intensely handsome man stood in the doorway wearing a pair of gray sweatpants and a powder blue Grateful Dead t-shirt, carrying a cup of steaming coffee.

"I didn't know how you liked it, so I added a little bit of everything."

He looked at her hopefully. His dark hair hadn't been combed and his eyes were ocean blue surrounded by dark lashes. He had dimples that looked more like deep, straight-line wrinkles—double on one side and triple on the other—and covered with dark morning stubble across his cheeks when he smiled.

The combination was mesmerizing, and not completely unfamiliar. An image of a dance floor kiss came to mind and Ginger dropped her eyes.

"Thank you, but I hope you don't mind if I pass. Feeling a little queasy. And embarrassed. Horrified, if I'm being honest."

"Tell you what," he said. "Let's start from the beginning. I'm Scott Everly."

An image smacked across her brain as he said his name. She'd seen this man before—before last night, that is. He was the man that she and Millie had seen in the laundromat weeks before.

Her father's words.

"I'm Ginger McCarthy," she said. "Mrs. Peter J. McCarthy. Happily married to a lieutenant in the U.S. Army and deeply ashamed of my apparent behavior."

"Well, Ginger. I wish to apologize to you as I, in fact, saw that you wore a wedding ring, I got the impression, however... Let's just say, 'I got swept up in your charms.'"

Ginger glanced uncomfortably around the room, not sure what to say next and wishing she were anywhere else.

"How about we get some fresh air," he said. "Mandy has a patio right around the corner."

"I'd really like to go home, but could I ask you a few questions first?"

Scott held out his arm and led her toward a back door and patio.

Grateful to move away from the unmade bed, Ginger followed. She realized she was in military housing similar to her own as she walked down the short hall and out the back door. The floor plan was larger and the flooring had a different pattern, but the style, the wall color and the windows were all the same.

The morning sun was already warming the patio and the air was crisp and welcoming. The corner-unit backyard was situated in a private alcove and she saw no one else on either side that might see them as they walked across the small patio.

The hideous taste of smoke and soured alcohol that filled her mouth hit her again. She rubbed her tongue across her teeth and cringed.

A wooden picnic table with an orange and yellow floral umbrella anchored through the center sat on the quiet patio surrounded by a small, grassy yard and fence. They sat opposite each other, and Ginger instinctively covered as much of her mouth as she could for fear of her offensive breath permeating across the table.

"So, I was with a girl named Lorna last night?" she questioned.

"Lorna Long Legs, the sorority girl from Duke," Scott said.

Ginger's offense was clear across her face. She started to stand.

"She had the bartender introduce her that way," said Scott, holding his hand out as if to calm her. "Before she did the dance on top of the bar. Do you remember her pink boots? Do you remember any of this?"

Ginger listened. "The boots, yes...." she thought. "And maybe a little of the dance on the bar... So where is she?"

"She left with a businessman from the other end of the bar. She told you she'd pick up her stuff when she could and not to worry about her."

"And I was...?"

"When I got there, you and Lorna had been drinking Harvey Wallbangers for quite a while with a couple of guys I know. Then about midnight, you and I were dancing, Lorna did her bar dance and the other guys started drifting away."

Ginger's head pounded deeper at the mention of Harvey Wallbangers. Much of what Scott was saying was beginning to come into focus.

"And I ended up here..."

"Well you didn't have a car—which you wouldn't have been able to drive anyway—and Lorna left her car in the parking lot when she left with the business guy and took the keys. I offered to bring you here and..."

Scott's wide neck and broad shoulders pulled at the worn t-shirt. The attraction was undeniable and quietly and reluctantly, she resolved herself to the fact that she was remembering more than she wished. Her guilt—mixed with a little stirring as her body reminded her of a few choice moments from the night—filled her neck and throat as she awkwardly worked to avoid his fabulous blue eyes.

"And I agreed?"

"Well you kissed me and tugged on the waist of my jeans. I took it as a 'yes.'"

Oh dear God, what have I done? This can't be happening. How will Pete ever forgive me?

She worked to swallow yet another lump that filled her throat as she focused on a toy truck that sat at the edge of the patio.

"Well, I was very wrong. I think I'd just like to go home now."

"Ginger, I hesitate to say 'I'm sorry,' because you're gorgeous and a lot of fun, but I am sorry you're upset. I'll be glad to take you home, but as for me, I've been crashing here with Mandy and William for a month or so while I'm in between construction jobs, but I'll be taking off for Charlotte in two days. I may seem like a cad, but if we had the chance to really know one another, I don't think you'd think so."

He pushed the untouched coffee toward her with a "maybe this will make you feel better?" look across his face. His straight-line dimples were fabulous.

She looked back at the toy truck and sighed.

"I guess I'm just saying," he continued. "Is maybe we can chalk this up to a night of serious primal attraction? And I won't be around to remind you."

The irony tugged at her brain in a perverted diversion.

What if I were single and really interested in this guy? Would it be worse if he just screwed me and then said, "See ya, I'm leaving town?"

"Yeah, I guess it's as simple as that," she said. *At least for you.* "Mandy offered to drive me home, though. I would really prefer that."

"That's cool. But for what it's worth, you are a gorgeous chick..."

She put her hand up to stop him just as Mandy appeared at the back door. Ginger stood and looked toward Mandy and nodded. "I'd love it if you could drop me off?"

"Sure," Mandy called. "Scott, please watch William for a few minutes."

He stood in front of Ginger. "Hug?" he asked.

Ginger looked at him hesitantly and extended her hand instead.

"Ouch," Scott said as he shook her hand and looked right into her eyes with a sheepish smile.

He was ridiculously attractive. Guiltily, she studied his face for one more look as the words, "My one-night stand," chanted through her head.

"Donut then? For the road?"

Ginger wrinkled her face, shook her head and walked to the door.

RACHEL: AUGUST 1998

After they left Peachtree Road Methodist Church, Poppy pulled the car up to the Harris Teeter grocery in his gold Impala. Rachel and Oodles reviewed the list they'd made along the margins of the church bulletin: cupcake liners, cake-decorating tools, powdered sugar.

"We'll be snappy, Van," Oodles said as she got out of the car and she and Rachel headed toward the grocery store.

Oodles pushed the buggy as Rachel tossed a half-dozen or so items into the shopping cart and they discussed their baking plans.

As as they exited with the groceries, they heard Poppy whistling a hymn from the morning's service from inside the car and shared a smile.

"We are going to make chocolate cupcakes, but we have some ideas to doctor them up a little bit," Oodles told Poppy as she closed the car door.

"Doctor up chocolate? I suppose if a good thing can get even better! Taste-tester extraordinaire at your service, of course ladies."

"It's for the church's youth group after all," Oodles said, ignoring him. "That Lorna may be crazy as a bedbug, but it will be fun to do something nice for them. And for Sarah, of course."

After a quick lunch, Rachel wiped out the cupcake pans while her grandmother pulled the sugar, flour, unsweetened chocolate, baking powder and other ingredients from the pantry and discussed plans for the cupcakes.

Oodles searched through a drawer and pulled out the apple corer and some waxed paper and a pile of various pastry tubes for cake decorating.

"After some of these bake and cool, let's experiment with coring out a hole and we can try injecting different things to add flavor."

The pair had picked up two flavors of instant pudding at the store and had also discussed trying a thick cream and even jams for their experiment.

"Here is the raspberry jam," said Rachel, pulling an opened jar from the back of the refrigerator. "What do you think about maraschino cherries? Here's half a jar."

"I wonder," said Oodles, turning back toward the pantry. "We might try some cupcakes where we layer our flavoring into the batter before we bake it..." She pulled out a can of almond paste and placed it on the counter.

"Great idea," Rachel said, understanding Oodles' creative mind with no more explanation than the shared thoughts that always seemed to bounce between the two women's heads. "Or peanut butter!"

"Bingo!" she said hugging Rachel. "Have you ever noticed how well you and I understand one another?"

"No one has ever understood me like you do, Oodles. Sometimes I think the two of us were melted together and divided in half zillions of years before we were born. It's why we make a good team!" she said pouring two glasses of milk and handing one to Oodles.

The two clinked glasses and set about mixing their batter and arranging the counter with the flavoring options.

Racks of cupcakes cooled on the kitchen table while the counter was lined with the puddings and fillings and the assembly line continued. Rachel filled the cups with batter while Oodles monitored the oven and transferring.

"Mother and Dad said they are planning to come for Thanksgiving this year. Did you talk to her about it?" Rachel asked.

"I did. She and your father called on Tuesday. They seem to really like the climate in New Mexico. I do hope Roxanne and P.J. will be able to come too."

"So, something else that happened this week..." Rachel segued.

Oodles stopped and turned toward her granddaughter.

"After I quit on Wednesday..." she added, drawling the words slowly. Oodles urged her on with her eyes.

"I went to see a fortune teller." This time the words were quick and Rachel's right brow arched while her left eye winced in anticipation of her grandmother's reaction.

"Oh, Rachel Jane McCarthy, you scared me for a minute! Well what did your fortune teller say was in store for you?" Oodles opened the oven and pressed her finger on one of the cupcakes. Satisfied, she pulled the pan from the oven and placed it on the cooling rack.

"She was a tarot card reader. Honestly, I was so uptight from storm-ing out of Quince that I'm not even sure I can remember what she said. There was something about three cups and three women. The Death card was one of them, but she said that had more to do with endings and new beginnings than it did with someone dying."

Oodles studied her face as she listened to her granddaughter. "I'm guessing nothing upset or surprised you, then. The endings and new beginnings certainly rings true considering you'd just quit your job. Had you told her that before you started?"

"No, she didn't know." Rachel struggled to remember more of Madam Sylvia's words. "She mentioned you, I think. She said one card meant I had a strong female influence in my orbit." Rachel put air quotes around the "in my orbit" part.

"I think that must have been me then," Oodles laughed. "I feel like I'm out in orbit most of the time anyway!"

"There was something about a change of finances, and then one card was upside down. It was the Temperance card. She said it showed an imbalance in my life."

"Hmm," Oodles said sadly. "'Chel, honey, Poppy and I will be happy to help you if you need money while you search for another job."

"No, I'm confident I'll find something quickly. Don't worry, but I promise I'll let you know." Rachel stood and went back to the mixer. "She also said a man with a mustache could be coming into my life."

"Well, now we're getting juicy! Did she say any more about this mustached man?"

"No, it's silly. Plus I don't like mustaches on men anyway."

"There are always razors, Rachel. Your Poppy had a mustache when I met him. I handed him a razor and gave him an ultimatum after our third date."

Rachel laughed. She debated telling Oodles about the guy she saw at the post office, but was interrupted as Poppy entered the room whistling, "Red, Red Robin."

"Anything you need taste tested?" he asked.

"We were just about to start working on our first set of fillings," said Oodles. "Why don't you make yourself useful and be our scribe." She ripped a stack of pages from a spiral notebook and then handed the book and a pen to Poppy. "We'll give you the quantities and details of what we put into each cupcake and you write it down so we have notes for how to improve on future cupcake efforts."

Then she placed the sheets across the counter and wrote "Vanilla Pudding" on the first one, "Raspberry Jam" on the next. "We'll use these sheets to keep track of which cupcakes are which."

Rachel carefully cored the cupcakes, keeping the part she pulled out to plug back in after she had squeezed pudding, cream or jam into the center. They kept each option separated on the notebook paper dividers and then started in on a batch of fillings that would be baked inside the cupcakes.

"We're filling these cups one-third of the way," said Rachel. "And then adding our fillings before adding the rest of the batter, so write that down, Poppy. In the peanut butter ones, I'm mixing a cup of peanut butter with two tablespoons of confectioner's sugar before I make the ball to make it roll a little easier. I'm making the balls about one-inch wide."

Rachel and Oodles spent the next two hours icing the cupcakes and practicing piping designs on each one while Poppy tested an assortment with a glass of milk. Out of time to decorate each variety differently, they created flags on toothpicks to identify each filling flavor and packaged the cupcakes in boxes to take to the church. They loaded them into the back of Rachel's Escort and came back to the kitchen to gather their bags.

"We make the perfect team, Oodles!" Rachel said. "That was such a fun day!"

"Oh, it was oodles of fun, Rachel. I enjoyed it so much, too. As for Lorna, we will probably never hear so much as a 'thank you,' but I know it will mean a lot to Sarah."

"Any more testing needed, ladies?" Poppy said rounding the corner of the kitchen.

"Van Hill, you have had three cupcakes already," Oodles scolded. "I saved you an almond cream-filled for after supper, so you just skedaddle. We are leaving to get these cupcakes delivered and will be back right after that."

Rachel's mind wandered as they drove toward the church and she tried to imagine how she would spend Monday and each day of the upcoming week.

"You know I just remembered," said Oodles interrupting her thoughts. "Your mother once had a friend who read the tarot cards."

"Really? I don't remember her ever mentioning that."

"It was a friend she met when they were in Georgia," she said. "At Fort Benning."

"No wonder I wouldn't remember. Fort Benning is where I was born."

As they pulled into the church parking lot, Sarah and Lorna were walking toward the fellowship hall entrance. Oodles pushed the button to roll down her window as Rachel drove nearby and sang out to them, "Oodles and 'Chel's cupcakes, at your service!"

Mandy: June 1972

The letter was from Adam.

It was dated May 20, four weeks earlier, and had been sent from the P.O.W. prison to Fort Benning. The top had been slit open and taped shut. An Army label had been attached to the top with the Sycamore Street forwarding address.

Mandy slid her finger into a small opening and ripped the envelope across the back.

She looked toward the house where she had left William watching television and then unfolded the letter, taking a deep breath as Adam's familiar handwriting came into focus. She steadied herself with one hand on the mailbox post.

My dear Mandy,

I pray this letter actually gets to you as I can only imagine how difficult it must be for you wondering what's happening to me. I received your letter and package dated May 10, so I know you know that I was captured along with two others and we are at a prison in North Vietnam.

Impossible as it must be, please don't worry about me. I know this letter will be fielded carefully so if it's ever going to get back to Georgia, I'll just say I'm doing all right. There are men that have been here much longer and they tell me they were completely isolated for many months at a time. Conditions have improved, so

I'm considering myself lucky as I do get to talk with other prisoners here and have actually made some wonderful friends. We get regular meals and even get a chance to exercise a little.

I know I've mentioned Roger Meehan in previous letters, and we have been told he was killed as he waited for us a few blocks away. He'd become a great friend, and when I get back home I want us to look up his family.

Mandy, I am so proud of you raising William on your own until I get back to you and I promise I'll make it up to you, babe. I can't wait to be a husband to you again and a father to our son. I think of the two of you all day every day and all night every night. Imagining the day I come back to you is what keeps me hanging on.

I think about that overcooked roast you made with the shriveled up carrots and potatoes every time I get something to eat and I would trade it in a minute. But mostly I think about the reason we forgot about the roast in the first place and I ache for you, babe. The chance to kiss and love you again is what keeps me alive.

I wish I could be there for William's fourth birthday, but I know you will make it special for him.

This war will be over soon and I'll be back to you. Please give William ten thousand kisses from me. I'm enclosing a picture of the three of us I drew for his room. I love you both so much.

The jerky and cookies and William's pictures were fabulous. Loved the books, too. Could use some Chapstick when you can.

Yours forever,
Adam

Mandy turned the paper over. There was nothing on the back and there was no drawing for William enclosed. She studied the envelope again and followed every stroke of the pen Adam had made. His penmanship was particularly neat and slanted at the same angle she had been taught in school. She liked the way he made his capital 'M's and studied the large, continuous loop he made in her name.

The war between North and South Vietnam was already two decades old and American soldiers had been held at Hoa Lo Prison since the mid 1960s. Prisoners released two years earlier as part of a goodwill gesture by the North Vietnamese, reported deplorable conditions within the prison including isolation and unsanitary living quarters, torture and even deaths. President Nixon's efforts in 1969 to force the North Vietnamese to adhere to terms of the Geneva Conventions gave hope that conditions had improved since that time.

Among many other provisions, the prisoners were supposed to be able to send at least one letter or postcard per month, and they were supposed to be able to receive packages that would be inspected to ensure they contained no weapons, explosives or poisons.

Twice a month, Mandy sent packages filled with beef jerky, nuts, toiletries, books and, of course, letters and pictures from William, but since his capture, there had been no proof that he had received them until this letter.

William was intently watching Mr. Do Bee, Romper Room's oversized bumble bee character when she entered the living room, so Mandy opened the cabinet where she hid her cigarettes, lighter and beanbag ashtray and slipped out the back door holding the screen door steady until it clicked with little sound. She'd only recently picked up smoking and was determined to quit before Adam returned, but she justified her habit as a means to calm her nerves when she was particularly on edge.

She reread the letter three more times, then came back inside, buried the cigarette butt and ashes in the trashcan and called Adam's parents.

"Thank God, Mandy. We have waited so long for a letter," said Sandra Rooks, a sweet but mousy woman who had spent every day since Adam's capture at the 7 a.m. Mass at St. Thomas More.

Mandy read her the letter, leaving off the paragraph about the roast.

"Ted has gone to fill up the car with gas, but he will want to hear it too. Mandy, I have a roast in the oven. What would you think about us bringing it over so we could read it and we could all have dinner together?"

By contrast, Ted Rooks was as charming and loquacious as he was corny and excessive. His jokes were silly but he was great with William.

"I'd love that," Mandy said. "William had a fall on his skates earlier today, so he'll be thrilled to see you."

She hung up the phone and heard the hostess closing the show with the familiar Magic Mirror bit.

"William, I have a surprise for you! Come here and see!"

William rounded the corner into the kitchen. His blond curls had grown long over his ears. Mandy realized her Army-man husband might prefer to see his hair cut short, but for now she was enjoying the soft curls and the way they made circles around his big brown eyes and round, pink cheeks. His milk mustache was crusty now and he had a line of chocolate sitting parallel across his cheeks at both sides of his lips and above the small scrape across his chin. The bandage on his left knee was already flopped and hanging from one edge.

"What surprise?"

Mandy stood and pulled a clean dishtowel from the drawer. She wet the corner and sat back down, pulling William onto her lap.

"Actually, Mr. William Adam Rooks, I have two surprises for you," she said as she wiped his face, uncurled his hands and rubbed the wet towel across his palms and fingers, being careful with the right palm that had been scraped in the roller skating fall.

"What, Mommy?"

"Surprise number one: Grandpa and Grandma are coming for supper tonight."

"Yay! Grandpa and I can play checkers!"

"Surprise number two: We got a letter from Daddy."

"From Daddy? Is he coming home?"

"Soon, baby. He says he loves you and he can't wait to see you."

"Can you read it to me, Mommy?"

Mandy thought about the missing drawing Adam had said he'd enclosed. She knew all correspondence would be reviewed and vetted, probably both at the prison and at the base in Columbus. No doubt someone pulled it out before it was mailed. She handed William the envelope and looked through the letter wondering what parts to read.

"Dear William and Mommy," she ad-libbed.

"I am very excited to see you both very soon. I know that William is growing up to be a very strong, brave boy and I am so proud of him. I wish I could be there for his fourth birthday party. I'll bet he's learning to skate and will be ready to ride a bike soon."

Her eyes were filled with tears but she could make out William's face as he clung to each word.

"Maybe when I get home we can all go to Lake Lanier and William can try waterskiing. Please be good for Mommy, William, and you two take good care of each other while I'm gone. The Army is working hard to finish this war for the United States of America, so all American soldiers can come home to their families. Remember to say your prayers and the Pledge of Allegiance, William, and know that I love you so much."

"Love, Daddy," she said choking on the words.

"Can you read it to me again, Mommy?"

Mandy worked to swallow the lump in her throat.

"Tell you what, why don't you go straighten your room and set up the checker board so you and Grandpa can play. I'm going to make some cornbread and we'll tell Grandpa and Grandma all about Daddy's letter when they get here."

"Yes, ma'am," he said. As he slid off her lap, the flopping bandage stuck to Mandy's leg.

"And before that, let's get you a fresh bandage on that knee."

After a fresh application of Bactine and a bandage, Mandy filled a bowl with water and arranged cuttings from the wisteria vine at the home's back gate around the bowl and placed it in the center of the table. The oven timer buzzed indicating the cornbread was ready at the same moment Mandy heard the familiar toot, toot from the Rooks' sedan.

"They're here, William! Go greet them!"

She pulled the piping hot cornbread from the oven, plopped a few pats of butter from the butter dish she had placed on the counter in preparation and moved toward the front window.

Ted and Sandra Rooks were both crouched in front of William as he pointed to each of his roller skating injuries. Their faces moved with exaggeration as he explained exactly how the accident happened and pointed to the area of the sidewalk that the incident occurred. As she opened the front door, she heard William add to the story, "I thought I saw a tiger in the bushes at Mr. Smith's house next door. I think that's why I crashed."

"A tiger, William? Wow I think I would have crashed, too, son!" exclaimed Ted laughing.

Mandy hugged Sandra and helped her pull a box holding her Dutch oven out of the back seat. "So good to see you, Mother Rooks. I'm glad you're here."

William had Ted by the hand and was leading him around to the other side of the car.

"Come here, Grandpa. I want to show you a hole I found in the ground. I think it's where some bunny rabbits might live."

Rachel and her mother-in-law laughed as Sandra pulled a tray of strawberries from the back seat.

"We're so happy to be here and really excited to see this letter," said Sandra. "I have prayed so hard for a letter and to see his handwriting. We will surely see the end to this horrible war soon."

Once inside, she turned Mandy's oven to warm and placed the Dutch oven on the rack. Mandy noted the silver bracelet with her son's name and capture date on her wrist. The war was always top of mind and it affected everyone she knew.

"That cornbread smells delicious. Now, where's that letter?"

Mandy handed her Adam's letter and peeked to watch her study the envelope and the letter carefully while she pulled a tray of ice from the freezer and filled two glasses for tea. She saw Sandra's eyebrow raise just a bit as she carried the refilled ice tray back to the freezer, probably reading the part about the burnt roast that she neglected to read while on the phone.

Sandra clutched her chest as she read and Mandy wrapped her arms around her mother-in-law as they read together.

She folded the letter and hugged Mandy. The women shook as they cried and Mandy pulled out chairs for them both to sit.

"And he drew a picture for William..."

"Except it wasn't inside when the letter arrived. I'm guessing it was confiscated for some reason. I didn't mention that part to William because I knew he'd be disappointed."

"I guess we just have to be grateful to get a letter at all. Oh my, will this war never end..." She closed her eyes and tipped back her head.

The screen door squeaked and William came running into the kitchen with Ted following him.

Sandra reached out her arms and pulled William onto her lap. She was nuzzling his head with kisses while she picked up the envelope and letter and handed it to Ted.

William giggled and wiggled in her lap, then turned toward his Grandpa who was intently reading Adam's letter.

"Will you read it to me, Grandpa?"

Mandy saw Ted glance down at William and saw his lips move into position, but she quickly interceded.

"Just a minute, William. Let Grandpa read it first then you can hear it again," she said. "How about some milk or a glass of Kool-Aid?"

"Yes! Kool-Aid," he said kicking his legs. Sandra slid him off her lap and back onto the floor.

Mandy poured another glass of tea and filled the Flintstone's cup with Kool-Aid, then turned toward Ted just in time to see him wipe a tear from his cheek.

"Yippee, grape is my favorite," William cheered. Now can you read it to me, Grandpa."

Mandy interceded again.

"At the table, son," she said and placed the cup in front of William's spot at the kitchen table.

She handed Ted a glass of sweet tea and looked at him carefully while rolling her eyes toward William. She took the letter from his hand and cleared her throat just enough to lock eyes with of both her in-laws before she began:

"Dear William and Mommy, I can't wait to see you again very soon. William, I know you are growing up to be a very strong, brave boy and I am so proud of you. I bet your birthday party was lots of fun. I'll bet you are learning to skate and will be ready to ride a bike soon. Please be a good boy for Mommy, William. Remember to say your prayers and the Pledge of Allegiance, William, and know that I love you so much. Love, Daddy."

She looked again at Ted and Sandra, wondering what they thought of her fabrication.

"You forgot to read the part about waterskiing!" William cried.

"Oh, goodness," she stammered, wishing she'd never started such a white lie. "Yes, it says, 'Maybe soon we can all go waterskiing when I get home.' Now, William, why don't you run and get your coloring book and crayons and maybe Grandma or Grandpa would like to help you color a page."

Ted looked at Mandy and smiled as if to acknowledge that such a white lie was perfectly understandable.

"But bring the picture your Daddy sent. I want to see that too," Ted called as William ran toward his room.

Sandra and Mandy both whirled around and glared at him, their ears tensed and their heads pulled back, shaking their heads as they willed his words to rewind.

William stopped and ran back to the kitchen. Ted looked confused.

"The coloring book, William. You can make a picture in your coloring book," Mandy said waving her arms and William back toward the bedroom.

Sandra lifted the glass of sweet tea and held it in front of his face. "Have some tea, Ted," she said, cocking her head and staring directly into his eyes.

Ted took the hint and sheepishly took the glass from her hand as he mouthed, "What did I do?"

GINGER: SEPTEMBER 1971

Once she slid the key into the front door, Ginger turned toward Mandy and waved. She saw Mandy wave back from behind the steering wheel of the white station wagon and pull the car into reverse. Their apartments were on opposite sides of the base, but just a short walking distance apart.

The room looked off kilter when she opened the front door of unit G-31. Ginger had worked to turn the box-shaped, no-frills military apartment into a home while she waited for Pete's return, and noticed immediately that the floral curtains that she'd sewn and Pete had hung across the main room window were pulled to one side. The pillows from the sofa were scattered on the floor. A half-bottle of Coke sat directly on the end table right next to the stack of coasters.

She turned toward the street to see the tail of Mandy's car pulling around the corner and out of sight. She took another scan across the room and saw an open bag of chips partially spilled across the kitchen counter alongside papers and the box where she kept Pete's letters. Leaving the front door open, she moved toward the box on the counter.

Two of Pete's letters were strewn across the counter and unfamiliar writing had been scratched across the back of one envelope.

Ginger, Sorry I had to break in. The window was latched but it broke easily when I pushed. Got my bag. Hope you had fun. That guy was cute! Lorna

Ginger's knees unlocked and collapsed. She fell against the counter as tears poured from her eyes and she studied the defaced envelope where Lorna had written her hideous, shameful message across the envelope of one of Pete's precious, very personal letters that she kept in a decoupaged cigar box. She had covered the box with a collage of photos of her and Pete, words from magazines that reminded her of him and pictures of places she wanted them to go. More, Lorna had clearly read one or more of her letters and hadn't even bothered to hide it.

But worse—so much worse—it was Ginger whose sin could not be forgiven.

Own your mistakes and learn from them, Dad always said. This time, I have crossed the line.

She stuffed the envelope with Pete's familiar handwriting under her leg and howled uncontrollably as she thought about what she had done the night before, searching the universe for a means to turn back time.

Barely audible over her own cries, she heard someone calling her name.

"Ginger? Ginger, it's Mike. Is everything okay?"

She saw the drab green pant legs and standard issue black boots and followed her eyes up to the head of her six-foot neighbor as he stepped into her kitchen.

"The front door was open and I heard you crying," he said as he put his wrists under her arms and lifted her to standing. "Did you fall? Are you hurt?"

"I'm fine, Mike. I'm so sorry you had to find me like this. Just a difficult day. That's all."

"Wendy just baked a pineapple upside-down cake. How about I send her over with a piece to cheer you up?"

Mike and his wife Wendy had a baby girl three months earlier and Ginger had heard Wendy's recount of childbirth more times than she could listen to again.

"No really, Mike. Thanks for your help getting me off the floor, but I'll be just fine."

She wiped her face of tears and spread a smile across her face as she walked Mike out the door but immediately locked the door and ran to the bed where she buried her face into the pillows.

By the time she recognized the ring from the phone on the kitchen wall and opened her eyes, the light in the room had moved to dusk. The end of a crisp fall day was growing clear from the golden glow and deep harvest sky she could see from the small window at the top of the wall, the bedroom's only source for natural light.

She rolled across the bed and stood, certain the effort would be moot and the phone would stop ringing before she could get to it, but she picked up the handset on the sixth ring.

"Toodle ooh, it's Millie," she heard before she could complete her greeting. "I'm fit as a fiddle again. Calling to see if you'd like to come over for lunch tomorrow."

"I'm afraid not, Millie," Ginger said. "I'm really not feeling very well myself. How about I call you in a couple of days?"

"Well let me bring you some soup then, Ginger McCarthy. My chicken soup can cure anything!"

"No, it's not that kind of sick. I think I'm really just missing Pete."

"Then there is nothing better than a little company when you're homesick or missing someone. Come on over tomorrow. I just watched Dinah Shore make a new dish on television and I want to try it. Trust me, I know how it feels to miss someone. We can talk it out."

"All right. I guess I could use a friend. Thanks, Millie."

"Yahoo. Come around noon. Maximilian and I will be ready when you get here."

Ginger rubbed her eyes and ran her hands through her uncombed and greasy hair.

A photo of Pete and her taken just a few minutes after their court-house wedding stung her eyes, so she turned it facedown on to the nightstand.

When the doorbell rang, she debated hiding and ignoring it completely until she heard Wendy's voice from the other side of the metal door.

"I know you're in there, Ginger. It's Wendy!"

Ginger surrendered and opened the door with a half-hearted attempt at a smile.

Wendy had a pink terrycloth sling wrapped around her neck and waist with the shape of a sleeping baby's back and bottom hugging against its folds. She was carrying a plate covered in tin foil.

"Oh, you didn't have to..." Ginger said. She reached to pat the sleeping baby's round bottom. "How's little Jennifer Marie?"

"She's such a joy. Smiling. Making funny noises."

"So sweet," Ginger said, rolling a fingertip across the baby's thin black hair.

"I brought you some pineapple upside down cake," Wendy said, handing her the plate. "Mike said you were having a bad day."

"Thanks, but I'm fine. Please tell Mike I'm sorry he found me crying on the floor. I'm okay, really."

"Is it morning sickness? I'm hoping Pete's visit means a playmate for Jenny soon?"

Ginger's hand flew to the doorframe and she steadied her legs to keep from buckling again. "No. That's not it, Wendy. But thanks for the cake. I'll see you soon, okay?"

She shut the door and ran to the coffee table and put down the cake. She picked up one of the throw pillows from off the floor as she flung herself across the sofa and buried her head into it.

Another round of sobs and heaves and Ginger forced herself to admit she'd been avoiding thinking about Pete for fear that one of her blue thought bubbles would travel around the globe and he'd find out what she'd done. Her mind traveled to the other thought that had been piercing at the edge of her subconscious all day too: What if she'd gotten pregnant while with Scott?

I don't know what to do. I have never felt so lost.

Once again, her father's words entered her head. As a high school math teacher, Ginger's father had shared many stories of his students over the family's dinner table. And presumably as a means to teach Ginger and Carlton lessons through the mistakes of the students he'd never name, his most consistent mantra was always, "Own your mistakes and learn from them. Use your setbacks as a launching point for surging ahead."

She walked back into the bedroom, picked up the photo from the nightstand and looked into Pete's eyes.

"Unfortunately, I don't think that Mr. Hill's advice is going to work in this case, Pete," she said quietly. "I can never admit to you what happened and it's going to haunt me for the rest of my life."

She set the picture frame upright and headed toward the shower.

Rachel: August 1998

The management office of Rachel's apartment building received two copies of the morning newspaper for the lobby and the manager on duty gave her permission to take a copy of the job classifieds each day.

She and her roommate, Cameron, were finding that they had a lot in common and were sharing a bottle of wine or going out for dinner several nights during the week.

She used the full book of stamps she had bought sending out resumes and cover letters, and had just typed another one and was headed to the post office for another book when the phone rang.

"Is this Rachel McCarthy speaking?" after she had answered with a simple 'Hello.'

"Yes. This is Rachel."

"I'm calling from Peachtree Paladin regarding a resume you submitted?"

"Oh, hi. Yes. Thank you."

After introducing herself as the Human Resources Manager, the woman gave Rachel a short description of a job that the company was interested in filling and asked if she could come in to the office for an interview.

As soon as she'd confirmed and completed a set of careful notes with the location, time and a list of items she'd been asked to bring, the telephone rang again with another request for an interview. The second one sounded even closer to the true marketing position Rachel was hoping to find. She confirmed the second one for 3 p.m. on Thursday, just four hours after the first scheduled interview, and hung up the phone.

"Yes!" she said to the walls of her apartment as she pushed a Spice Girls CD into the stereo player.

She was dancing and singing at top volume when Cameron walked in. She turned down the volume on the stereo when she couldn't get Rachel's attention.

"You look happy," she said, placing a Styrofoam box in the refrigerator. "Good news?"

"Two interviews this week. I got calls from two of the companies I sent resumes to within minutes of each other."

"Awesome. We should celebrate."

"I'm game."

"I have some friends going to Tongue and Groove tonight."

"Sounds great."

"I'm going to crash for an hour or so, but I have some leftover pasta I just put in the fridge if you want it. I'll be ready to go around nine?"

"Yep, I'll be ready," Rachel said, opening the refrigerator and dumping the fettuccini into a dish and placing it in the microwave. "And thanks for the pasta."

Rachel was dressed in a short, plaid school girl skirt, crop top and little cardigan sweater when Cameron emerged from her room wearing a black spaghetti strapped dress with a red bustier showing from underneath.

"Oh my God, Rachel, you look amazing," said Cameron. "So Cher Horowitz. I have the perfect knee socks for that outfit."

"And you're so Posh Spice, Cameron. With a little Madonna added in."

Rachel pulled on the knee socks and a pair of Mary Jane heels and they locked their apartment door and headed toward the Buckhead dance club in Cameron's Honda Civic.

The summer sunset provided an orange, pink and lavender background to the city skyline as the girls drove south on Peachtree Street. They were dancing in their seats as the English version of Ricky Martin's "La Copa De la Vida" came on the radio.

"I am so happy we have started hanging out together," said Cameron when the chorus ended. "You weren't a lot of fun when you were working all the time."

"I know. Of course, I hope I'll be working again soon, but I'm sorry I was such a dud roommate for a while. I'm happy we're hanging out, too."

The chorus came on again as Cameron stopped the car at a traffic light. The roommates belted the lyrics at the tops of their lungs: "The Cup of Life. Al-lay, Al-lay, Al-lay!"

They were laughing and dancing when a dark blue Isuzu Trooper pulled up next to them. The sun's glare placed a star-filtered light on the driver that was swaying and singing at the top of his lungs to the same song. The girls screamed with laughter as they watched him bring a fist to his mouth as if it were a microphone.

Sensing their presence—or perhaps hearing their laughter—he stopped singing and looked to his left. Cameron and Rachel unsuccessfully suppressed their smiles but couldn't hide the fact that they were both looking directly at him as his eyes darted between the two girls. He pushed the radio button to turn it off and offered a guilt-ridden smile.

He glanced toward the traffic light and Cameron and Rachel could read the disappointment on his face when he realized it was still red. He hesitated just a second and then turned back to the girls as his window seamlessly slid down into the driver's door.

Rachel's heart pounded. All at the same time she realized he was going to speak to them, Cameron pushed the button to lower the passenger's side window. Rachel recognized his face.

"Gotta love Ricky Martin, right?" he said to the girls.

His curls had been combed into a more professional style than the

last time she'd seen him and his collared shirt and tie proved an equal-
ly pleasant alternative to the faded blue t-shirt that had tugged across
his shoulders and upper arms.

"The Cup of Life!" Cameron screamed from the driver's seat.

His eyes, though, were focused on Rachel as the two locked eyes.

"You're the juggler," she said, almost to herself.

She could tell he understood her though as he glanced at the light,
saw it was green and turned back to her.

"'O' for three, Red," he said. "And that was a wasted guess because
you already tried juggler."

A short toot of the horn from the car behind them sent both cars
traveling through the intersection.

"You know that guy?" Cameron screamed. "Oh my God, he's so
cute!"

Rachel watched the lane to her right and realized he was going to
maintain half distance behind Cameron's car so she couldn't see him
without craning her neck to the back. She looked ahead to see if they
would be catching another red light.

"No, but I've seen him before. He was at the post office when I was
there last week and we talked for a minute."

Her mind was reeling as she tried to recall their full post office
conversation when Madam Sylvia's face and short, slit smile filled
her head. The image faded into the large graphic mustache that was
spread across his chest in the blue t-shirt when she heard Cameron say,
"We've got another red light!"

Both cars slowed and then stopped at the intersection of Peachtree
and Lenox Roads. Rachel worked clever comebacks through her head,
but Cameron beat her to it as she yelled across the passengers seat,
"We're going to the Tongue and Groove. Can you meet us there?"

He shook his head. "Working. Got a courier package that needs to
get to a law firm downtown by 10 p.m. I guess some of us get to dance
to Ricky Martin and some of us have to work."

Rachel cringed as Cameron yelled, "So, you're a lawyer?"

"Nope, just a moonlighting courier delivering the package," he said.

The light turned green and he looked directly at Rachel. He smiled and waved before slowly accelerating through the intersection.

As the two cars traveled south, Rachel sensed that he was hesitating at lights hoping to catch another one, but the lights stayed green until they reached Lindbergh and Cameron turned toward the Tongue and Groove.

Mandy: July 1972

Napalm bombs, made from gasoline and a thick combination of two acids—naphthenic acid from crude oil and palmitic acid from coconut oil—created an inexpensive and powerful weapon. Napalm could be shot long distances and its gel-like state allowed spreading and an adherence to surfaces that could destroy a target even with imprecise aim.

Mandy made certain to read stories from all sides of the controversial war. The U.S. government's quest to sustain an independent, noncommunist nation for southeast Asia transformed into internal war between the North Vietnamese and the South Vietnamese. And contrary to the military directions made, many believed that it was a war that not only could not be won, but also one that the United States had no business of being a part of anyway.

Adam's father and grandfather had been high-ranking officers in the Army, and his patriotism ran deep, but for many others, the mandatory draft was an unfair inconvenience to their lives. And for a growing number of military personnel as well as civilians, the Vietnam War was in direct conflict to a new peace-loving, anti-war, anti-government mantra that was spreading rapidly through the country.

Now Adam was a prisoner of that war and she had no way of knowing if he would ever make it home. Her own resolve toward supporting her husband's work was waning as she listened to the protests each night on television and even in the streets as marches continued all over the country and to parts of Atlanta that she traversed with their young son. Just the week before, picket signs and protesters calling for an end to the war lined Peachtree Street as she took William for his four-year-old check up. She was glad that he was young enough that she could limit conversations about the war to how brave his father was as he protected their country, but she knew it was a matter of time before he'd sense the discourse that was growing by the day.

Mandy studied the double-framed photos of her with Adam that sat atop their black and white Zenith console television that the couple had purchased with money her parents had sent for their wedding. The photo on the left was taken at their wedding in Atlanta. Mandy's newly shorn pixie was haloed with a headband of tiny baby's breath blossoms and miniature roses. Adam wore a rented tuxedo and a short military haircut. It was the only time she'd ever seen him in a bow tie. On the right, was a photo from their single days when they'd hitchhiked to California for a three-day concert. Mandy's long hair and hippie clothing was crowned with a headband she'd made from dandelions and ribbons. She had a hard time remembering Adam's baby face as she studied his long hair and tie-died shirt. Both photos seemed so distant and so uncomplicated.

She pulled the silver power pin on the television and more images of actress-turned-activist Jane Fonda came into focus on the screen. For weeks, Fonda's controversial trip to North Vietnam had been all over the news. She pleaded to the U.S. soldiers over North Vietnamese radio to stop the bombings and the use of napalm that often destroyed homes and fields of Vietnamese civilians.

Back in the states, some were calling her a traitor and scorned her for abetting the enemy. For many, a photo of Fonda with North Vietnamese soldiers sitting on top of an anti-aircraft missile used to shoot American planes out of the sky was the last straw and earned her the name, "Hanoi Jane."

Mandy was grateful to be away from the Army base as the discussions never seemed to wane and she was happy to have William to bring diversion to her life. And she knew that everyone at Fort Benning would have a strong opinion about Hanoi Jane. It was just as well she was in Atlanta and isolated from the controversy in their tiny rental home with her son.

She watched what seemed like the thousandth aerial video of another bombing and fire rushing across a field, but quickly turned off the television when she heard William shuffling down the hallway, awake from his afternoon nap.

No longer a toddler, her four-year-old was looking more like a boy than he was a baby. She could see Adam in his eyes and mouth and the way he stood with his legs and arms akimbo.

"If Daddy can't come home, why don't we go there to see him?" he asked. William's cowlick, accented by the nap, had curls sprouting from the top of his head like a fountain.

"I wish we could, sweetheart," Mandy said pulling him into her arms. "But we are just going to have to wait until his job is finished and he can come back to us. I know he'd like to come home, but he will be here as soon as he can."

"Do you think he will remember us?"

"Oh, yes, he will remember us, William. Just like we remember him."

"Does Daddy like to skate?"

"I've never seen Daddy skate," Mandy replied. "Let's write him a letter and ask that question."

GINGER: SEPTEMBER 1971

After a night of sleepless worry, Ginger was reeling through all that happened since Lorna had come two days earlier.

She was grateful she hadn't seen her again. She wondered what Lorna might tell her Aunt Sarah and what her parents might hear from her, but let it pass as the least of what she might be facing.

She thought about the conversation she'd had with Mandy on the short drive between their two base apartments. They had compared details about their husbands both deployed in Vietnam and their southern roots, and had even exchanged telephone numbers. Mandy didn't seem to have any interest in judging her behavior. Ginger was hopeful that their commonalities would outweigh their embarrassing introduction. At the same time, though, she couldn't shake what she'd done with Mandy's brother from her thoughts.

She lay in bed as she saw the sun moving higher in the sky casting an image of the grids on the wall across from the room's only window and wondered how she might cancel her plans for lunch at Millie's when the phone rang.

She assumed it would be Millie, but was surprised to hear Mandy identify herself and say, "Wanted to check on you."

Ginger sat up and picked up a hairbrush and pulled it through her tangled hair as she talked.

"I'm okay. I'm glad you called."

"I know this has been awkward, but I also know my brother..." she said. She hesitated as if unsure whether to continue the thought, but Ginger finally heard a deep breath and, "Scott has offered to take William to the zoo in Atlanta today before he leaves for Charlotte, and I wondered if you were free for lunch? Maybe we could get to know one another a little better. I was thinking about our conversation and how seldom I get a chance to spend time with another woman."

"Actually, I do have plans, but I would be thrilled if you'd join me for lunch with my friend, Millie."

"Maybe we should just try for another time," Mandy offered.

"Nonsense," said Ginger, happy to be in control. "She loves meeting new friends and I think the three of us could have a lot of fun together. I'll call her right now and let her know you'll join us and I'll call you right back."

As expected, Millie was thrilled and Ginger called Mandy back with confirmation.

"Give me your apartment number though. I didn't make note of it when I was there, and I'll pick you up at noon."

"Perfect. Scott and William just left. I'll be ready."

Ginger meandered the Vega hatchback down the road that led to Millie's long, gravel driveway. "I met Millie just a few days after Pete was home on leave," she explained. "She's quite the character. I know you'll like her."

She saw Millie and Maximilian at the end of the street and slowed down to make the turn. Millie was waving green and yellow crepe paper streamers in the air as Maximilian sat at her feet with his eyes at half mast.

"Toodle oooh," she sang as Ginger stopped the car. The window was rolled halfway down, but she cranked the handle to open it completely when she saw Millie wearing a floral housedress accented with a polka dotted scarf trying to put her face through the window and into the car. "Hello! It's always a good day when you meet a new friend. I'm Millie LaMurphy," she said speaking over Ginger to Mandy in the passenger's seat.

"Hi, Millie. I'm Mandy Rooks," Mandy said extending her hand. "Ginger said I'd like you and I already do."

Millie moved a bouquet of dandelions from to her left hand and palmed it around the crepe paper streamers to shake Mandy's hand. "Welcome to my home, Mandy Rooks. We're going to have a wonderful visit."

Ginger could smell Millie's strawberry Chapstick as she turned her face and attention to the driver's seat and blew a kiss to Ginger.

"And this here's Maximilian LaMurphy, also goes by Maxie Pie." Millie gestured toward the tree where the hound dog had fallen asleep and was snoring with a cadence of deep inhales followed by three short puttering spurts into the damp air. "Park the car, Ginger, and let's get started. Let's go Maxie Pie," she called.

Millie unwrapped the scarf from her neck and dangled the fringe across Maximilian's nose singing, "Company's here Maxie Pie. Time to put on the dog, as they say."

The dog ignored her. She pulled on his loose skin and bandana collar until he gave in to the nudging and followed Millie and her guests to the front door of the trailer where he lay back down on a dusty rag rug and closed his eyes. Millie placed the bouquet of dandelions in front of his nose and stepped on to the wooden stoop.

"I'm making something special for my new friends. I watched Dinah Shore make it on television," she said as she gestured the two younger women into the trailer.

Mandy took in the strings of lights, the mismatched furniture, a small RCA television, and the aquarium that sat atop a makeshift bookshelf of cinder block and wood in Millie's home. "You're sweet to include me, Millie. You have a lovely home. I spend my days and nights with a three-year-old, and while that can be fun, this is a welcome diversion."

"Any friend of Ginger McCarthy's is a friend of mine," said Millie as she opened the oven door and a waft of cooked ham filled the room. "Have a seat ladies. Who wants sweet tea?"

The table had been set with a yellowed, once-white lace tablecloth, cloth napkins and full-sized plates in blue and white.

"Oh, this is lovely Delftware, Millie," said Mandy picking up one of the plates and turning it over. "My grandmother had this peacock design. I always loved it."

"Are you talking about the plates? They were my mother's. I just thought they were plates."

"They're Dutch," said Mandy. "And there are a lot of similar plates like this. The style is called transferware because of the designs that are baked into the plate." She brought the plate to Millie and showed her the back. "See this stamp indicates the artist's initials and date code and certifies it as Royal Delft."

Ginger studied Mandy's face as she talked and swallowed hard with the realization that with all that she and Mandy had in common, she was outmatched in worldliness and maturity though she was only two years younger than Mandy's twenty-five.

Millie shrugged and said, "Well I'm hoping you like what's on top even better," as she pulled out a pie-shaped dish and placed it on the table. "It's called kwish! Let's eat!"

"Kwish?" Ginger asked.

"It's a pie crust, but you fill it with beaten eggs and ham and cheese. You can add vegetables too, if you like. Dinah Shore made it look so delicious."

"Actually Millie, I think it's pronounced 'keesh,' with a long 'e' sound. It's spelled q-u-i-c-h-e," said Mandy.

"Oh long 'e', short 'e', quash, quish, quokkas, it's all the same to our tummies. Now how about that sweet tea?"

"Yes, please," Ginger and Mandy said in unison.

The three women sat. Millie folded her hands in prayer and the other two followed.

"Heavenly Father and Jesus our Savior, please bless the food we are about to eat and let it nourish our bodies as we nourish our souls with new friendships. And God bless Maxie Pie, O'Ray, Ray Senior and the hard-working, far-away husbands of these pretty ladies that have joined me today. Amen. Let's eat!"

Millie cut the steaming pie into four wedges and placed one on each of the three plates as they chatted about their respective families and plans.

"A quokkas, by the way, is a small wallaby native to western Australia," Millie said in the middle of the conversation. "We had one in the petting zoo outside the circus tent. Bet you're glad I'm not serving that." She took another bite and changed the subject, "Mmmmm. Dinah Shore was right!"

Mandy steadied her eyes on the lace tablecloth, clear in the message she'd just been sent. "My Millie," she said. "It is delicious! Is it hard to make?"

"Oh, it's a little complicated," said Millie. "But I figured it out! By the way, ladies, would either of you be interested in a tarot card reading after lunch?"

"I didn't know you could do that, Millie," said Ginger.

"Just something I picked up while working in the circus," she said. "My friend Sylvia gave me lessons and a set of cards. She was good at the tarot and palm reading and crystals, but the tarot cards always fascinated me the most."

"Well sure, I'm game," said Ginger.

"I've got another couple hours at least," Mandy shrugged. "Why not?"

RACHEL: AUGUST 1998

Rachel noted the faded "T&G" stamp still visible on her hand from the night at the Tongue and Groove as she pulled a blank journal from her nightstand to make a shopping list for the bakery items.

"If we're going to do this, we need to be very careful to include all of our hard costs and then add a fair fee for our time prepping, baking, packaging, delivering and even cleaning up," she'd explained to her grandmother earlier that day.

A customer at the church bake sale had been so impressed with the raspberry jam-filled cupcakes that Rachel and Oodles had made, that she tracked down Oodles via Sarah and asked if they could make six dozen for a party for her husband's fiftieth birthday.

She turned back to the front page and scripted "Oodles and 'Chel's" in her best fancy handwriting across the page. She added "Baked Delights," then "Cupcakery," then "Cupcakes and More" underneath as a reminder of ideas to discuss with Oodles.

"Her name is Mrs. Gaston and she'd like them delivered to her house in Buckhead. It's not far from here at all," Oodles had said, carefully reading her notes over the phone to Rachel. "She's asking for three dozen chocolate and three dozen yellow or vanilla. And she'd like half of each flavor to have the vanilla cream inside and the other half with the raspberry jam. I told her we'd have to get back with her regarding the price. She said that wouldn't be a problem at all."

Both of Thursday's interviews had been successful. Rachel knew she was perfectly qualified for both positions and felt she'd interviewed well. Both seemed like jobs she could enjoy. And both company representatives had promised to be in touch with a next step by the end of the month, but Rachel was surprised how intrigued she'd been with the idea of a cupcake business. She'd been thinking about it since she and Oodles had discussed the catering request.

After gathering all the groceries and talking the man behind the bakery counter at the grocery store into giving her three large bakery boxes, she headed to Oodles and Poppy's to prepare for the Friday night party. Poppy met her at the front door.

"Oodles is full of great ideas for this new business of yours," Poppy teased. "I think she may be ready to come out of retirement, Rachel."

"Oh, Poppy, it's just one order," she said kissing him on the cheek and handing him one of the grocery bags. "But I have to admit, I could see a cupcake business working in Atlanta. Let's make these six dozen and see how it goes."

"Don't forget to make enough for taste testing," he said. "I've got a gallon of milk ready for cleansing my palate in between flavors."

"Gotcha covered, Poppy. We'll make plenty for your taste-testing role."

Oodles was wearing a yellow chintz apron and searching through the bottom drawer of the kitchen hutch when Rachel entered.

"Here it is, business partner," Oodles said, standing. She handed Rachel a blue chintz apron with a similar pattern and gave her a kiss on the cheek.

"Oodles, it's just one order," Rachel said, immediately regretting her words when she saw Oodles' embarrassment.

"Oh, I'm just teasing," she said. "But I admit, I am a little excited. It makes me feel young to think about starting a business with my granddaughter."

"Well, I've been thinking about it too, Oodles, and it's not a completely crazy idea."

They set out all the ingredients on to the expansive kitchen table and discussed their plans for the cupcakes. Rachel clipped the grocery receipt to a page in the journal and then opened it to the first page and showed it to Oodles and Poppy.

"If I don't find a job soon," she said. "And if we really *did* think about starting a cupcake business, I think 'Oodles and 'Chel's' would be the perfect name for it. It sounds kind of French, don't you think?"

Oodles clapped her hands but was careful not to say more. "Tell us about your interviews," she said instead.

The three chatted about the interviews while Poppy transcribed his original notes from the first cupcake baking experience into the new journal and Rachel and Oodles dictated measurements and quantities for the new order.

Once all six dozen cupcakes were iced, boxed and labeled, they pulled out a calculator and discussed how to assign costs for each ingredient and totaled the hours that they had each spent.

"If we charge one dollar per cupcake, we are covering our costs and then between us we'll split about $46 for our time," Rachel calculated. "We certainly couldn't make a business work with those kinds of numbers. Will people pay more than a dollar for a cupcake?"

"For 'Oodles and 'Chel's' cupcakes they certainly will!"

Rachel laughed. "Well even so, we will need to spend more time figuring out how this kind of business could scale, but for today, I think we should charge $1.35 each. We aren't doing this just for fun after all."

They spread the boxes across the back seat of Rachel's Escort and drove to the address of the party. Mrs. Gaston squealed with delight when she opened up the first of three boxes and didn't blink when Rachel handed her the bill.

"How should I make out this check?" she asked. "I'm certain you'll get more business from the party tonight. Do you have some business cards I can give guests if they ask?"

Rachel and Oodles looked at one another with regret that they hadn't thought about some kind of marketing piece to leave behind.

"Please write the check to Rachel McCarthy," offered Oodles. "And

I'll write down our phone numbers for you in case anyone asks for them."

After settling back into Rachel's car, Rachel started the engine and looked at Oodles.

"We could have charged more for those cupcakes," she said.

"They are stuffed with filling, after all," said Oodles.

"And she's feeding dessert to about sixty guests for right at $100. That's a really good deal."

"And we could get even fancier with our decorating and charge even more."

"Next time, we'll get this right," said Rachel, just as her cell phone started ringing. "I do think Atlanta could support a specialty cupcake business. Maybe we're on to something."

She pulled her mobile phone from her purse. It was Cameron on the line.

"Rachel, where are you?"

"I'm with my grandmother. We're in the car. Why?"

"I just found a note on my car. It's from the guy we saw on Peachtree Street the other night. The one that was singing to Ricky Martin."

"What? Where was your car?"

"At our apartment!"

"How did he know..."

"Let me read it. It says, 'Civic and Red...'"

"Civic and Red? Oh. Your car, my hair. Okay, go on."

Rachel could tell that Oodles could hear both sides of the conversation from the passenger's seat because she was looking at Rachel with wide eyes and exaggerated facial expressions. She held her fingers over her upper lip and pantomimed, "Did he have a mustache?" as she listened to the conversation.

Cameron continued reading, "We met on Peachtree the other night. I was in the blue Trooper. I know I'm taking a risk by leaving this on your car, but don't worry, I'm not really a creepy stalker. I wrote down your license plate number and a friend's brother works for the motor vehicles department. It was kind of easy to figure out where you live, but I'm harmless. Really. I throw darts every Monday night at the Beer Mug. They don't play a lot of Ricky Martin, but maybe I'll see you there sometime. It seems we're destined to meet. Third time's a charm? Someone said that anyway."

"That's it? Is it signed?" Rachel asked. "Is there a number?"

"It's signed 'LW.'"

"Oh my gosh, Cameron! LW? Larry? Lance? Luke?"

"It just says 'LW.' Maybe it stands for Letter Writer. Whatever, I think we should go Monday night. Even though I think he's interested in you, since you're the one he'd be seeing for the third time!"

"I'll be home in about an hour. Let's talk about it then."

She hung up the phone and asked Oodles, "What made you think of the mustache thing?"

"You told me about the fortune teller and the man with a mustache entering your life. Just wondering if the guy that left a note had a mustache."

"No. Well not exactly," she replied.

She wanted to tell Oodles about the graphic on the t-shirt and the two times she'd run into this blond, curly headed guy, but she was struggling to make sense of it all herself. Then Madam Sylvia's words rang through her head, *Three is a significant number.*

MANDY: OCTOBER 1972

In October, the National Security Advisor Henry Kissinger promised, "Peace is at hand," as he announced plans for a peace settlement between the United States and North Vietnam leader Le Duc Tho.

The plan called for a cease-fire of the fighting and bombing and withdrawal of American troops from North Vietnam in exchange for the release of the American prisoners of war.

Mandy got a call early in the morning from a staff member at Fort Benning's internal communications division and the sound of her own heartbeat nearly drowned out the initial part of the message: "Mrs. Rooks, don't be alarmed. The situation regarding your husband's imprisonment at Hoa Lo Prison is status quo. The Chief Communications Officer has requested that we contact all families to check on any needs that they might have and to re-establish and update our records to ensure that our contact information is correct. Is this the best phone number to reach you while you're in Atlanta?"

The extra long phone cord could stretch from the kitchen wall to the living room or out the back door to the bench on the back porch. Mandy found herself on the back porch bench before she even realized it.

"Yes, thank you, it is," Mandy said. "I hear there is news on Dr. Kissinger's settlement?"

"The situation is progressing, ma'am."

"Is there any news about when the prisoners will be released?"

"No official word at this time, ma'am, but the U.S. Army will be in touch when there is a message or instructions for families. In the meantime, are there any needs that we might help you with? And can you confirm your address on Sycamore Street?"

Mandy gave him the address and added, "No particular needs, sir. Just very anxious, as you can imagine."

"Of course I can imagine, Mrs. Rooks. I'd also like to update contact information for additional family members and close friends who would always know how to reach you."

Mandy moved back into the kitchen and pulled her address book from the drawer. She confirmed the address and phone number for Adam's parents. "Yes, Ted and Sandra Rooks," she said as he repeated back the contact information.

"Other family or close friends?"

"My parents are in upstate New York," she said. "Charles and Eve Everly," and read their address and telephone number from the address book. "I have one brother. He works construction and moves around a lot. I don't have a current address or number for him."

Changing the subject, she asked, "Do you have an idea on the condition of the prisoners?"

"Not that I'm authorized to report, ma'am. Please let us know if you need anything, and immediately update us should your contact information change. We will be in touch just as soon as possible."

GINGER: SEPTEMBER 1971

Millie cleared the quiche plates and tea cups from the table and piled them next to the sink as she instructed Mandy to turn off the lamp and Ginger to pull out the velvet tablecloth from the bottom drawer of her hutch.

"Let's start with Ginger first," Millie said smoothing the velvet cloth across the round table and pulling a cloth-wrapped package from her apron pocket. She carefully placed a stack of cards on the table, refolded the cloth and tucked it back into her pocket.

The cards were just a little smaller than a paperback book and had colorful but unfamiliar designs across each one.

"I learned to read the tarot when I was with Oscar and working in the circus," Millie said. "My friend Sylvia taught me to read the cards in the mornings before our shows. She came from a long line of for-tunetellers. Her mother, grandmother and great-grandmother were all clairvoyants."

She placed three cards face down in a horizontal row across the middle of the table. "We spent a lot of time together when I was preg-nant with O'Ray and had to quit the lion act. She taught me palm reading, too, but I always liked the tarot best."

Millie motioned to Ginger to hover her hands over the cards. Then she closed her eyes and took three deep breaths.

"There are many ways to read the tarot, but my favorite is this sim-ple means using three cards. From left to right they represent past, present and future."

She turned over a card and placed it at the left side of the table.

"Ginger, you can put your hands back now," she said and Ginger pulled them to her lap. "We start with your past, Ginger. And lordy loo, look at this... we have The Sun card."

"Is that good?" Ginger asked.

"The Sun Card is often called The Children Card. As you will see the child on the horse pictured on this card has his arms wide open and appears to be full of joy." Her voice was steady and almost entrancing. "There are two types of cards in the tarot, twenty-two major arcana cards and fourteen cards in each of the four minor arcanas—cups, pentacles, swords and wands—for a total of seventy-eight cards. The Sun Card is one of the most positive cards in the tarot deck."

The mature, confident and professional change in Millie's demeanor as she explained the tarot was evident to both Ginger and Mandy and they exchanged a quick glance.

"This would indicate a happy childhood, perhaps security with your home and evidence of sanctuary. The Sun card can also be an indication of growth, success and happiness."

Before Ginger could comment on her childhood or confirm the card's message, the trio was startled by a single, quick bark from Maximilian sitting just outside the trailer. Ginger looked at Millie, surprised to realize it was the first time she'd ever heard the dog bark.

"Must have seen a rabbit," Millie said, shaking her head to indicate she wasn't worried as she turned over the center card. "And the Nine of Swords in the center."

She hesitated a moment before continuing. "At the present position, the Nine of Swords represents anxiety."

Ginger studied the illustration of a person, with face hidden, sitting up in bed. Nine swords were drawn horizontally across the top of the card, the bottom three behind the man or woman.

Anxious. Can't sleep. Guilt. That couldn't be more true.

"It's easy to see the man or woman depicted on the Nine of Swords looks sad and concerned," Millie said. "While this could indicate tension and worry, also note the colorful quilt that lays across the bottom of the bed and across the lap of the figure. Because he or she is covering their eyes, they cannot see the zodiac symbols on the quilt alternated with bright red roses. The roses are a symbol of love and hope and offer a positive sign toward the future."

Ginger could tell Mandy was staring at her, but she was afraid to raise her eyes. The sound and words Millie used sounded surreal and dream-like. Almost scary.

"The final card is the future card," Millie began again as she flipped the card over. "And now we see the Three of Cups!"

The picture on the card showed three women, each barefoot, standing in a circle and holding cups in the air. They appeared to be dancing in a circle in celebration.

"The perfect card for three new friends," Millie said. "You see how the three maidens are dressed in different colors. The one in white indicates strength, the woman in the crimson robe represents justice and the third woman links the two by wearing both colors and is representative of temperance. The Three of Cups is associated with the element of water. You'll note that two raise their cups with their right hands while the other toasts with her left hand showing that they both give and receive with joy in their hearts."

"I like that one," Ginger said.

"And while the Three of Cups indicates vitality, balance and perhaps even three friendships, it can also represent the feminine principal in the sphere Binah, which is the tree of life in three aspects of the goddess: maiden, mother and crone. So, either an indication of the three stages of your own life or even perhaps indication of the relationship of you with your mother and perhaps a future daughter."

Ginger sat back and took a deep breath, unsure that this had been a good idea, but intrigued by Millie's demeanor. She rolled the portions of her reading that resonated strongest through her mind.

"It seems like there is a lot of personal interpretation with all this," said Mandy. "With all the different various meanings to each card, you could easily find a way to make portions of it true for anyone."

"It's your prerogative to be skeptical of the tarot if you wish," Millie said. "And you are correct. There is a lot of room for interpretation. Are you interested in a reading, Mandy?"

Mandy looked at her watch. It was three o'clock and she wasn't expecting Scott to get back to Columbus with William until dinnertime.

"I am, Millie," she said. "And I have to admit you're good at this. I might be skeptical, but I'm impressed too."

"Well then," Millie said stacking and shuffling the cards and cracking a slight smile. "Let's get to gettin' on, as they say. Place your hands on the deck and take three deep breaths."

Mandy obeyed. Ginger watched her close her eyes as she pulled three deep breaths in as she was told, then slammed her eyes shut when she saw Millie look her way.

"If you'd prefer, we can use the tarot to answer a question," Millie said.

"My husband is fighting with the Army in Vietnam like Ginger's," Mandy said. "I'd be afraid to ask anything too specific about that."

"I understand."

"Maybe something about my son?"

"Certainly," Millie said spreading the cards in a fan shape face down across the table. "With your left hand, you'll select three cards. Mandy, please make your first selection."

Ginger opened her eyes and watched Mandy point to a card with her left hand. Millie picked it up and placed the card below the others.

"Each card of the tarot has 'yes,' 'no,' or 'neutral' meaning in this type of reading. We will ask the question three times, as a single 'yes' or a single 'no,' is not always certain. There are a few exceptions to all this as well, which I'll explain if one of the exception cards should surface."

"Okay. How about 'will Adam and I have more children?'" Mandy asked.

"Will Mandy and Adam have more children?" Millie repeated as she turned over the first card. She drew in her cheeks and held her lips tight together before she spoke. "The Five of Pentacles is a 'no' card."

Ginger looked quickly at Mandy. Her face was crestfallen, but Millie quickly interceded, "But we use three cards with this reading for exactly the reason I mentioned. Not every card provides a definitive answer. Mandy, please select a second card, again with your left hand."

Mandy pointed to a second card.

Millie picked it up and turned the card over next to the first selection as she said, "Will Mandy and Adam have more children?"

At first glance, the card looked like it was upside-down in the deck, but at the bottom of the card were the words, "The Hanged Man." Ginger's eyes widened as she studied the face on the card of a man with a halo around his head hanging upside-down from a tree.

"The Hanged Man is a neutral card," said Millie. "So it indicates neither 'yes' or 'no' to your question. By its name, you may assume that The Hanged Man indicates negativity, but in fact, you'll note his face appears perfectly calm as he hangs upside-down from the tree of life. You'll note the tree is budding with new growth indicating hope and promise."

"I'm not sure this was a good idea," Mandy said, placing her hand across her face. "I really don't want William to be an only child, and this whole thing is scaring me now."

"The fact that your second card was neutral shows that the tarot is not offering a definitive 'no,' Mandy, and you said yourself there are lots of ways to interpret the meanings that are presented with the cards. Why don't you pick your final card?"

Mandy looked over the remaining cards carefully. After long consideration, she pointed to a card and said, "Will William have any brothers or sisters?"

Millie picked up the card, turned it over and placed it to the right of the first two as she repeated Mandy's words, "Will William have any brothers or sisters?"

"The Seven of Wands," she said. "The Seven of Wands is one of the exception cards I mentioned. With this card, the answer is 'yes,' but you must fight for your prize. The Seven of Wands indicates struggle. Getting to your goal requires conviction, persistence and courage."

Mandy's low-cast eyes stared at the velvet tablecloth for a long period of time before finally offering, "Well that was fun, Millie. I'm not sure what I think of all that, but I thank you for inviting me today."

Ginger studied both women carefully and finally offered, "You are good at this Millie. You almost seem like a different person when you explain the tarot."

"Let's do it again soon!" Millie said brightly. "Ginger knows I'm always up for fun."

"The quiche was delicious," Mandy said. "And I'd love to get together again soon. I'll need to bring William, of course."

"The more the merrier. I'd love to meet your son," she said, her voice cracking at the end.

Both women were silent as Ginger backed the car into a flattened clearing and then pulled away from Millie's trailer. She stopped before pulling on to the main road to allow a grey rabbit to hop across their path.

RACHEL: SEPTEMBER 1998

It was raining on Monday night and when Cameron called to say that she would be working late, Rachel was grateful. As much as she wanted to finally talk to the blond stranger with the mustache shirt, she was concerned about appearing too eager. He'd used Cameron's license plate to stalk out their address, and as flattering as that felt on one level, it also felt a little creepy.

Instead, she called her mother and father to talk about her job options.

"'Chel, honey," her mother said when she picked up the phone. "I'm so glad you called."

Rachel was shocked when her eyes filled with tears upon hearing the nickname that she typically only heard from Oodles. She hadn't seen her parents since Christmas and she was surprised at the wave of homesickness that rushed through her stomach and chest.

"Your father is watering the grass. Let me see if I can get this phone cord to stretch far enough to get his attention."

Rachel wiped her eyes, poured herself a glass of water and laughed as she heard her mother calling, "Pete! Pete, pick up the phone in the bedroom. Rachel's on the line."

She and her mother were chatting when she heard the second phone click.

"I've had two interviews so far and I feel comfortable that I'll be offered at least one of the two. And I have another interview this week.

All are marketing positions," she said.

"How are you doing on money?" her father asked.

"Hi Dad," Rachel said. "A little better now. I made one phone call to the secretary at Quince and my final paycheck showed up in the mailbox two days later. I've budgeted out all my expenses and I should be fine if I find a job by mid October."

"Let us know if you get into a bind, Rachel," her father said.

"I'm pretty sure one of these jobs will come through. And besides, if it doesn't, Oodles and I are playing around with the idea of a cupcake business."

"Cupcakes? As a full-time job?" her mother said.

"We did a catering order for a fiftieth birthday party last weekend. Just a crazy idea we are tossing around."

"Crazy, I'll say," said her father.

"You and your grandmother are two peas in a pod," her mother said. "By the way, it looks like Roxanne and P.J. will both be coming to Atlanta with us for Thanksgiving."

"I heard and I'm so glad. We haven't been together for so long. I'm getting homesick to see you."

"Are you dating anyone special, Rachel?" her mother asked.

Rachel looked at the clock. *9:15*. Probably the perfect time for throwing darts at the Beer Mug.

"No, Mom. No boyfriend. No dates. My roommate and I have been hanging out though, so my social life is improving a bit."

"Well good then. I'm not sure about the cupcake idea, but I will hope to hear some good news about your interviews. Please call us as soon as you hear."

"How about your car, Rachel?" her father said. "Are you changing the oil, regularly? Make sure you have your tire pressure checked every month or so, too."

"Thanks, Dad. All good. Love you both and I'll call again soon."

She hung up the phone just as the apartment door opened and Cameron came in tossing her bag onto the sofa.

"Work was horrible!" she said. "I'm ready for a beer and some darts."

"Seriously? Now?" Rachel looked at the clock again.

9:20.

"Why not?" Cameron asked.

"Do you think we'll look too... available?"

"I'm available and ready for a beer and a game of darts," Cameron said. "LW Letter Writer, who may or may not even be there, doesn't have to be our only reason."

"Well, my next interview isn't until Wednesday..."

"Let's go. I'll drive."

Peachtree Street was quiet even for a Monday night. The drizzling rain had kept the pedestrians away and the late summer sky was showing hints of the season to come as the Atlanta skyline came into view at Brookwood Station. Less than two dozen cars filled the small parking lot, so they easily found a spot, parked the car and headed for the door.

Televisions lining the ceiling played the first Monday night game of the football season, a baseball game and a tennis match, but few people paid attention. Most were gathered around small tables or chatting with the bartender.

"Let's get a beer," Cameron said. "Then we'll look around."

Rachel followed her to two bar stools and took a seat. Cameron's confidence and quick decisions intrigued her. She'd always been sure of herself, quick-witted and considered herself fun to be around, but Cameron seemed to be even better at all that.

I'm going to need to up my game.

"I'll have a beer on draft," Cameron told the bartender.

"We have a special on a local brew called Sweetwater," said the bartender.

Cameron looked at Rachel and the two nodded.

"Two, please," Cameron told him.

They sipped their beers at the bar while both took furtive glances around the bar.

The bartender caught Rachel's eye and offered a raised-eyebrow nod toward her beer.

"Yes, it's great! Thanks for the recommendation."

Cameron tapped her back. "So let's find this mystery man it seems you're destined to meet," Cameron said, sliding off her stool. Rachel followed just as a loud cheer came from an adjoining room partially separated from the main bar.

They shared a look and followed the cheers.

The room was quiet again and all of the eight people in the room were facing the back wall. One of only two women prepared to throw her dart as the rest of the group watched.

Rachel picked out the tall blond right away. He was wearing a pair of madras plaid shorts, a red t-shirt and the same cheap flip flops he'd been wearing at the post office. He was standing next to the woman ready to throw and it appeared the game was between the two of them.

The woman threw her dart and the crowd roared again.

All moved toward the dartboard and then debated among themselves before determining her to be the winner. The small crowd clapped, high-fived, hugged and picked up their glasses to cheer the two of them.

Rachel watched as LW and the woman both moved to the dartboard and pulled darts from either side of the rim of the center hole.

As they turned back toward the center of the room, Rachel ducked behind a wooden column and looked around for Cameron. She was sitting at a high-top table watching her and waved her over.

"Do you think they're together?" Rachel asked.

"I can't tell yet. Why don't you sit across from me and I'll watch."

"If they are together, we are going to dash for the door, so figure it out quickly."

Cameron provided a discreet play-by-play as the roommates pretended to be deep in conversation.

"Bingo," she said. "The woman just walked over to the guy in fatigues and the wife beater and they kissed. Now he has his arm around her."

Rachel sighed. "Yes!"

Then, just as quickly, "Mayday. Mayday. LW has spotted us and he's headed this way."

"Oh, shit." Rachel grabbed her beer and took a big swig.

"Ladies?" He put his beer on the table and placed his elbows on either side. As he rotated his head slowly between them, Rachel realized his impish smile and brown eyes were even more fabulous than she'd remembered. "I'm glad to see you're dart fans."

"Well if it isn't LW," Cameron said.

He laughed. "I'm glad you didn't think I was a creepy stalker finding your car like that."

"Oh we do," Rachel said. "But we also found the Ricky Martin song into the fist pretty fascinating."

"Plus, who doesn't come out on the town on a Monday night?" Cameron teased. "We're regulars here."

"Shocking it's taken us so long to meet then," he said smiling. He took a sip of his beer and smiled at them both without offering an introduction.

"So, we've been calling you 'Letter Writer.' Does the 'LW' have any other meaning?" Rachel asked.

"In fact it does. I'm Liam Wilson."

"Liam Wilson," Rachel said, mulling the name in her head. "So, you're not a lawyer or a juggler..."

"Or a professional dart player or a pop singer," he said. "But I can't give away all my secrets yet. Tell me about you."

"I'm CC," Cameron offered. "Cameron Clark."

"Cameron Clark," he said shaking her hand. "Blue-eyed Cameron Clark who drives a baby blue Civic. And you're a diver? I saw the license plate on the front of your car."

"Well, once. In the ocean," she said. "I got my certification at Dynamo and I've been on one dive in the Bahamas. So, sort of."

He nodded and turned to Rachel who extended her hand.

"I'm RM. Rachel McCarthy."

"Well it's about time we actually meet, Rachel McCarthy. I've been looking forward to this."

Rachel studied his face and tried to picture him with a mustache, but was glad the image didn't work. Despite his killer smile, he had a baby face and she noted a patch of freckles across his nose and cheeks. A small raised scar across the bottom of his left eye looked like he'd likely had stitches. His eyes were the color of a Hershey's bar.

Rachel searched for her next words, but he began again, "I've always liked red hair, by the way."

"I like to call it auburn," she said, pulling her hand to tuck her hair behind her ear. "But thanks. My mother is a redhead—hers is more strawberry blonde—so I come by it rightly."

"And Rachel McCarthy has a lovely Irish-sounding lilt to it," he said.

"Well, that too, so I guess I was destined.. In fact my mother's first name is Ginger. How's that for the perfect name for a redhead?"

A waitress stopped at the table and Liam pulled a stool to the end of the table and sat. They ordered another round and the trio laughed, shared stories and introductions. One by one, groups of Liam's dart-throwing friends dropped by the table to say "goodbye." He introduced them to Rachel and Cameron. Soon they realized they were the only ones left in the small side room.

They each looked around and then at each other. "It looks like it might be time for us to go home," Rachel said.

"Anyone got a pen?" Liam asked.

Cameron pulled one from her clutch and Liam wrote a phone number on a cocktail napkin and pushed it to the center of the table.

Rachel took the napkin and wadded it in her hand. "Better idea," she said taking the pen from his hand and pulling another napkin from the silver dispenser. "Here's our number at our apartment," she said as she wrote. "Your move next."

"You're on," he said.

Cameron raised her glass and the other two did the same. "La Copa De La Vida! The Cup of Life!" she cheered.

"Al-lay, al-lay, al-lay!" Liam and Rachel sang in unison.

MANDY: JANUARY 1973

Hopes faded a few days after the initial announcement of Kissinger's peace agreement.

South Vietnam's President Nguyen Van Thieu was angered with the details of the secret negotiations that had not included him and felt that the treaty's conditions would jeopardize his country making it vulnerable to attacks from the Viet Cong.

Frustrated, President Richard Nixon ordered B-52 bombings of North Vietnam's Hanoi and Haiphong. The attacks—named Operation Linebacker II—began in late December and lasted several weeks. A ceasefire and a pledge of nearly one-billion dollars in military support for South Vietnam from the United States brought the four sides back to the negotiating table in mid January of 1973.

Then finally on January 27, 1973—after nearly five years of negotiations—the Paris Peace Accords were signed by representatives of the United States, North Vietnam, South Vietnam and the Viet Cong's National Liberation Front calling an end to the nearly thirty-year war.

Mandy was glued to the television. A ceasefire of all forces would begin the next day, and all sides would have sixty days to release their prisoners and remove all troops. Vietnamese citizens were to be given the choice for their own political future and reunification of the country would happen via peaceful means.

While the news reports offered a cynical mix of jubilation by most and contempt about the war itself from many others, Mandy's heart soared with excitement. She rubbed the engraved letters across the silver P.O.W. bracelet she wore on her wrist. The indentation was familiar. She could read each letter with the tip of her finger as it traveled across the cool metal: LT. ADAM J. ROOKS USA 4-7-72. Adam had been held captive at Hanoi's Hoa Lo Prison for more than nine months and now he was finally coming home.

William was down for a nap and, and wishing there was someone to celebrate the news with, Mandy had just begun a letter to Adam.

She heard four knocks on the door and stood to walk toward it. As the knock's cadence replayed in her head, an ominous feeling filled her body. She turned the knob, but made a notable hesitation before pulling the door into the small foyer. The sun was setting and offered an eerily bright backdrop to the two uniformed officers standing at the door.

"Amanda Everly Rooks?" the taller man asked.

"Yes." Her eyes darted back and forth between the two men.

The shorter man introduced himself as Army Chaplain Captain John Mixon from Fort Benning, then said, "I'm here today with Major Paul R. Palmer. Major Palmer serves as the U.S. Army's Casualty Relations officer." He handed Mandy two cards with the U.S. Army seal across the middle. "May we come in?"

No. Please just go away and make this not true.

"Yes, of course," she said.

"Is there anyone here with you, Mrs. Rooks?"

"My son. He's four. He's napping."

"Do you have parents or siblings close by?"

"My husband's parents live just a few miles away. Is there news about my husband coming home? I just heard that the prisoners would be released..."

"Yes, ma'am. But I'm afraid that's not why we are here..."

The world was celebrating the end of the war and the news of the return of the P.O.W.s, and she was here with these two men that seemed destined to crush her world and the world of her son.

"Mrs. Rooks, I'm afraid we have some very bad news for you."

The silhouettes of the officers seemed to pulse in and out of Mandy's vision as did the sound of Major Palmer's voice as he continued. "We have learned and confirmed that Lieutenant Rooks died at Hoa Lo Prison."

Mandy made no movement.

Major Palmer continued, "Our intelligence has confirmed that your husband died from complications of a staph infection. The Army has determined the date of death to have been January 22."

"A staph infection?"

"We do hope we can provide more thorough details as the weeks progress, but as you might assume, the Vietnamese have provided minimal medical assistance to prisoners that have needed attention. We understand that this infection may have started in a wound that Lieutenant Rooks received on his right calf. The Army will do everything possible to provide you with a thorough report."

Mandy nodded slowly.

"The good news, Mrs. Rooks, is that we have been able to secure the body and it is being transported to the United States as we speak. The U.S. Army will make all arrangements for a formal military burial. If you are in agreement, you will be contacted by a member of the Army's Civil Affairs division to discuss the arrangements later this week."

Mandy managed a second nod.

"Is there anyone you would like us to contact for you, Mrs. Rooks?"

"No. Thank you."

"On behalf of the Vice Chief of Staff and the entire Unites States Army, I offer our most sincere condolences, Mrs. Rooks. Your husband was a brave and loyal soldier for his country during this difficult crisis and his sacrifice is duly noted and deeply appreciated."

Her head throbbed and her chest felt as if it were filled with slow drying cement.

"I think I just want to be alone," she managed.

"Would you allow me to say a prayer before we go, Mrs. Rooks?"

said Captain Mixon.

"Yes. Of course."

Mandy bowed her head but Mixon's words had no meaning as visions of Adam dying on a cold, concrete floor roared through her head.

The body is being transported back the United States as we speak.

She noted a reference to William in Mixon's words and her stomach turned over to the point she felt a retch gathering momentum at the pit of her stomach.

William will never know his father. And Adam will never know William.

"In your name we pray," Mixon said. "Amen."

"Amen," Mandy said, and then took hold of a burst of strength that enveloped her body. "Gentlemen, I know this is difficult on both sides. I thank you for your graciousness and your sincerity, and would request that I be left alone now."

"Of course, Mrs. Rooks. You have our numbers. Please call with any needs you might have."

She closed the door and moved to the window to watch the two men walk down the concrete walkway to a dark sedan parked across from her rented house on Sycamore Street.

She walked into the kitchen where she kept her cigarettes and beanbag ashtray. She fumbled for the lighter then changed her mind. She turned, slipped off her shoes and tiptoed into William's room and lay down beside him in his twin-sized bed. He grunted and moved slightly with his back to her so that she was able to curl around him.

GINGER: SEPTEMBER 1971

Ginger brought banana bread, a thermos of iced tea and three plastic tumblers when she met Millie, Mandy and William at the community garden three days after the quiche and tarot reading. Mandy brought her camera and took photos of William walking around the raised garden plots and of Ginger and Millie weeding the beds and filling Millie's baskets with squash, collards, radishes and lettuce. Once they were finished, Millie piled the baskets in the back of the truck bed and brought out a thick winter quilt and spread it across the grass.

The trio of new friends stretched across the blanket and enjoyed the early fall sunshine as William played in the nearby sandbox. The two younger women sat cross-legged, while Millie stretched her legs across the top of the blanket with her gauze skirt fanning more than half of the woolen quilt.

"Tell us about your husband, Mandy," Millie said. "Adam, is it?"

"Yes. Adam Rooks," she said. "Adam was stationed at Wunder Beach along the Vietnam coast but he's been transferred to Long Binh Post. His job is working with the Army's logistics and supplies. I got a letter from him yesterday. He sent a Polaroid photo of him with the guys in his barracks."

"He was here in May over William's birthday," she continued. "But that's the only time William has seen him. I was seven months pregnant when he deployed."

"How did you meet?" Ginger asked.

"Well that's a little crazy, actually," Mandy said. "Adam likes to tell his friends I was naked when we met."

Both Ginger and Millie let out a little scream and the three of them instinctively looked toward William whose attention they had attracted from the sand box.

"Everything's fine sweet pea. We were just laughing," Mandy yelled, and William went back to his work.

Mandy continued, "I was skinny dipping with some friends in a backyard pool in Atlanta. There were three other women and two men in the pool—the guys were both boyfriends of two of the women. Adam came into the back yard with another guy and we were introduced."

"Did he skinny dip, too?"

"No, we told him and his friend to turn around and a couple of us got out of the pool and got dressed before he turned around. Plus," she added. "I had really long hair then and it was kind of dark. He really couldn't see anything. He just thinks it's funny to tell his friends."

"And it was love at first sight?" Ginger asked.

"Pretty much. We shared a lot of music interests and we were both kind of borderline hippies at the time. He's very quick-witted and funny. I was attracted to that right away. That, and his cleft chin and broad shoulders and sexy buns."

Millie laughed and held up her iced tea cup in a toast. "To sexy buns," she snorted.

"Mmm," said Ginger. "I'd love to meet him. And I can't imagine you with long hair. It's so precious short."

"It was down to my waist. I chopped it off a few days before our wedding."

"Did you both grow up in Atlanta?"

"He did. I grew up in Rome, in northwest Georgia. Adam's parents still live in Atlanta, but mine transferred to New York after my brother and I graduated from high school."

Ginger's eyes dropped at the mention of Scott.

"I spent some time in Rome, Georgia, myself," Millie spouted. "Our circus stopped there when I was still helping Oscar with the lion act. We set up camp right along the Coosa River."

"That's not far from where I grew up at all."

Mandy's delicate nose and tiny, chiseled cheekbones were contrasted by oversized, round, chocolate brown eyes. She wore small silver hoop earrings in her ears and a lightweight V-neck sweater that looked like it could have been Adam's or her brother's. A tiny cross on a thin silver chain sat in the base of her neck.

"We both started college, but it's on hold until he gets back from Vietnam, of course," she added. "He wants to get into Georgia Tech and study engineering. I need just a few more semesters before I can get my nursing degree. Adam is a very sweet and gentle man. He's going to be a fabulous father if this damned war will ever end."

She smiled at her new friends. "Tell me about Pete. And, Millie I'd love to hear more about your time in the circus. And your son, if that's not too sensitive a subject," Mandy said.

"Ginger first," Millie squealed. "Tell us about Pete McCarthy."

"It won't surprise me if Pete stays in the Army even after the war," Ginger began. "He's mentioned it many times and I think he was cut out for a military career. He's patriotic and driven and I know he'd make a great Master Sergeant or Command Sergeant some day."

The natural streaks in Ginger's strawberry blonde hair looked even lighter as the autumn sun bounced across it and were perfectly contrasted by her clear, pale jade-colored eyes. Mandy had mentioned the unique green color to her several times and referenced her mother's Celadon pottery collection.

"He grew up in Indiana but we met in Atlanta when he was in basic training. I'm from Atlanta, a neighborhood called Garden Hills. My parents are still there. His father passed away when he was in high school, but his mother is still in Indiana."

"Were you naked when you met?" Millie said and then laughed with a high-pitched snort at her own joke.

Mandy looked toward William who was still busy in the sand box.

"No. We were both fully clothed," answered Ginger. "We were standing next to one another in line at a bank when we met. Nothing as exciting as Mandy's story."

"And how did you turn a wait in the bank line into a relationship?"

"While we were talking, we realized we had a mutual friend. He got my number through him and called the next week."

"How long since you've seen him?" Mandy asked.

"He was here for two weeks at the beginning of August. He was in Panama for seven months after we married last November. Now he's at Camp Eagle in Vietnam. For now, they tell us he'll be home next August."

"Other kin?" Millie asked.

"Well, besides my parents, I have an older brother. His name is Carlton."

"Is he in the service?" Mandy asked.

"He did four years in the Air Force, but never went to 'Nam. He was based in California for a while and then in Alaska for three years."

"Lucky," Mandy muttered.

"Yep."

"Do you and Pete plan to have children?" Millie asked.

Another wave of guilt rushed through Ginger's body and she felt her insides shudder.

What if....?

Ginger raised her eyes to sneak a peek at Mandy who seemed sincerely curious as well, and like their first meeting, showed no judgment.

"We definitely want children," Ginger said. "Some day," her voice trailed.

She wondered if she would feel just as guilty if Mandy's presence wasn't a constant reminder of her unfaithfulness.

Of course I would. God, how could I have been so stupid?

"I think you'll make a wonderful mother someday, Ginger McCarthy," Millie snapped as if sensing her melancholy.

"Thanks, Millie. Me too. Now, tell us about the circus."

"The Billings Brothers Circus came to Columbus when I was seventeen," she said. "I still had another year of high school, but I had ants in my pants to do something different, if you know what I mean."

She looked at her two new friends, both half her age, and winked. They smiled and she continued. "A woman at the circus was selling tickets from the side of a red and white striped trailer. I introduced myself and asked her if there were any jobs I might apply for. She said, 'Honey, if you'd like to sell tickets, I'm leaving after this shift. I met a fella who wants to marry me and take me to Florida to be a part of a water show with real mermaids down there.'"

"I said I would like to do that and how can I apply, and she said, 'Just come back after we close up tonight and I'll introduce you to Sid Billings. I haven't told him I'm leaving yet, so he won't have any choice but to hire you.'"

Millie cocked her head and picked up her glass of tea. "So I did. And I started working there the next morning. After a week I told my Daddy when it was time for us to pack up for the next city."

"And you never finished high school?"

"Nah. Don't 'spect I missed too much though. I learned everything I've ever needed to know in the circus."

"And that's how you met Oscar?"

"Yep. Oscar had six trained lions and had joined Billings about four years earlier. I didn't know him, but I'd seen him around the food tent and the campsite a few times, and lordy loo, was that man 'sizzle-your-pants' handsome!"

Rachel and Mandy laughed and urged her on.

"One night after a really big show in Anniston, Mr. Billings treated a bunch of us to dinner at the Howard Johnson's for their all-you-can-eat fried clam night. There were about forty of us, so we couldn't all eat at the same table. After I finished, I went outside to wait on the rest of the folks that hadn't finished yet."

Millie halted her story and nodded toward the sandbox as she saw

William wandering over toward the blanket.

"Mommy, I'm thirsty," he said.

Mandy poured iced tea into his sippy cup and gently swatted the sand from his hands and legs as he drank. "Why don't you put your head down on my lap and take a rest?" she said. He snuggled into her lap and Mandy stroked the back of his curls while Millie continued.

"So, the Howard Johnson's had this big porch in the front of the restaurant with a long row of adriatic chairs."

Mandy and Ginger looked at one another. "Wait, Millie, do you mean 'Adirondack' chairs?" Mandy asked.

"Exactly. The ones with the low seat and the high arm rests." Millie demonstrated by holding her arms out to the side and front as if she were sitting in the chair.

"Anyway, I was sitting in one of those chairs just watching the cars go by when Oscar Swift sat down beside me and introduced himself. I already knew who he was, but I didn't tell him that. I think I charmed him that very first night though, because he started finding a reason to hang around the ticket booth every day while I was setting up and counting money."

Ginger watched William's brown eyes as his lids dropped lower and lower. After a dozen or so slow flutters, they finally closed and his breathing deepened.

"He's out, Mandy," she whispered, nodding toward the three-year-old sleeping boy.

Mandy looked down at her son and smiled. She picked up the camera and handed it to Ginger with a nod. Ginger understood and steadied the lens until she had Mandy and her sleeping son framed with a small bit of the blanket below and the gardens behind them to tell a story of their afternoon. She snapped the photo and handed the camera back to Mandy.

"Thanks," she mouthed to Ginger. Then, "Tells us more, Millie."

"After that I started spending time with him at practices and I got to where I really loved his lions—Zeus, Satyrs, Apollo, Leda, Aphrodite and Pan. He made me a part of the show until my pregnant belly got too big for the costume and I went back to the ticket booth."

"And the baby traveled with you?"

"Absolutely. There was a childcare center that was part of the circus, where the kids stayed while the parents were performing. O'Ray—that's what we call him—Oscar Ray Swift, Jr., grew up with the lions too. He helped with practice and feeding from early on."

"And what about school?" Mandy asked.

"Well that turned out to be our problem. When it was time for O'Ray to go to school, I wanted the three of us to stop touring and find a job in Columbus where we could put O'Ray in a traditional school and settle down. Oscar wouldn't quit the circus, so I suggested that O'Ray and I move to Columbus and he could stay with the circus and visit us on the off-season. Well, that's when Oscar took off with him. I suspect he switched to one of the other circus companies because I haven't seen hide nor hair of either of 'em for about five years."

"Wow. I wish we could help somehow," Mandy said. "What have you done to try and find them?"

"Lots of letters. Sometimes I address the letter to the Billings management staff and sometimes to some of the friends I had there. I've sent letters every month for more than five years, but I've never got a reply. If they ever get close enough to Columbus, I'll go myself to find them, but I don't really even know if they've stayed with Billings Brothers or not."

"Do you think your friend who taught you the tarot reading is still with the circus?" Ginger asked.

"Sylvia? I'm not sure about that either. I sent a letter to her just last month."

The wind picked up and Mandy looked at her watch.

"Well, this has been a great afternoon. It's already after five o'clock."

"I've had a great time, too," said Millie. She picked up her near-empty cup of ice tea and raised it in the air. "To us!"

Mandy and Ginger raised their matching Tupperware tumblers

and the three clinked their plastic cups.

"To the Three of Cups!" Millie shouted. "Mandy, Ginger and Millie. We're just like the goddesses on the Three of Cups tarot!"

Rachel: September 1998

A digitized '3'—the three parallel lines and the two vertical lines on the right—were flashing red on the answering machine Rachel and Cameron shared when she returned home from a run Thursday morning.

It was her second day of a commitment to exercise, something she never felt she had time for while working full time, and she was hoping she'd begin to enjoy it before she found a job that offered another excuse.

She tossed her keys on the counter, picked up the notepad and pen ready to make notes of any messages for Cameron and pushed the button.

"Hi 'Chel, honey." It was Oodles' voice. "You won't believe it, but we've had another request for our cupcakes. This time it's for a children's party and they are wondering if we could decorate the cupcakes like those little Teletubby creatures that are on TV. You know what I mean? One's yellow. One's red. One's purple, I think? Call me back and let's talk about this. Love you, sweetheart."

She'd already spent two afternoons researching what they'd need to start a cupcake business and was meeting Audrey for happy hour later in the week to pick her brain about the idea. Audrey's concierge position made her a terrific resource on most every subject and she was a creative, out-of-the-box thinker. Rachel filled a notebook with calculations of costs and volume needed to cover overhead. With her own background in the dot-com arena, she was confident that she could create a website for their business that would allow for on-line orders and would expand reach much further than Atlanta. She'd even researched packaging and shipping options that she felt could work. The biggest hurdle was that to get licensed, they would need a commercial kitchen, and the little bit of research she'd done for rentals swayed the numbers to a point she couldn't get comfortable.

When prompted, she pressed the button to erase the message and a new voice came from the tape recorder.

"This is Kate Richardson from ERG Global calling for Rachel McCarthy. We'd like to schedule a second interview for you to meet with our CEO and CFO. Could you please return the call and let me know of your availability for Tuesday next week?"

Rachel wrote the number and details. ERG Global was the position she was most interested in. She'd been impressed with the woman she would be reporting directly to and was excited at the opportunities the position offered for travel. The company's headquarters were in San Francisco and she'd already learned there would be a two-week training there.

A great chance to see my sister and brother.

This time she pressed the '2' to save the message, just in case she misplaced her note or needed to hear it again.

The third message was from the one person she'd unsuccessfully tried to put out of her mind, fearing he wouldn't call. She felt her face flush when she heard his voice.

"Hello ladies, it's Liam. You may remember me as 'Letter Writer.' I hope you're having a great week. Had a great time shooting the breeze with you Monday night. I'm having a few friends over on Sunday to watch some football and order pizza. Would love to have you two come by. Call me and I'll give you the address. Your move now. Here's the number."

This time Rachel pressed '3' to repeat the message and pressed it two more times before writing down the number and then saving it for Cameron to hear.

Rachel ran to the stereo, turned up the volume and began dancing around the apartment before it occurred to her that she forgot about the other two calls. She turned the stereo off and returned the call to Kate Richardson and confirmed the Tuesday interview.

She dialed her grandparents' number and Poppy picked up.

"Hi sweet pea," he said. "Your grandmother is at the hairdressers."

"Oh of course, Thursdays at ten. Should have thought of that," Rachel said. "Poppy, I won't be able to come over this week for dinner so be sure to tell Oodles. I've been invited to a football party."

"Well don't make missing Sunday night dinners a habit, young lady. You know it's my favorite part of the week."

"Definitely not. I'll be there next Sunday for sure, Poppy. But also tell her I got her message about the Teletubby cupcakes and we can definitely do that. Tell her to accept the order and we can talk later."

"I'm writing it down right now. 'Teletubby,' you say?"

"They are crazy little guys with televisions in their bellies, Poppy. It's a British show for kids."

"Doesn't sound like my bag. Is that the right word?"

Rachel laughed. "A couple of decades ago it might have been, but you're right: Teletubbies wouldn't be your bag. Love you, Poppy, and I'll see you soon."

Rachel hung up the phone and thought about the party.

Is this three-way invitation a prelude to a real date, or is it too awkward for him to single me out at this point? What if he likes Cameron instead? What if Cameron likes him?

After wrangling the questions in her mind, she slid her feet out of her running shoes and decided to spend her day sending another batch of resumes.

Cameron was excited about the plan when she got home from work. "Awesome. The Falcons are playing the Eagles on Sunday," she said. "Let's tell him we'll be there."

On Sunday, Rachel dressed in a red cashmere sweater tucked into a pair of cinch-waist jeans. She added a red patent-leather belt and a pair of high-top sneakers. She pulled her hair into a ponytail and added simple pearl studs in her ears.

Cameron came out in her bathrobe and fuzzy pink slippers.

"Get in the shower, girl," Rachel shouted. "The party starts in thirty minutes!"

"I'm sorry, Rach," I'm not going to be able to go after all."

"What? Why? What's the matter?"

"I think I'm coming down with something."

"Like what? I have a whole medicine cabinet of stuff in my room. What do you need?"

"No, Rach. I really don't think I should be going. I could get everyone sick."

Rachel's heart sank. She couldn't go alone and she didn't want Liam to think she wasn't interested. And she'd been so excited about it.

"Bum," she said, sinking into the living room club chair. "Well, if you're sick..."

"It doesn't mean you can't go, Rachel. You should. It will be better this way anyway. I'd really just be a third wheel."

"It's a party, though. He said he had other friends coming. And who knows, maybe you and Liam would be a better match than me and Liam. Or maybe we'd all just be great friends. Or maybe there will be another cute guy there," she said. "Besides, I'd never go without you."

"What do you mean, you wouldn't go without me? Of course you can! You should! He's adorable and I know he thinks you are too."

"First of all, you don't know that. And second, I'm just too big of a chicken."

"First," Cameron said. "I do know that. It's written all over his face. And yours isn't suppressing any signs of crush either, if you want to know the truth."

Rachel blushed, but didn't argue.

"And second, you're not too chicken. Take your mobile phone and call me once you get there to let me know everything is cool. If it's not, I'll come right over and get you out of there. He seems like a great guy, Rachel. You really need to go."

"You're not really sick, are you, Cameron?"

"No, not really. But do call me as soon as you get there for a safety check. I think this guy's worth an afternoon."

"I really can't. I am a chicken."

Cameron pulled Rachel out of the chair. She turned her toward the door and placed her hands on Rachel's shoulders. "You can. And you're not," she said. "Give this guy a chance. What have you got to lose?"

Mandy: February 1973

"Mommy, don't leave me!"

William's reddened and teary face was smashed against the screened door as Mandy got into the back seat of her father-in-law's car.

"Ted, just go on," Mandy said. "It breaks my heart, but my mother and father are taking him to the park. He'll calm down soon."

"Maybe I should stay here," said Sandra.

"I really think it would be best if he got to know my parents without you or me around, Mother Rooks," Mandy said. "I don't expect he'll be able to jump into the kind of relationship he has with you two, but they will like one another once they've had the chance."

She watched her mother pick William up and turn away from the door as Ted backed up the car, but she could see his legs kicking and her mother put him back down again and watched as the door closed.

Ted and Sandra were quiet as they drove to Fort Benning's GRS office. The chaplain John Mixon who had come to Mandy's home five days before had called to schedule the 10 a.m. meeting.

"You'll be meeting with two Mortuary Affairs officers at the Graves Registration Service," Mixon had said over the telephone. Mandy cringed at the department names, while he continued. "I would imagine Lieutenant Rooks' parents will want to be there, but of course I'll leave those details to you."

"Yes, of course," she said. "There will be the three of us."

Mandy was grateful for the quiet as she leaned her head along the cushion of the back seat of the car and stared blankly out the window. William had always been an easy child and had never cried when Mandy left before, but the past week had changed them both. William's numbness when he heard about his father's death was understandable. He was too young to understand death, but the fact that he'd only had a handful of actual memories with his father, made it even more difficult to imagine him grieving. For William, it was Mandy's behavior that scared him. As hard as she tried, she couldn't hide the hollowness she felt, even in front of William.

At twenty-six, she was a widow. For four years she had raised their son on her own, working hard to be a perfect mother and a father to him, so that she could share him with Adam when he returned, and he could see first-hand what a wonderful and amazing child they had made together. Now, the enormity of raising their son through childhood, puberty, the teenage years and into adulthood all alone crushed across her shoulders and hammered through her muscles and back. Worse, she couldn't shake the image of Adam dying on a cold, concrete floor, likely knowing full well that the untreated infection was killing him, yet he never even mentioned the injury or the pain to Mandy.

Her parents had never met Adam and had seen William only once before. Almost three years earlier, they'd scheduled a stop in Atlanta on their way to Miami for a Caribbean cruise and drove one night from the airport to Columbus for an afternoon visit. They'd peeked in on him while he napped and then saw him for an hour or so while Mandy was bathing him and getting him ready for bed. Mandy was certain that he was just days from walking and was hopeful they might witness William's first steps, but even though she offered her bed, they opted to stay in a hotel that night and drove back to Atlanta early the next morning for the second leg of their flight.

They were quick to come when she called this time, though. They agreed to stay in her room and Mandy and William would share his twin bed. He'd always been such a good sleeper, she worried that this could cause a setback for him, but she justified the plan by putting him to bed every night as usual and then slipping in beside him after he was fast asleep.

Her parents flew down the day after she called and left their return flight open assuring Mandy they would stay as long as she needed them. Her mother was fixated on the irony of the timing—dying of a staph infection the same week that the war had ended and the prisoners were finally set to go home. The timing—and the irony—hadn't missed Mandy either, but she had finally, the night before, asked her mother to stop bringing it up.

Just an hour or so later, though, Eve Everly was reading the baby book that Mandy had been keeping for William and made note of the date of William's first steps.

"Oh, darling, little William started walking on June 9, 1969," she called to Mandy from the living room. "That's the same day our cruise ship took off from Miami when your father and I went to Jamaica and the Virgin Islands."

"I remember," Mandy said, rounding the corner from the kitchen. "Remember you saw him for the first time the night before? I remember telling you I thought he was just days away from walking."

Eve laughed. "Isn't that ironic?"

As soon as she realized she'd used the word again, Eve looked at her daughter to see if she'd hit a nerve.

"Ironic, Mom," Mandy said as she headed back to the kitchen.

Satisfied that she hadn't, Mandy's mother continued chatting, as she perused more pages of the baby book. "I'll never forget that date because your father got such a kick out of the 6-9-69 reference as we headed to all those romantic islands."

The words swatted just as idiotic the second time as Mandy recounted the conversation in her mind and Ted turned the car toward an unassuming one-level office building. And just like the night before, she'd felt a surprising release of pressure from her shoulders as resolve filled her head, "I can do this," she said loudly inside her head.

"And I can do this on my own."

"Well, it looks like this is where we're going," her father-in-law said taking a long, steady look at Sandra and a second one at Mandy in the back seat. "And we're right on time. Ready, ladies?"

The trio took a collective sigh and opened their car doors.

GINGER: OCTOBER 1971

Ginger remembered before she'd even opened her eyes on Monday morning: The deadline day she'd imposed for herself had arrived. She reached between her legs to see if there were any signs of dampness on her panties.

No.

"Okay," she said inside her head. "I'll get up and go to the bathroom and then I'll know for sure."

Inside the bathroom, she held her breath as she checked for any signs of her period, and she let it back out slowly when she found none.

She walked back to the bedroom and pulled the calendar out of the bedside table and checked the tiny star marks she'd made again.

Albeit light, she'd had a period that started nine days after Pete left to return to Vietnam. She had five little star marks on the dates she'd had blood. She'd found herself in Mandy's brother's bed—with Scott Everly if she dared to think his name—on a date fourteen days after that, and now it had been twenty-two days since then and she still hadn't started her period.

Oh, God. I'm so stupid. This can't be happening.

And again, she counted the months from the date twenty-two days before. Nine months would be June. Late May if she was lucky. But nine months from Pete's leave during the summer would be early May. Or even late April.

What do I do? Should I see a doctor and get a date? Should I tell Pete I'm pregnant and hope the dates work out? Should I tell Pete the truth?

It's not a good idea to tell him the truth now, she justified. He's got to keep his mind on his job, and on staying alive.

Should I see the Army's doctor on base?

No. Not a good idea, she decided. She pulled out the welcome manual that she and Pete had received when they moved into the base's family housing. She knew there had been a list of Columbus area shops, vendors and medical specialists in the back.

She thumbed through the pages and found two names under obstetricians: Mark J. Cohen and Rhuben Z. Schwartz. She called the first number. After providing her name and address and more information than she'd really hoped to share on the telephone, the receptionist asked her reason for needing the appointment, followed by a long list of questions about the dates of her period and best guess as to date of conception.

"I really don't remember," she lied. "But I know it's been thirty-six days since my last period."

"Okay, honey, why don't you give us a call back in about a month and we'll schedule an appointment to see the doctor in December," she said. "It's much too early for the doctor to give you any real diagnosis now and the tape measure won't be able to determine any due date this early. In the meantime, eat well and take it easy. Remember, you're eating for two! Hard lemon candy may help if you experience any morning sickness."

"Yes, ma'am. Thank you."

She hung up the phone and reeled through another round of questions.

Should I tell Pete that I'm pregnant now or wait?

If I wait, he might find it odd that I kept it from him for so long. What if I told him now and then miscarried? That would be more devastating to him than not knowing. But then again, who am I really trying to protect with that reasoning? Pete or myself?

Ginger paced the floor, went back to the bathroom to check again, and went back to pace the floor.

I can't talk to Mother about this. And I can't keep this to myself.

She thumbed through the hand-me-down copies of *Redbook* and *Good Housekeeping* that she'd picked up at the base book exchange. She turned on the television. She took a shower. And then she did what she knew she would do all along: She drove to Mandy's apartment.

Mandy put on a pot of coffee and they sat in the living room to talk.

I'm ten days late," Ginger said once they were settled. "And you're the only one I can talk to."

Mandy looked confused, but just as quickly, an uneasy understanding filled her face.

"So.... Pete's been gone too long for it to have happened then..." Mandy said.

"Right," Ginger said. "He went back mid August."

"You're worried that if you're pregnant now..."

"I'm ten days late, Mandy."

"It's still an *if.*"

Ginger looked at her achingly and Mandy conceded.

"*If* you're pregnant, it would have to be from the night with my brother."

Ginger gave her a slight nod, her eyes heavy and searching for a sliver of hope, resolve or help.

"Okay," said Mandy, simply to stall.

Ginger's face was drawn and hollow. Her usual luminous green eyes were glassy and strained.

"Option one." She winced before continuing, "Abortion?" she said with a non-verbal cower.

"No way," said Ginger.

"As I suspected," Mandy said straightening her back and taking a deep breath. "So that's off the table. Option two: Tell Pete the truth."

"How?" Ginger wailed.

"With honest, sincere words."

"That would kill him, Mandy. He's got enough to do just trying to stay alive through this crap-ass war. Plus, he'd never trust me again."

"Well, do you love this guy?"

"Do I love who?"

"Scott Everly."

"Of course not!"

"Is he the man you dream of at night?" Mandy asked, her voice growing more dramatic with each question.

"No! I love Pete! Peter James McCarthy."

"Do you hold one iota of anything real for this Scott Everly fellow?"

"No!"

"So, let Pete know that!" Mandy shrugged. "You made a mistake. A big mistake, but it doesn't change anything about the two of you."

"Mandy, is this your free-love, hippie lifestyle talking? Because I'm pretty certain it won't resonate well with Pete McCarthy."

"Okay, then," Mandy said. "That leaves us with option three."

"And that is..."

"Have this baby and raise it as Pete's."

"How could I possibly keep *that* secret?"

"Well, who knows so far?"

"You."

"Stop there."

Ginger sat still for a long time without moving.

"Really?" she said finally.

Mandy shrugged.

"What about the dates? Won't he figure it out?"

"That remains to be seen, I guess. You were with him only about three weeks before. Depending on when this baby shows up—*if* there really is a baby, Ginger—I suppose you'll have some explaining to do then if he questions it, but maybe it will be nothing but joyous elation. You and Pete have been wanting a baby, and here he or she is!"

"You make it sound so simple."

"Well it doesn't have to be complicated, Ginger."

"But if it's not his baby, maybe he'll find out," Ginger bewailed. "Even if it's not because of the dates, maybe because of another reason."

"If you can't tell him the truth up front—and I understand how you feel about that, truly I do—then you need to be prepared for that happening some day," she said. "But maybe that someday never comes. You have the whole rest of your life to prove that Pete is the only one for you."

"You make it sound so easy."

"Well, it was *one night*."

Ginger sighed, deflated. "And you make it sound like that was nothing either."

"Well it wasn't anything but carnal attraction, right?"

"True. But it was also betrayal. And I'd never expected to take part in betrayal. And I wouldn't expect Pete to forgive me for betrayal any more than I'd want to forgive him for a such a betrayal."

"Maybe I *am* thinking like a free-love hippie," Mandy sighed.

"Yep, but I was feeling option three, Mandy. You almost had me convinced."

"Well is there an option four?" She thought for a while, then offered, "Have the baby. Give it up for adoption without telling Pete. I know that's no good."

"No. Mandy, I'm stuck here, and I think option three is my only choice."

"Okay. Option three: you have the baby and raise it as Pete's. You and I alone will hold this secret through eternity. Sometimes we have to adapt to what's less than ideal to create the best option we have."

Ginger pondered the idea for a long time, certain it wouldn't have passed her father's "honesty is always the best policy" exhortations.

"Do I tell him that I'm pregnant now, or wait?"

"How do you know you're pregnant, Ginger?" Mandy asked.

"I just know it. And I'm ten days late."

Mandy thought for a moment and said, "And if you don't tell him now, he will think it's odd, because chances are you would have already written him with the news if you'd gotten pregnant while he was in the states."

"Exactly," Ginger said. "And I would have been elated and giddy and bubbling all over the page. How do I justify telling him three months after he's gone, and with only moderate elation?"

"Okay, I see the problem," Mandy said, thinking.

Finally she offered, "Write him with the news and tell him you wanted to be sure of the pregnancy before you told him. Get excited because this is what you've both been wanting. Pray the dates work out. And you and I will be the only ones that know anything different."

"Come on, Mandy."

"Do you have a better idea?"

Ginger thought for a long time before speaking. "I don't," she said.

Rachel: September 1998

"Cameron, I'm in the parking lot," Rachel said from the car. "It's still twenty minutes until game time and I don't want to be too early."

"But it's perfect timing for when he said the party would start. You're good. Quit worrying, girl. You've got this."

"I don't know..."

"Rachel, for God's sake! It's time you got some confidence. You're fabulous. Go find out if he is."

"Oh, wait," Rachel said. "I see some people going into his apartment."

"Male or female?"

"Both."

"How do they look?"

"Nice. He's carrying a little Playmate cooler. Should I have brought something?"

"No. I think you're good. He invited you. I'm sure he'll have something to share."

"He invited *us*. Are you sure you won't come over here?"

"I'm sure. But tell me where you are. I have the address, but tell me how you got there, and I want you to call me within fifteen minutes to let me know everything is okay."

"Peachtree and then right on Collier. The complex is on the right. It's a beige building and he's in P-8, the far-right unit."

"Got it. Now get in there and have fun. And don't forget to call me."

Another car pulled up with two guys and one girl. Rachel watched them get out of the car, knock on the door and wait on the small porch in front of his apartment door. She saw Liam greet the friends and once they entered the apartment, he stepped out on the porch and looked around the parking lot. She tried to duck behind the dashboard, but she saw his eyes linger on her car and then he held up his hand to wave her in.

Shit. No going back now.

When she didn't open the door right away, he stepped off the porch and started walking toward her car.

Crunch time. Time to prove I can do this.

She opened the car door, stood and waved.

He walked toward her car with a big, devilish smile across his face.

"You *are* a Falcons fan, right," he said.

"Oh, are the Falcons playing today?" she teased.

"Eagles fans are welcome too, but they have to sit on the floor. And they have to bring their own pizza," he said with a smile.

Sounds from the apartment were lively as they approached and he opened the door and extended his arm to welcome her in. The apartment was simple but spacious. A two-sided sofa and two mismatched recliners had three women and three men sitting, while two more men sat on stools behind the back of the sofa. Most all were holding red plastic cups and talking as if they knew each other well.

After trying to get their attention a couple of times to no avail, Liam put his fingers to his mouth and screeched a caustic, deafening whistle. The chatter stopped.

"Yo, Adrian," he said as the group looked his way. "Everyone, meet Rachel."

"Hellos" and "hi, Rachels," and raised cups were conventional, but friendly.

"Rachel McCarthy, this is Jay, Greg, Lizzie, Tim-bone, Melody, Nadia, Sam-I-Am and Frankie." He pointed to each as he said their names. "Now repeat that back."

The crowd laughed as Rachel blushed.

"Falcons or Eagles?" the guy named Frankie asked.

"Reeves over Rhodes 17-14," she said, thankful she'd read the morning sports page to learn the name of Philadelphia's coach and review both team's standings.

"There we go," Frankie said raising his glass. "You're gonna fit in just fine, Rachel."

"Can I get you a beer, Red?" Liam asked, and cocked his head toward the kitchen where a pony keg was sitting in a bucket of ice on the floor.

"You're serious here at Unit P-8," she said, looking at the keg. "Please."

He grabbed a red Solo cup from the stack and pumped the keg a few times.

"So where's your roommate? I thought Cameron was coming," he asked.

Rachel tried to quickly analyze the phrasing of his question.

Disappointment or a simple question?

She felt her face blushing. "Yeah, something came up and she asked me to tell you she was sorry."

"Bummer," he said.

Her face burned as she studied the top of his head while he filled the Solo cup with beer.

I shouldn't have come. He's interested in Cameron. Oh, God, this is embarrassing.

Liam stood and handed Rachel the beer. Then reaching toward the counter, he picked up his own and held it up as if to offer a toast.

"But I'm glad you're here," he said smiling. "Red's always been my lucky color."

He tipped his cup toward hers and she clinked back.

"Kickoff," someone yelled into the kitchen.

Grateful—and flattered—by his corniness, Rachel relaxed and they headed toward the living room. The group on the sofa saw them come in and shifted to the left to make room for Rachel to sit on the edge. Liam stood behind the sofa and the group cheered, fussed at the referees and coached from the stools and reclining chairs.

The first quarter was down to seconds when Rachel remembered she hadn't called Cameron. She popped off the sofa and scurried over to her purse she'd left on a kitchen chair.

"Do you need another beer, Red?" Liam said, following her into the kitchen.

"No. I mean, yes," she said looking into her nearly empty cup and handing it to him. "But I forgot about a phone call I need to make. I'll be right back."

She pulled her orange Nokia phone from her bag and dialed Cameron's number but the background noise was drowning out the sound, so she looked toward the kitchen. When she didn't see Liam, she opened the front door and stepped on to the porch.

Cameron picked up. "Please tell me you just forgot to call," she said.

"I just forgot to call. I'm sorry."

"Well I'm pulling in right now, on my way to save you," Cameron said.

"Oh, no!"

She looked up and saw Cameron's blue Civic enter the parking lot, turn toward the building and slow down in front of her.

Rachel hung up the phone and walked guiltily toward the car. She laughed when she saw Cameron behind the wheel of the car, wearing no makeup, an inside-out sweatshirt and a "you've-got-to-be-kidding-me" smile.

"What exactly were you going to do to save me?"

"First I was hoping I'd find a window to peek in. I figured I'd see you inside having fun and I'd leave. If that plan didn't work, I was going to ding-dong ditch and hide behind a car to see if anyone opened the door. If no one opened the door—or if it opened and I didn't like what I saw—I was going to call the police to come crashing down the door."

"I'm so sorry, Cam."

"Let me guess: He's wonderful, and you're having a lot of fun, and he realizes you are wonderful too, and he's sharing his beer with you."

"Something like that," she said smiling.

"Big crowd?"

"Eight or nine."

"Go back. Have fun."

"Thanks roomie. I owe you."

"Take care o' you," Cameron said, pointing at Rachel and repeating a line from "Pretty Woman" they'd watched together the week before.

As Cameron took her foot off the brake, Rachel turned and walked toward the apartment, just in time to see Liam coming out the door.

"Was that Cameron's car?" he asked.

"She'd left her wallet in my purse," she lied. "She just came by to get it."

"We're ordering pizza. Do you like anchovies?"

"Actually I do."

"No way."

"Yes. I have a brother on the west coast and he introduces me to something new every time we're together. I like anchovies on pizza."

"Well, we're not ordering that. We didn't have any other anchovy takers inside. We're getting sausage and green pepper, a mushroom and pepperoni and a cheese only."

"That works, too."

"But it gives me a great idea for a place to ask you out sometime, Red." Then added, "If *that* works."

Rachel felt herself blushing again and internally cursing her fair skin. She turned her face away from him. "Could," she managed.

The second quarter started and Tim stood as she entered. "Here, Rachel, sit here. I'm going to stand for a while."

Rachel took his seat between Melody and Lizzie and when action in the game slowed, the three chatted about what they did, where they lived and where they were from.

"My company could have something you'd be interested in," Melody told Rachel when she said she was job hunting. "And my roommate is in HR with Rollins-Hope. I'll give you my card and you can call me tomorrow."

"That would be awesome."

"I need five dollars from everyone," Liam roared above the voices and television. "Pizza will be here by halftime."

Then he lowered his voice and bent behind Rachel's ear, "Except for Red. I've got you covered."

Rachel turned and blushed again. "Are you sure? I'm happy...."

"Got you covered, Red. Relax."

The group fumbled with their wallets and handed their money to Frankie who was calling himself "the banker." Melody walked to the foyer and came back to the sofa with her oversized Louis Vuitton bag.

Hers looks real, Rachel thought.

Melody pulled a five from her wallet and passed it to Frankie, then pulled out a business card and handed it to Rachel. "Here's my number and my email," she said. "I'll be in all day Monday so let's talk." She placed her bag in front of her feet.

They pulled their eyes back toward the game until the doorbell rang. The group collectively yelled, "Pizza!" as Frankie headed for the door. Liam dropped a roll of paper towels and a stack of thin paper plates onto the coffee table and gathered Solo cups from the ladies with offers to refill.

"Second half one minute, forty seconds," he yelled. "Guys, get your own."

Frankie talked with the delivery boy about the score of the game and then carried the stack of pizza boxes toward the crowd. "I'm just going to pass these boxes around. Take what you want and keep passing."

Liam entered the room cradling three Solo cups full to the top with beer between his outstretched hands. Just as he turned toward the sofa, a deafening crash sounded from the front end of the apartment. The floor moved beneath them, lamps shook and flickered off, a set of candlesticks on the coffee table rattled, the ice around the beer keg sloshed, the television went black and ten human gasps were almost simultaneous. And at the same moment, Liam tripped over Melody's purse hurling the three cups of ice-cold beer squarely onto Rachel's lap.

Her mouth flew open as the shock of cold hit her legs, stomach and quickly rushed between her legs.

Rachel sat frozen as Melody and Lizzie leapt off the sofa, both splashed, but mostly spared.

"What the... Oh my God! Rachel! I'm so sorry," he said, pulling her off the sofa while Melody gathered the cups and pulled her bag safely away from the mess.

"What was that sound?" someone cried.

"Was that an earthquake?" another voice said.

Tim and Frankie ran to the front door and out toward the street. Tim came back inside and quickly reported, "It was the pizza van. It hit the side of the building."

Everyone but Rachel and Liam ran out the front door.

Liam stumbled over apology after apology, blushing himself as he pushed dry towels toward her soaked jeans and she worked to sop the cold liquid.

"And to think I once took you for a juggler," she said.

His tensed facial muscles softened. He looked at her and smiled, "I hope I can make this up to you, Red. Klutz-man wasn't the impression I was going for."

"Maybe we'd better go see what happened when your building met the pizza van," she said.

"Good idea," he said and they headed out the door.

The teenaged pizza delivery boy was talking with Frankie and Jay. The rest were talking with a group of neighbors that had come out of their apartments.

"He left the van running and hadn't set the brake when he brought our pizzas," Tim reported when Rachel and Liam joined the circle. "He saw it take off as he was stepping off your front step. Looks like it's pulled all the electric and cable wiring out of the building, too."

Liam groaned and walked around the corner to investigate.

"Are the police coming?" Rachel asked.

"Lizzie called," Tim answered. "They're on the way. She's calling Georgia Power now."

As Liam walked back toward the group, Tim called to him, "Who do you use for cable, Wilson? Looks like you're gonna be out for a while."

"Damn it," Liam said, shaking his head.

"The game," whined Greg. "And our pizza."

"Beer Mug," Sam and Tim-bone said at the same time. Then repeating the idea, they sounded almost in song.

The rest of the gang heard and confirmed the plan.

"Beer Mug. Beer Mug," they chanted.

Liam dropped his head and looked at Rachel from the tops of his eyes, "Could I interest you in watching the rest of the game with me at the Beer Mug?"

His brown eyes and remorseful baby face warmed the coldness she felt across her lap.

A mustache would never work for him.

She looked down at her cashmere sweater and pulled the fine soaked wool from her skin.

"You know, I think I'll pass," she said. "But I haven't had an anchovy pizza for a while. I might be hungry for one soon."

"Do you think you might be hungry for an anchovy pizza on Friday night?"

Rachel cocked her head and raised her eyebrow.

"I think Friday night is exactly when I'd love an anchovy pizza." Then she surprised them both by standing on her toes and presenting him with a quick kiss on the lips. "For now, though, I think I'd best get my purse and go home for a shower."

The rest of the guests were inside scarfing down pizza and rallying to head to the Beer Mug for the rest of the game.

She said her goodbyes and Melody reminded her, "Call me tomorrow, Rachel."

"I hope we'll see you again," Frankie called.

"I'll call you this week," Liam said, as he walked her to the car.

Rachel drove back down Collier and Peachtree roads and thought about the cross shape formation that Madam Sylvia had placed the tarot cards and the creepy Death Card she had turned up on the left.

"The Death Card can be a reminder of our own vulnerabilities and frailties," she'd said. "...often indicates endings and new beginnings... perhaps the opportunity to let go of what you no longer need... or the entrance of something or someone very new."

The images from that day continued to roll through her head and she remembered Madam Sylvia's final card flip onto the black velvet table.

"The Three of Cups," Madam Sylvia had said.

"Now that's appropriate," Rachel said out loud and laughed as she turned into her apartment complex. The image of three Solo cups full of beer hurling toward her lap put another cold chill across her body.

MANDY: FEBRUARY 1973

A chilly wind blew through the February sky as Mandy saw Ginger pull up to the church parking lot. It had been eight months since she'd seen her friend and she was grateful to see she'd arrived in Atlanta early. With more than an hour before the funeral would begin, they would have some time to catch up. She noted the sweater set and black skirt Ginger wore as she stepped from the car and that she was still carrying a few pounds of pregnancy weight. Pete had returned to Fort Benning and she knew from their letter exchanges and telephone calls that he and Ginger were enjoying their baby daughter and making plans for a career in the Army. The dark color washed out her fair complexion and strawberry blonde hair and it occurred to Mandy that she'd never seen her friend wear black before.

Mandy watched Ginger crook her purse at her elbow, hesitate and then come toward her for a welcomed embrace.

The two hugged and cried for a long time and then laughed for a moment when they separated and Ginger's hair was tangled around Mandy's pearl necklace.

"Thank you for coming," Mandy said.

"Oh for heaven's sakes, of course, Mandy. You're my closest friend," said Ginger. "And I am so, so, so very sorry."

"I know."

"Pete sends his regards, but the Army is relocating us to Fort Dix New Jersey and he had some meetings he couldn't get out of. He knew it would give us a little more time together, too. We leave a week from tomorrow."

"I would have loved to finally meet him," Mandy said. "I know how much you are enjoying having him back safe and sound."

"I do. Military life will have its challenges, I'm sure, but I know it's the right decision for Pete. And he's completely enamored with Rachel. And she adores him."

"I wondered if you'd bring her today."

"Wendy's watching her. Today is not the day for fussing over the baby."

Mandy nodded, remembering Ginger's neighbor in family housing who had kept William for her so she could be at the hospital with Ginger when Rachel was born.

"Did you bring William?" Ginger asked.

"No, a friend from the Rooks' church is keeping him until after the service. We thought it would just be too much."

Mandy took Ginger by the elbow and they turned to walk up the concrete pathway to St. Thomas More. "This is their church," she said. "And it's the church Adam grew up in."

"Adams parents are here, of course," she continued. "Lots of their friends. My parents are here. And Scott is here."

Ginger shuddered and looked toward the floor.

"Don't worry, Ginger. You've got nothing to worry about."

"There's never been any conversation or mention..."

Mandy cut her off. "Nope. All good."

"The guilt is still so debilitating," Ginger said. "I wish I had your confidence."

Then she stopped herself. "I'm sorry, Mandy. This is not about me. Please forgive me."

They stopped at the front door and Mandy looked deep into Ginger's celadon-green eyes. "You're my closest friend, too. And just knowing that you're on my team is helping so much," she said. "I wish we could spend some serious time."

Ginger hugged her friend again. "You know you're the strongest person I know, Mandy. You are going to survive this."

Mandy's eyes filled with tears. She nodded quickly and turned her head before the two walked into the church.

"I need to be in the family room when the church starts filling, but first come to the back with me. The Army returned Adam's personal items stored in his barracks and the prison, and I want to show you."

"Is the rest of the family back there?" Ginger asked, unsuccessfully trying to mask her fear of seeing Scott.

"Probably just Adam's parents, but don't worry. This will just take a minute."

The two walked into a room with a metal sign engraved with "Bereavement" on the door. The room was empty of people and Mandy guided her to a cardboard box on the table.

"They sent his wallet." She opened it and showed Ginger photos of William as a baby and a wallet-sized picture cut from a snapshot of their wedding to fit the plastic sleeve. "And here is our only family photo. You've seen it, of course at my house, but this is the copy I'd sent Adam. And here are all of the letters his mother and I sent him."

She picked up a tall stack of letters bound in twine in Ginger's hands.

"And then there are some miscellaneous things," she said as she held up a hat, a pair of shoes, a small vase with Vietnamese writing on the sides and his dop kit with a razor and a toothbrush inside.

Mandy took the letters from Ginger and placed them back in the box, and handed her a silver chain with an Army-issued dog tag. "And this, they got from his body. He was still wearing it in the prison."

Ginger held up the chain and turned the tag over to read: Roger R. Meehan. She looked at Mandy with confusion.

"It's not his!" Mandy cried. "It belongs to his friend Roger R. Meehan who was killed the day he was captured."

Ginger blinked with confusion as Mandy continued.

"Adam mentioned Roger many times in his letters. They were close friends. The day he was captured, he and four others from their unit were together. At some point, Meehan was alone in the jeep and was ambushed and killed. The other three—including Adam—were taken to Hao Lo."

Ginger studied the tag and looked at Mandy with concern. "Are you saying there was mix-up in the identification of who was who?"

"No, no, no. The Army officials tell me that it happens all the time. The guys trade tags—totally defeating the purpose of having them, of course. Evidently they rarely have the right set of dog tags to return to the family."

"So, what *are* you saying, Mandy?"

"Just that Roger's widow may have Adam's dog tags. I'd like to try again to find her and trade tags," she said. "Adam had mentioned her to me in letters and said that he hoped we might spend time with Roger and Susan when the war was over. I sent her a letter when Roger was killed, but I'd like to try again."

"I see," Ginger nodded, surprised and perplexed that her friend had found the strength to even think of the idea. "You should."

They were interrupted when two men and two women opened the door and walked in the room.

"Oh good," Mandy said. "Everyone, I'd like you to meet my friend from Fort Benning. This is Ginger McCarthy. The older couples nodded and smiled.

Then she turned to the two couples and said, "Ginger, these are Adam's parents, Sandra and Ted Rooks. And these are my parents, Eve and Charles Everly."

Ginger shook hands and exchanged how-do-you-dos with the Rooks and the Everlys and then turned to Mandy. "I'll get out of your way. I'll be sitting toward the back if you need me." She hugged Mandy before walking out the door.

A few minutes later, Scott entered the bereavement room with a quizzical look on his face, but Mandy didn't question its meaning.

Entering the church, Mandy walked with her brother, followed by the Rooks and then her parents. She saw Ginger sitting at the back as she entered, but was not able to catch her eye.

As planned, the service was a stately combination of military precision and the pomp and circumstance of the Catholic Mass. One high school friend, whom Mandy had never met, had asked to offer a eulogy to include Adam's early years. He kept his message short and smartly avoided silly stories of adolescence, which would have clashed with the austere tone of the service. Rather, the presentations focused on his bravery, his service to country, and his love for his wife and son.

I don't even know this man they are talking about.

Mandy fidgeted as she worked to rearrange herself on the front pew. None of the words meant to chronicle felt like a description of the Adam Rooks she knew any more than the words of comfort felt directed toward her. Other than a couple of Adam's Atlanta friends that she'd met early in their relationship and her in-laws, no one among the entire congregation knew both Adam and Mandy as a couple. And even the passionate descriptions of how Adam Rooks loved and adored his wife and nearly five-year-old son felt contrived, disingenuous.

She felt a hand on her shoulder and turned slightly to see Sandra Rooks sitting in the row behind her with Mandy's parents and Scott. Though she didn't turn in the other direction, she assumed it was Ted's hand steadying her shoulder.

Yes, Adam loved me. And yes, Adam loved our son. But not in the ways anyone here could understand.

For the Rooks, though, the atmosphere was exactly as they would have scripted. Ted and Sandra stood regally at the church's narthex exchanging stoic pleasantries with friends and guests for almost an hour following the service. Both wept off and on, but seemed perfectly comfortable with the descriptions presented of Adam and his short twenty-five years on earth.

Where is Ginger? Did she leave already?

She calculated the weeks she and Adam had actually spent together as husband and wife as she watched the Rooks chat with the preacher and Army chaplain: Only fourteen. Even prior to the wedding they'd been together less than a full year.

Adam had seen William only twenty-one days in his entire life.

Adam loved us for what was ahead. He loved what we were to become once his service in the Army was complete. All the years of duty were simply meant as pre-payment for the chance to live and dream together at its conclusion. He didn't ask to be a part of the damned war; he just did what he had to do. And it killed him.

Ginger was suddenly beside her with her arm around Mandy's shoulders. She whispered, "I can't stay. I need to get back to Columbus and pick up Rachel."

"Where...?"

"Sorry, I've been hiding in the bathroom until I could be sure you were alone."

Scott.

"Be strong, my friend," Ginger said.

Mandy watched as Ginger walked to her car and then pulled out of the parking lot. She turned back to the church vestibule and made polite conversation with the dozens of Army officers and unfamiliar faces that surrounded her as long as she could and then retreated to the bereavement room to pick up the box of Adam's things.

The Vietnam War robbed us of our conclusion.

She untied the stack of letters and sat down on the room's only cushioned chair. Her face was wet with tears she hadn't even noticed, and she was still reading when the Rooks came in and found her an hour later.

"Your parents and brother went on back to the house. Are you ready to pack up and get back home?" Ted asked.

Mandy looked at her watch.

Ginger should be back in Columbus by now. She and Pete will transfer to Fort Dix and start the lives they've been waiting to live together with their new baby. The life they pre-paid for with four years of service.

Mandy sighed. "Yes, I'm ready."

GINGER: OCTOBER 1971

Ginger pulled the unsealed envelope from the pages of the paperback book on her lap and unfolded the letter she'd begun. The conversation she'd had three days before with Mandy rolled through her head again as she sat in her favorite Naugahyde chair in the base commissary commons sucking on the last lemon drop from the box.

Could I possibly keep this secret from Pete? Is this the best conclusion or am I just hiding from my mistake? Is Mandy right?

The queasiness had passed for the day, but she was enjoying the Lemonheads and found herself mindlessly pulling them out of the box as she skimmed through her paperback and through the letter she had written to Pete. She made mental notes to thank the receptionist for her suggestion of the lemon candy when she was able to get her first doctor's appointment and to pick up another box on her way home.

She was on her third day of morning sickness and had noticed tenderness in her breasts when she showered and put on her bra.

As the days passed, she became more convinced that she would never be able to tell Pete anything other than a baby was on the way and he or she would be here when he returned from Vietnam in the summer. No other scenario was better.

Just like Mandy said, this is the best option given the circumstances and I'm going to have to live with it.

She had worked carefully to craft her letter, being vague about the dates and assuring Pete that she'd have more details once she met with the doctor. She rewrote the letter three times to intensify the excitement in her words and prayed that soon anticipation and excitement about this baby truly would eclipse the guilt, worry and remorse that she couldn't shake.

She tried to imagine his facial expressions as he read the letter and wondered whether he might call his bunkmates over to celebrate the news or if he'd immediately sit down to write her back. She imagined how much harder it might be for him being so far away when the baby was born, but also hoped that the anticipation of meeting their baby would make his return from war that much sweeter.

Finally satisfied, she licked the envelope and pulled a stamp from her wallet to adhere to the corner. She kissed the letter, as she did every letter to Pete, and walked toward the wall of mail slots and post office boxes.

She pushed it partially through the chrome mail slot and held it for a long time as pangs of guilt pounded across her temples. She counted slowly in her head, and when she got to ten, she dropped it and heard it ping, slide and then go quiet.

An imaginary blue bubble began forming in her head, but its message was empty.

What do I want Pete to know? I'm sorry? Please forgive me? I hope you believe my deception?

"Hi, Ginger!"

Startled, she whirled around to see her neighbor Wendy walking toward her pushing a navy pram.

"Wendy!" she said, almost out of breath. "Hi."

"Jennifer and I are just out for a stroll."

Ginger steadied herself with one hand on the metal wall, then walked around to peek at the sleeping baby. "Oh, she's so sweet. How old is she now?"

"Four months on Tuesday," Wendy said smiling at the baby. "Mike and I are already thinking about number two."

Ginger nodded and forced a smile.

"Oh, Ginger, I'm sorry. I hope I didn't say the wrong thing. I know there are only a few of us lucky enough to have our husbands stationed on base."

"No, you're fine," Ginger said. "I'm happy for you and Mike."

"You do look particularly pretty today, though. You look like you're glowing, in fact."

Ginger wiped the top of her hand across her forehead and tugged on her hair. "Well that's sweet. Thank you."

"You really do," she said. "I'd almost think *you* were pregnant."

Shocked at the words, Ginger's eyes opened wide.

Do I look different? Is it showing on the outside?

Seeing Ginger's puzzled face, Wendy stammered, "Oh Ginger. I've done it again. I always say the wrong thing. I'm so sorry..."

"No, really, Wendy..." she said, but Wendy had turned the pram and was hurriedly walking away. "I'm so sorry," she stammered again as she hurried off.

Oh my God, is this really happening? Do I look like I'm pregnant?

A new and sudden rush filled her body.

Pete and I have prayed for this.

"I'm having a baby!" she said to no one.

She strolled toward the base apartment and realized she had been smiling for a long time. She touched her face and hid her eyes in her hands and let out a muffled scream.

She thought about Pete and how excited he would be when he received the letter. Their baby would be here by early summer and Pete would be home in August. They'd be a family and they'd all be together.

She pulled her keys out of her pocket to open the apartment door, but stopped and instead turned toward her car parked just a few feet away.

I want to tell someone that Pete and I are having a baby!

She thought about her parents but realized she wanted Pete to know before she shared the news with their parents or her brother.

Suddenly chilly, she untied the sweater that she'd had tied around her waist and pulled it onto her arms and over her shoulders and got into the car.

"We're having a baby," she sang as she started the car. "We're having a baby!"

She pulled out of the parking lot and drove toward Millie's.

RACHEL: SEPTEMBER 1998

"What are the chances that two anchovy lovers would find themselves in the same place at the same time just weeks apart, have the same taste in draft beer, and then be in the same room when a pizza van tries to mow down the joint?"

Rachel laughed. "Must have been in the stars," she said, flattered at Liam's insinuation but reminding herself to avoid the Madam Sylvia-mustached man story at all costs.

Way too early to share.

"So anchovies for sure," Liam said. "You pick a second topping and I'll pick a third. If either of us croak at the other one's choice, we'll assume we're doomed. If we both agree, we'll discuss another date at the end of the night."

"Deal," she said. "Italian sausage."

"Whoaa. Can't croak at Italian sausage. Nice choice."

Rachel blushed but the banter was easy and fun with Liam. She gave him a "your turn" nod.

Liam picked up the menu. "Before I make my choice, I want to know what I'm up against. Look over this list and tell me how many of these are croakable to your palate."

He handed her the menu and pointed to the list labeled "You-Pick Toppings."

Rachel took the menu and studied the list. She handed the menu back to Liam.

"Four," she said.

"Hmmm," he said perusing the list. "Eighteen toppings to pick from... the odds are good, but the stakes are high..."

"Mushrooms," he said, snapping the menu on the table.

Rachel winced and dropped her head.

"What? You don't like mushrooms? Who doesn't like mushrooms on a pizza? And a perfect choice with Italian sausage and anchovies, I might add."

Rachel lifted her head. "It's a texture thing. And the fertilizer."

"Oh man, I really thought we were safe with that one. What are the other three?"

"Green olives, black olives and banana peppers."

"Ouch," he said, then "Okay, quick, we need to find some more common ground. Did you read Harry Potter?"

"Quidditch. Privet Drive. The sorting hat. Neville Longbottom..."

"And we're back in the game," he said raising his glass. "Raiders or Star Wars?"

"Hmmm," Rachel said. "Too close to call, but Harrison Ford..."

"Mmm. All right. Let's just call it a win anyway," Liam said.

They clinked glasses and Rachel said, "You say you're not a juggler or a lawyer. I know you work as a courier but what's the part you've been vague about?"

"Not vague, just a little scattered. I do research and prep work for a law firm twenty hours a week. I go to law school Tuesday and Thursday nights at Georgia State. And I work for a courier service a couple of nights a week."

"That's quite a schedule. How much more school do you have?"

"One semester after this one. And if all goes as planned, I'll be hired as an associate with the firm I'm with now."

"Nice. Where's your family?"

"Also scattered. My parents are in St. Louis. I have two brothers. One lives in Memphis and the other is finishing college at UT in Austin."

"Did you grow up in St. Louis?"

"Mostly. I was born in Georgia though. What about you?"

"I was born here too. I have a younger brother, P.J. in Oregon, and a sister, Roxanne, in California. My dad is career Army and we lived all over the world growing up. My parents are in New Mexico now, but this will be their last Army move."

The waitress brought another round of beers and took their pizza order.

"What brought you back to Georgia then if they are all out west?"

"I went to college at UGA. And my grandparents have always been in Atlanta. They've been the constant to our crazy military moves. And I'm very close to them."

Liam asked about the job search and Rachel told him about the Tuesday interview and updated him on the other positions.

As she finished, the pizza arrived.

"Medium pizza with Italian sausage, green pepper and chopped anchovies," the waitress said as she placed the steaming pizza between them.

"Looks awesome," Rachel said. When the waitress left, she added, "Meanwhile, though, my grandmother and I have been doing some baking. We've had two catering orders for our stuffed cupcakes."

"What's a stuffed cupcake?"

"We add pudding or jam fills or even bake in an almond or peanut butter ball. We were just experimenting one day, but we've come up with some pretty good combinations."

"Sounds cool."

"Actually we have played around with the idea of doing it as a business."

"A business of cupcakes?"

"It's just an idea. And I'm kind of convinced it could work. We're playing around with the numbers at least."

Liam took a sip of beer and was quiet for a moment before announcing, "Hey, you could call it 'Little Reds,' kind of like 'Little Debbies,'" he laughed. "And your logo could be a picture of Little Red Riding Hood and the grandmother!"

"Very funny," she said. "We actually have a very French name for the business: "Oodles and 'Chel's. I'm picturing an Eiffel Tower in the logo."

"*What* and *what*?"

"Oodles—that's what we call my grandmother—and 'Chel's because that's what she calls me."

"To Oodles and 'Chel's," Liam toasted. "And to a delicious anchovy pizza and the deal we made."

Rachel lifted her glass and clinked with Liam.

"Deal?"

"That we'd make plans for another date."

Rachel could feel her face beginning to burn but quickly recovered. "Assuming no more beer in my lap, I'm in."

MANDY: MARCH 1973

Mandy pointed out a few daffodils popping through the ground as she and William walked through the park with their blanket and tote bag filled with a Tupperware pitcher of lemonade and a stack of paper cups.

"I've got one for you, William," Mandy said.

He stopped and looked at his mother.

"What did the big flower say to the little flower?"

William smiled and shrugged.

"Hi there, bud," she said.

William laughed. "Miss Maisy told you some good jokes when you were little, Mommy."

"She did indeed. Do you remember any of the other ones I taught you?"

"What kind of flower grows on your face?" he said smartly.

Mandy pretended to forget the punch line. Then at the same time, mother and son pointed at each other and shouted, "Tulips!"

"Ha, good one!" she said as they approached the swing set area.

"Will Johnny will be here today, Mommy?"

"I don't think so sweet pea. Remember his mommy said they were visiting his grandmother for a few days. He should be back tomorrow."

As they rounded the corner and the park swings and slide came into view, they saw two little girls on the swings that William had played with before.

He turned to Mandy and shrugged, then ran off toward the slide.

Mandy placed the tote bag on the ground and spread the blanket. Then she pulled her pen, paper and a paperback from the side of the bag to write her letter to Ginger.

Dear Ginger,

I hope that by the time you receive this letter you are settled in New Jersey and ready to truly begin your adventures as a family. Thank you for being at Adam's service and for sending the photo of Rachel. She is such a gorgeous baby! Looks like she's got your amazing green eyes. I bet she'll be pulling up onto furniture any day. I know you and Pete are so proud.

All is as expected here. Adam's parents have been wonderful and though many days I just can't bear to get out of bed, I try my best to hold those feelings to Wednesdays and Saturdays because Sandra and Ted have been taking William for full days and sometimes at night to help me out. Sometimes I spend the day just crying. Other times I go to the park and read or go shopping, but I'm grateful for the time because I can just "let go" and not let William see me down.

William is handling it just as you'd expect an almost-five-year-old who has only a slight memory of his father would, I suppose. A boy his age moved in about a block away, so he has a new playmate. He mentions Adam in his prayers every night, but I'm struggling with how I'm going to be able to keep his memory alive for William.

He's already got a loose tooth and he's so proud of that! He says he's certain he'll be able to sleep with one eye open so that he can peek at the tooth fairy. I've even been able to convince him to nap every day this week just in case it falls out before bedtime.

Ginger, I don't want you to think I'm wallowing in depression, so please don't worry. I know I'll make it to the other side of this, but the nights have been harder than I expected. It's funny because Adam and I have been apart for more than five years, but I never felt like a single parent until now. It's only now that my dreams have turned to nightmares. I often wake up shaking with visions of him alone in that horrid prison.

For awhile I think we will stay in the rental since it's close to the Rooks and they are so very helpful. I made some calls about re-enrolling to finish my nursing degree, but the program doesn't start again until fall, so I'm trying to see if I can take a few core classes at the community college this summer and then transfer them. William will start school in the fall too, so that will also help. Once I've finished, I don't know if I'll want to stay in Atlanta or not. My parents have suggested that I move to Rochester near them, but I can't think of anything worse than that idea. I guess I'll follow the job opportunities.

Adam was gone all those years, but I never thought of myself as alone. Now that I truly am, the thought is terrifying. Everything feels so different. But please know I'm just venting because you're my closest friend. Don't worry. We are going to be okay. Your letters and encouragement definitely help. Keep them coming!

Please send photos of you and Pete and Rachel when you have some. And write when you can too. I miss you! Maybe some day William and I will drive up to visit you and I can finally meet Pete and see you and Rachel again.

Love,
Mandy

Once finished, she stuffed it in the pre-addressed stamped envelope she'd brought, sealed it and tucked it in the back of her paperback.

"William, would you like some lemonade? Bring your friends and have a drink," she called.

William and the two girls came running over. Mandy handed each of them a cup.

"William, did you introduce yourself to your friends?" she asked.

"I'm William," he said looking their direction briefly and then dropping his eyes to the ground.

"And I'm Mrs. Rooks, William's mother," she said pouring the lemonade as they held their three cups toward her. "And who are you two young ladies?"

The girls shyly introduced themselves and then held out their cup for more when they saw William do the same.

After they'd finished and Mandy had gathered the cups from them, one of the girls offered, "Thank you, Mrs. Rooks."

"Thank you, Mrs. Rooks," the other repeated.

"Thank you, Mommy," said William handing her his cup.

The children turned and ran back toward the swings. Mandy heard William ask, "Do you girls know what kind of flower grows on your face?"

GINGER: JUNE 1972

Knowing the long-distance rates would drop after six o'clock, Ginger waited until after the evening news to call Mandy in Atlanta.

"It's all set," she said. "Wendy will watch William at her apartment for as long as needed. When I think it's time, I'll call your number with a collect call for Ginger McCarthy and you'll just refuse the charges. That will be the signal and should give you time to drive to Columbus, drop William at Wendy's and get to the hospital."

"I'll be there," Mandy said.

"The doctor says it could be this week," Ginger said.

"Don't be nervous. It's going to be fine. They will probably give you twilight sedation like they did me when William was born. And I'll be there—in the room or just outside the door—wherever they will let me. Don't worry."

"I'm not. Thank you, Mandy. For everything."

She hung up the phone and picked up the stapled pages of steno paper with baby name ideas that she and Pete had traded back and forth in the mail. It was simple if it was a boy. They'd both agreed that they'd name a boy after Pete: Peter James McCarthy, Jr.

"We could call him 'P.J.,'" Ginger had suggested.

Pete said he'd think about that idea.

The girls' names, however, filled two pages front and back. Ginger had started the list by sending Pete a list of her favorite names with subset lists of suggested middle names. Pete had sent the list back with stars by his favorites and a line crossed through a few suggestions. He'd marked three stars by several of her suggestions: Michelle, Heather, Melissa and Rachel. Then he'd added in a few of his own: Jennifer, Stephanie, Jane.

"Jennifer" was already taken by Wendy and Mike's baby next door. Though she didn't expect to remain friends after their time in Columbus, she marked that suggestion off the list. "Stephanie" she couldn't consider because of a mean girl that had dated her brother Carlton in high school and broke his heart. She was surprised and intrigued, however, by the simple "Jane" he'd written on the page and sent back to her.

Pete hadn't commented on the middle names, other than to say that he'd leave that to her. She made a final list using their combined favorites, but after counting the days on the calendar, she realized there would never be enough time for the names to reach Pete, for him to respond and for his letter to get back to her.

It could be weeks before this baby gets a name if I do that.

Instead, she started a new list of their favorites along with her picks from the middle name suggestions: Michelle Marie, Michelle Leigh, Heather Leigh, Heather Jane, Jane Marie, Melissa Marie, Melissa Ann, Rachel Marie, Rachel Jane, Rachel Leigh. She practiced writing each name in traditional printing and in cursive. When she'd finally made her selection, she circled it and went to bed.

The next morning, she was watching shadows dance across the bedroom wall before she got out of bed when her lower body cramped and her arms went numb and her chest clamped in pain. Once it was over, she sat up in bed and waited. When she didn't feel anything new for a few minutes, she got out of bed and headed for the bathroom.

Another few minutes with no cramping, she changed into one of the maternity dresses Mandy had passed on to her, brushed her teeth and splashed water across her face. As she walked to the kitchen, the cramping hit again and she dropped to a chair to wait it out.

As soon as it passed, she called the doctor and left a message with the receptionist, called Wendy who promised Mike would be ready right away to drive her to the hospital, and called the operator with Mandy's telephone number and the collect call request as code that she was in labor.

She slid on a pair of shoes, grabbed the suitcase she had pre-packed, and waited for Mike's tap on the door. The next few hours were a blur: short-lived consciousness in the hospital waiting room; traveling on a gurney through the hall; and a brief conversation with a nurse once she entered the delivery room. Hours later she woke up in a hospital room covered with blankets. Her best friend sat in the chair next to the bed reading an article from *Life* magazine.

Mandy looked up when she felt Ginger's eyes on her. "Well hi there, sleepyhead. You were a champ!" she said.

"Is there..."

"You've got a baby girl, my friend. And she's beautiful."

Ginger smiled. "Where..."

"She's in the nursery. I'm sure they will bring her to you soon," Mandy said. "I watched her get a bath from the window. She's loud and proud to be here. Congratulations."

Ginger closed her eyes and pictured a blue balloon flying out of her head with a message to Pete: *We have a baby, Pete. She's here.* She imagined the balloon flying around the earth and melting into Pete's head on the other side of the world. She smiled and opened her eyes.

"Her name is Rachel. Rachel Jane McCarthy."

"I love her name, Ginger. It's beautiful."

There was a knock at the door and Millie walked through the door wearing a pink muumuu dress and carrying a vase of daisies from her yard. "Toodle ooh, I hear there's a new mother in this room," she sang.

"Millie! So sweet of you to come," Ginger said.

"I came as soon as I heard. Mandy called me this morning and here I am."

"What day is it anyway?" Ginger asked.

"It's Monday," Mandy said. "Mike brought you here about nine o'clock yesterday morning. The baby was born at 8:10 last night, June fourth."

"June fourth," she said quietly.

Rachel: October 1998

"You're getting great at piping, Oodles," Rachel said. "I think we will need to designate you as the VP of Decorating."

"Well that's fine by me since this will just be a once-in-awhile thing."

"I'm glad you're not disappointed," Rachel said. "I was a little worried."

"Relieved, actually. I did my thirty-two years teaching sixth graders," Oodles said. "It sounded like fun at first, but I like my retirement too much to go back to work."

Rachel and Oodles packed the Teletubbies cupcakes—one dozen each of the four characters—into white bakery boxes and spread them across the kitchen table.

"We couldn't get licensed without a commercial kitchen, but I'm happy to keep filling occasional orders from here if you are," Rachel said. "We make a great team. But I have to say I'm excited about this new job, too."

"Are you starting next week?"

"No, they want me to start two weeks from Monday. Their office is in Buckhead, so close to home, and close to you and Poppy."

"I'm just thrilled for you, Rachel. This is all working out for you."

"I'll have training in December in San Francisco, so maybe Roxanne or P.J. can meet me there."

"Wonderful. And Thanksgiving is just around the corner. It looks like we'll have all the McCarthys in town for the holiday. It will be so nice."

"I know. It's been a long time," Rachel said. "By the way, there's something else I wanted to tell you about too..."

"I'm all ears," Oodles said smiling and placing her hands next to her ears and waving them up and down.

"I'm liking this guy I met a lot. Do you remember me mentioning Liam Wilson?"

"I do, indeed. He's the one that left the note on your roommate's car."

"Yes! I forgot you knew about that..."

"And you don't have to tell me you like him, 'Chel, honey. It's written all over your face."

Rachel blushed. "We've been out four times in two weeks and the law firm that he works at part time is having a new partner reception Friday night and he's invited me to that. He's even set up a blind date between one of the other interns and Cameron, so we'll all go together."

"He's a lawyer?"

"Actually a law student. He's doing some part-time research work there but thinks they'll offer him a position when he finishes school."

"And no mustache, right?"

"No mustache, Oodles, but there is a funny story about the first time I met him."

Rachel told her about the post office conversation and the boxes he was holding.

"I waited in my car to see him come out and his shirt had a large drawing of a mustache across the chest."

"What kind of shirt was that?" Oodles asked.

"It was a college fraternity and sorority party. The back of the shirt gave the name of the party; something like mustache and pearls, white gloves and cigars. They do themed parties like that all the time."

"And it was soon after you'd seen the fortune teller who'd mentioned a man with a mustache, right?"

"Exactly. I haven't gotten the nerve to tell him that story yet."

"Are you going to?" Oodles asked.

"Some day, I'm sure. If this turns into something."

"Smart girl, Rachel."

They heard Poppy's whistling long before he opened the back door after a morning at the barbershop. He entered the kitchen with a bag of groceries.

"How about hug for your Poppy," he said putting the bag on the table, kissing Oodles on the head and then putting his arms around Rachel with a big bear hug.

"Hi, Poppy. You're looking chipper today. Did you get a hair cut?"

"Nope."

Rachel and Oodles both looked at him quizzically.

"I got 'em all cut!"

"Oh, good one Poppy," Rachel said. She rounded her fingers and thumbs into an 'O' shape and held them up to her eyes. Poppy followed by doing the same and they said in unison as they peered at one another with faces just inches apart, "See ya in the funny papers!"

Poppy beamed and pointed at Rachel with a grateful and nostalgic smile.

"I almost forgot about that," Rachel laughed. "I'm not sure we've done that since I was little."

"Such a wisenheimer, you are Van Hill," Oodles said, brushing some lint from Poppy's jacket. "We saved you a TinkyWink cupcake, and Rachel has some great news about her job.... And a new fellow in her life."

She looked at Rachel with a guilty smile, but Rachel's face was giddy.

"Well I suppose I won't even ask what's in a TinkyWink cupcake, but I'll give it a sample," he said taking off his jacket and putting his arm around Rachel. "Let's hear this good news."

Mandy: May 1973

William arranged his dump truck, his favorite stuffed rabbit and the duffel bag he and Mandy had packed with coloring books, crayons and snacks of Space Food Sticks and potato chips across the back seat of the station wagon. He placed his pillow on the floor and tucked his blue flannel blanket over his lap.

"I have a thermos up front with some Kool-Aid if you get thirsty," Mandy called, craning her neck to look at him from the driver's seat.

"Just lie across the seat when you get tired because we'll drive through the nighttime to get there."

"I'm not sleepy."

"Maybe not yet, but it will be dark soon. If you're awake, I'll let you know when we get to North Carolina."

"New Jersey, you said, Mommy."

"We'll be in New Jersey by lunch time tomorrow. First we have to drive in North Carolina and Virginia and Maryland and some other states. Would you like to go to the bathroom one more time before we leave?"

William shook his head and Mandy opened the map of the eastern United States to study it again. She'd clipped notes to the side of the map with the names of cities where she would change roads and had tucked a mason jar with quarters, dimes and nickels into the glove compartment for the toll roads they would need to travel.

Once she was satisfied, she started the engine, but then turned it off.

"I think I'll go to the bathroom one more time before we go," she said to William. "Are you sure you don't want to try?"

"Nope," he said, cranking the bed of the truck up and down.

"Then I'll be right back."

When she returned she reached into the back seat and held up her hand for William to grab it. "Here we go, William. It's William and Mommy's big adventure! Are you ready?"

"Ready," he said.

"Me too," she said, working to convince herself. "Let's go."

Mandy cranked the car and pulled out of the driveway of their house on Sycamore Street headed for a visit to see Ginger and Pete McCarthy and their baby Rachel at Fort Dix in New Jersey where they would stay two nights in their apartment. Mandy would sleep on a rollaway in Rachel's room with William in a sleeping bag on the floor, and Ginger and Pete would move Rachel to their room. From there, Mandy and William would drive to Philadelphia to meet Susan Meehan, the widow of Roger R. Meehan. Susan was planning a light lunch and they could visit and exchange Adam's and Roger's military dog tags. That night, she and William would stay at a Howard Johnson's Hotel in Richmond, Virginia, and then drive home the next day.

"William and Mommy's big driving adventure," she said mindlessly several times as she traversed toward Interstate 85. "Let me know when you're hungry for a peanut butter and jelly sandwich, sweet pea."

It was dark by the time they got to Charlotte, North Carolina, and William slept stretched across the back seat all the way into Virginia, just outside of Washington, D.C.

Though she'd stopped twice for gas and coffee during the night, she hadn't dared step into the restroom and leave William in the car alone, so she was happy to see his ruffled curls pop up from the back seat as the sun began to rise.

"Well good morning, partner," she said. "You did a good job in the co-pilot seat. We are almost to Washington, D.C.!"

"I'm thirsty, Mommy."

"Perfect, because I'm ready for a break too. Let's stop and get some breakfast and freshen up a little."

After a breakfast of pancakes and strawberries, they washed their faces and brushed their teeth in the restaurant bathroom and got back in the car. By two o'clock, they arrived at the Maytown Apartments outside of Fort Dix. Mandy's eyes were heavy and her second wind had waned by the time Ginger met her at the door with Rachel in her arms and big hugs for her and William.

Mandy reached for Rachel, who she hadn't seen since she was an infant, and squatted to let William meet her and make her laugh with patty cake and funny faces.

"Pete won't be home for another three hours, and Mandy, I know you're exhausted after driving all night," Ginger said, showing her around the small apartment. "I have the rollaway bed ready for you. Why don't you lie down and sleep and I'll take Rachel and William to the park for a few hours. I have the stroller all packed."

William looked at his mother with concern, but Ginger immediately interceded with, "And I hear you, William Rooks, had a birthday last week."

"I'm five," he said holding up both hands, fingers spread.

"Rachel has a present for you. Something you might like to play with at the park."

She handed William a small box with a card taped to the top. He handed the card to Mandy and grabbed the paper of the box ready to open.

"Wait just a minute, William," Mandy said laughing. "Let's read the card first."

He tapped his foot as Mandy read the card's message.

"We are so happy you have you come to visit us," Mandy read. "With love, Mr. and Mrs. McCarthy and Rachel."

Inside the box was a plastic pail, shovel and rake. Despite little recollection of Ginger, William's concerns about going to the park with

Ginger and Rachel passed and he jumped up ready for the sandbox.

Mandy was grateful for the invitation to sleep. She watched Ginger push the stroller away from the apartment. William held onto the stroller with one hand while he swung the pail in the other. When they reached the sidewalk she headed to the rollaway bed and fell asleep within minutes.

It was after six o'clock when she woke up and meandered through the apartment until she found Pete and Ginger sitting at a picnic table on the back lawn while Rachel held on the chairs and tried taking steps from one to the next. William hovered over her trying to help.

"Well I finally get to meet the famous Mandy Rooks," Pete said, rising from his chair and greeting Mandy with a bear hug.

He was just as Ginger had described. Tall, blond, freckled and full of charm. An image of Adam filled her head and she pushed it away quickly, wanting to avoid emotion at all costs on their getaway adventure.

"Mommy!" William came running and hugging her legs.

"I'm having a beer and Ginger has a Sidecar. Can I get you something?" Pete asked.

"I'll have a beer, please," she said.

"You got it," he said, opening the screened door.

"He's fabulous," Mandy mouthed to Ginger as she pulled her knees under the picnic table and lifted William to her lap. "And he adores Rachel, I know."

Ginger nodded with a conceding smile. "It's so wonderful to have him home. And we are so happy to be a family. He's never even questioned the timing, but I try hard to never think of it anyway. We're happy, Mandy."

Pete opened the screened door and placed a glass in front of Mandy and handed her the bottle of beer. "I wish I'd had the chance to meet Adam," he said looking squarely into her eyes. "Your husband was a brave man, Mandy, and I can tell you from experience, he thought of you and your son every single second he was there."

A lump filled Mandy's throat. She gently pushed William off her lap and he ran toward a soccer ball in the grass.

"I wish you could have met him too," she said. "Thank you."

Ginger brought Rachel's highchair outside and placed it next to the picnic table and then went back inside for the baby food dish, a bib, two jars of baby food and a spoon. "If you and William and Pete can wait until I'm finished feeding Rachel, I have a lasagna in the oven that is ready any time," she said.

"Sounds perfect," Mandy answered.

They all cooed and made faces at Rachel as she ate her dinner of chicken and noodles and bananas, and then Mandy set the picnic table with paper plates, napkins and forks as Ginger brought the steaming lasagna to the table.

The next day, Ginger and Mandy packed Mandy's station wagon with a picnic and blankets and the kids and headed to Cape May. William strolled Rachel around the picnic blanket and found a new friend to play with on the slide and teeter-totter while Rachel napped. Ginger and Mandy talked for hours.

"Any news from Millie?" Mandy asked.

"She is definitely missing the two of us," Ginger said. "She invited Pete and me to her trailer for a send off our last week in Columbus. She served quiche, of course. And one night she stayed with Rachel at our apartment while we went out to dinner."

"Still no answers to her letters about O'Ray?"

"Not that I've heard since we moved. I sent her a letter last week with our new address."

"Did you tell her about Adam?"

"I did."

"I'd like to stay in touch with Millie, too," said Mandy after a short pause. "Maybe later this summer, William and I will venture down to Columbus for a visit."

"Do you think you'll stay where you are in Atlanta for awhile?"

"I think so. I've registered for some core classes that start in late

August at the community college nearby. And I have applications in to several nursing programs. All that will be a lot easier with Adam's parents close by."

When Rachel woke from her nap, Ginger fed her while Mandy and William packed up the picnic and the car.

The next day was Saturday. With tears streaming down both of the women's faces, they said their goodbyes. Mandy and William waved to Pete, Ginger and Rachel out the windows of the station wagon until they turned at the end of the street and could no longer see them and then headed south toward Philadelphia.

Mandy checked the map as she exited I-295, then pulled into a gas station to have the tank filled while she reread the directions.

When they pulled into the driveway of the address Susan Meehan had provided, a dark-haired woman about Mandy's age was watering pots of flowers in front of a yellow one-story ranch. She put down the watering can and walked toward Mandy's station wagon with a smile and wave.

"You must be Mandy! And William!" she said peeking into the back seat.

"Yes. Hi, Susan," Mandy said, opening the car door.

The two women hugged.

"Please come inside. I'm happy to have the chance to meet you and talk about our husbands," Susan said.

Inside, the tiny home was neat and sparsely decorated. A large wedding photograph hung behind the sofa. Mandy walked toward it and studied the faces of Susan and Roger Meehan.

"What a beautiful picture," Mandy said.

"Thank you. We were high school sweethearts, and together since we were both fourteen. Married just ten months though when Roger was killed," she said sadly.

William grew bored and started pulling on Mandy's arms.

"I brought some coloring books, or maybe there some cartoons still on TV that might keep William entertained while we chat?" Mandy asked.

"Sure," she said turning on the console television across from the sofa. "This antenna is a little persnickety, though." She moved the antenna around and changed the channel. An H.R. Pufnstuf rerun came on the screen and both Mandy and William let out a little cry.

"Pufnstuf!" said William.

"That will be perfect," Mandy said.

Susan adjusted the antenna until she was satisfied the picture was as clear as it was going to get. "William, would you like a pillow and a blanket while you watch the show?"

William looked at his mother.

"That might be nice," Mandy said, nodding toward Susan.

Once William was settled, the two women went into the kitchen and Susan started a pot of coffee. They shared stories about meeting their husbands and their marriages cut short because of war.

Mandy stood to peek at William who had fallen asleep on the sofa.

She picked up her purse and pulled out two envelopes and a small velvet jewelry case. "I brought two letters that Adam had sent which he mentions his friendship with Roger. I thought you might like to see them."

Susan picked up the first letter and Mandy pointed to the part she wanted her to read.

"I'm on the bottom bunk in a four-man room," she read. "A big guy from Philly is above me. Roger Meehan has got to be one of the funniest guys I've ever met. He has me laughing all the time."

Mandy handed her the second letter and pointed to a paragraph for her to read: "Can't wait to get back to the states and be a normal working stiff and away from this place. I want us to stay in touch with Roger Meehan though. We've become great friends and I'm guessing you'd like his wife Susan. The way he describes her, I think you'd get along. The guy is a scream. Keeps me in stitches non-stop."

Susan smiled. "Roger was naturally funny. He was named 'Class Clown' of our high school senior class."

She handed the letters back to Mandy.

"Thank you for showing me those," she said. "I have something for you too."

She pulled a small envelope from the kitchen drawer. She opened it and pulled the dog tags and chain and a Polaroid photograph from it.

"Roger sent this with one of his letters," she said, handing Mandy the photograph. "I thought you'd like to have it."

It was a grainy picture of Adam and Roger standing in front of a metal building. Both were wearing Army fatigues and black boots. Both were smiling and Roger had his hand on Adam's shoulder. The bumper of a jeep was in the corner of the photograph.

As she studied it, Mandy realized that it was the most recent photograph she had seen of Adam. "I'd love to have this, Susan," she said. "Are you sure?"

"Absolutely I'm sure."

"Thank you," Mandy said, still studying the photograph.

"Thank you for reaching out to me after Roger was killed," Susan said. "I'm sorry I didn't respond to you then."

"I understand."

Mandy picked up the velvet box and pulled out the dog tags for Roger R. Meehan and handed them to Susan. Susan looked them over quietly.

She handed the dog tags in front of her to Mandy.

Mandy fingered the metal tags and chain and ran her finger over the imprinted name: ADAM J ROOKS. Underneath was his social security number. Under that, the words: A POS for his blood type. The second tag was identical to the first and both hung on a beaded silver chain.

Mandy looked up at Susan and noted a tear running down her cheek. At the same time, both women pulled the chains over their heads and patted the tags hanging at their center chests.

"I'm glad we did this," Susan said.

"Me too," said Mandy.

Susan served a tuna noodle casserole for lunch that William picked at.

That night they stayed in a hotel room in Richmond and the next morning, headed home to conclude their big adventure.

GINGER: AUGUST 1972

Everything was different once Rachel was born. Every day, Ginger was surprised all over again how difficult it was to squeeze in a shower or an actual meal, though she'd experienced the exact same thing the day before. Feeding, burping, changing, sleeping, waking, bathing all ran together. But as difficult as it was, the sixty-five days between the day that Rachel was born on June 4 and the day that Pete returned from war flew by.

On Thursday, August 10, she set her alarm for four-thirty a.m. She got in the shower, shaved her legs and spent more than an hour with her makeup and clothes before Rachel woke just before six in the morning. Then she took her time feeding and dressing their baby in her nicest outfit in preparation for Pete's return scheduled just before noon.

Early in her pregnancy, once her morning sickness passed, she had experienced an invigorating rush of energy. She spent time nearly every day with Millie, Mandy and William during her second trimester, but it was at the beginning of her third trimester that Mandy's husband had been captured as a prisoner of war and the Army moved her to Atlanta.

Ginger was devastated. As much as she wanted to give Mandy's heartbreak her full attention, her pregnancy and Pete's return took her first thoughts, and Mandy's move accommodated it.

Their daily get-togethers ceased and Ginger depended solely on Millie for companionship. She couldn't share the secret she and Mandy shared with Millie so she did her best to focus on the baby she and Pete would raise and push her concerns that Pete would suspect out of her mind. She checked off the months that turned into days, then hours before Pete would return from Vietnam.

It's finally here.

Right on time, the plane landed on base and sat like a silver-sphered illusion as it rested on the tarmac. Ginger was surrounded by children, parents and other wives waiting on the inside of the glass wall that separated them from the soldiers they had waited so long to see. It felt like forever as she paced back and forth. She wanted Pete's first look at Rachel to be perfect and rocked and patted their baby in her arms praying she wouldn't get fussy before Pete saw her as she exchanged shy smiles with the other women.

Once the door opened and a set of metal steps unfolded from the door of the plane, a collective gasp filled the room as soldiers began to emerge one-by-one down the steps across the asphalt toward the windowed room that separated them. Ginger didn't realize she was counting until number fourteen reverberated through her head and she saw Pete's lanky, beautiful body emerge from the plane. She saw him squint toward the window and sprint across the tarmac.

It was then that she noticed the rise in decibel that had enveloped the room as soldiers were reunited with their wives, children, parents, siblings, friends and more. She pushed through the crowd and panicked that she wouldn't make it to a spot that Pete could see them as soon as he entered the room.

But he did. He spotted them through the crowd and gave Ginger a smile and nod as he stepped back to allow for reunions to happen around him. He patiently kept his eyes on Ginger and Rachel until he was clear to move their way. When he was just a few feet away, he dropped his knapsack and made a quick push through the remaining crowd to put his arms around his wife and daughter. He met Ginger's lips and didn't let go for a long time. When he finally did pull away, his eyes found the eyes of the wide-awake baby she held in her arms.

His face grew soft, an audible exhale released in his chest, his shoulders relaxed and remained motionless as he looked at Rachel's eyes. Rachel blinked and looked right back at him. She blew a tiny bubble from her mouth without taking her eyes off of his.

Ginger smiled and placed their baby in Pete's arms.

"So this...." he said quietly, "...is Rachel."

Rachel looked at him as intently as he looked at her. He only blinked when she did.

After a long while, he pulled his eyes back up to Ginger and tears instantly fell from his eyes. "Oh my, God, babe. This feels so good."

I'm falling in love all over again, Ginger heard herself think.

"Let's get out of here," he said.

It wasn't until Ginger passed the keys to Pete and she was in the front seat holding the baby in her arms that Pete realized that he'd left his knapsack. She waited in the car with a smile spread across her face until he returned with the bag and threw it into the back seat of the Vega.

"Time to start our life," he said. He turned to Ginger and kissed her again before starting the car. His hands and arms were shaking as he backed out of the parking space.

RACHEL: NOVEMBER 1998

"Cameron went out with your friend Dave again last night. Did he tell you?" Rachel asked.

Liam's head popped from the bathroom door. A toothbrush was dangling from the side of his mouth. "He said he was going to call her," he mumbled unintelligibly.

His head disappeared and Rachel heard spitting and rinsing.

"Sorry," he said popping around again. "He thinks she's really cute."

Rachel didn't respond but stored the information to share with Cameron later.

It was the second time she'd spent the night at Liam's apartment. They had made it through the awkward conversations about HIV testing, birth control options and exclusivity, and had found the initial clumsiness worth the effort.

Twice last night and once this morning worth it, she thought.

"So when will you leave for St. Louis?" she asked, sitting up in bed and fluffing the pillow behind her.

"I have a flight on Tuesday night," he said, stepping into the room wearing nothing but a pair of grey sweats. "Thanksgiving dinner will be at my parents' house with both of my brothers and I return Saturday morning around ten."

"Okay," she said, wondering if she should ask the question she'd been pondering.

"What about you?" he asked. "When does your family get in town? I'd love to meet them if it could work out."

"You would!" she said, fearing she sounded a little too excited. "I mean, I'd love for you to meet them. They won't leave until Sunday night, so maybe we can plan on Saturday night?"

"Perfect. Will I get to meet your Oodles and Poppy too?"

"Of course," she said. "Roxanne will be at my apartment most of the time, but everyone else will be staying at their house. Oodles will plan a meal of some sort and she'll be excited to meet you too. They all will," she added.

"Then it's a plan," he said, leaning onto the bed to kiss her. "Put on some music and I'll try my culinary skills and see if I can make us an omelet."

"Really? Sounds fabulous."

"Don't get too excited. It's an experiment, but I'll do my best."

"Deal," she said, swinging her legs to the side of the bed.

After brushing her teeth, washing her face and pulling on a pair of jeans and a t-shirt, Rachel perused through Liam's collection of CDs and cassette tapes.

"Is James Taylor too mellow?" she called.

"Your choice," he called back.

"Well it is a rainy morning after all," she said to herself as she put the CD into the player and pressed the power button.

She looked through his stack of books and found one she wanted to take a closer look at. On top of the book, she pulled down a cubed plastic display box with a silver bracelet inside. The name ADAM J. ROOKS was imprinted across it.

Liam walked toward her with a glass of orange juice and saw her looking at the box.

"What is this?" she asked.

"It's a P.O.W. bracelet. For my father."

Rachel looked confused.

"My biological father died as a prisoner of war during the Vietnam

War," he said. "I was four when he died and had only seen him once when I was three. I really don't remember him at all."

Rachel had a vague memory of seeing a similar bracelet among her mother's things, but was confused by Liam's story.

He continued, "The bracelets were worn in support of the soldiers that had been captured and held as prisoners by the Vietnamese. The intention was that people would wear the bracelets until the prisoner was released. Unfortunately, my father died in the prison. Just a few days before the Vietnam War ended, in fact."

Rachel handed the box to Liam and took the glass of juice from his hand. She sat on the sofa and he joined her.

"So, Rooks..." she began.

"My mother remarried a man named Glenn Wilson," he explained filling in the answer to her question before she had the chance to ask it. "He's the only father I've really ever known and he adopted me, so my last name has been Wilson for as long as I can remember."

"Wow. I'm sorry," Rachel said.

"Me too," he said kissing her head and placing the box on the coffee table. "I'm going to get working on my omelet though."

Rachel's favorite James Taylor song, "Don't Let Me Be Lonely Tonight" came through the speakers. Feeling mellow with Liam's story and the music, she curled up on the sofa.

After breakfast, Liam pulled a small box from the hall closet and set it on the coffee table in front of Rachel. He opened up a framed photograph and studied it, then handed it to Rachel and plopped down beside her.

"This is me and my Mom and Dad when he was on leave during the war. Soon after, he was captured as a prisoner."

She looked at each face carefully. Liam was on his father's shoulders and swinging an oversized sucker. His curls were blonder and longer.

"Was this at Six Flags?"

"Yeah. I was three. He was home for my birthday that year."

His dad was broad-shouldered like Liam. He was wearing aviator-style sunglasses and had a smile that looked familiar. His mother was cute. Her sassy short haircut emphasized her big eyes and she wore short white shorts and a halter top.

"Your mom is adorable," she said. "And you look a lot like your dad, too. He's very handsome."

"I wish I remembered more about him," he said. "And by the way, you didn't even mention how cute I am in this picture!"

"Goes without saying, dude. You're hot—and a little gooey it looks like. Look at that sucker you had!"

Liam pulled a stack of loose photos from the box and handed her the first one.

"This is my family before Ben was born. My dad—he's my adopted dad, but I just think of him as Dad, and this is my Mom and my brother—technically my stepbrother—Will. Will was eight and I was seven when Ben was born, so Mom might have been pregnant in this picture."

He handed her several more: Liam in his football uniform; Liam and his Mom licking batters while making a cake; the three Wilson boys in an Olan Mills sepia-toned photo.

"Why don't you display some of these?" Rachel asked.

"I guess I'm just not much of a picture guy," he said, putting the box back into the closet.

He picked up the shadow box and reread the inscription before placing it back on the shelf.

"Not much of a decorator I guess," he added. "Anyway, what do you want to do today?"

MANDY: JANUARY 1974

Mandy stretched clear tape across the box of Christmas decorations and then pushed the box into the hall closet of the house on Sycamore Street. Then she spread out the coats and starched tablecloth that hung there to cover the box until the next year.

She knocked on the window and waved to William who was seated in the backyard playing with his trucks. He waved back. It was a warm day for January and the sun was glowing across his blond curls as he played. The two of them had enjoyed the small Christmas tree they'd picked out together and decorated with popcorn strings and ornaments she'd bought at the dime store. Taking it all back down felt more hopeful than she expected—like an opportunity to start anew.

She pulled down the handful of Christmas cards and photos from the cabinet where she'd taped the holiday greetings that had been mailed to the house and stacked them neatly. Then she tucked the card and photograph Ginger had sent inside a tablet of paper and headed toward the sofa. It was full of so much information that she felt she needed a quiet and lengthy opportunity to answer with a letter and update.

She studied the photo. Rachel was eighteen months and cute as she could be. She stood in front of Ginger and Pete holding a doll with long red hair in one hand and a doll that Mandy recognized as Baby Beans in the other. Ginger was wearing a green halter-style jumpsuit and platform shoes. Pete was wearing a sports jacket and grey pants.

She could tell they were standing in front of the window in the living room of their New Jersey apartment when the photo was taken. They looked happy.

She reread highlights from the note that Ginger had written on both sides of the inside and the back of the card:

> ...Looks like the Army will be moving us again. Texas this time. I'll send our new address when I know details. Our biggest news, though, is that we are expecting another baby in April.

Mandy studied Ginger's body in the photo. No signs that she was showing when this photo was taken. She picked up her pen and started her letter:

> Dear Ginger,
>
> I love the green jumpsuit. You're a knock-out in it and I certainly can't tell you're pregnant in that get-up! Pete and Rachel look wonderful, too. Congratulations on baby #2!
> A move to Texas? Sounds like a great place for William and me to visit once you're settled.
> We had a nice and quiet holiday. My parents flew us to New York for Thanksgiving, which was a big treat for William to fly on a plane. Me too, for that matter; it was only my third time flying. My brother came too.

She stopped and considered whether or not she should scratch out the last words. She'd studied Rachel's face carefully in the photograph when it had arrived before Christmas and had looked at it several times since noting the resemblance to Scott across the eyes and forehead.

I would never say that to Ginger, of course. She's so sensitive at the mention of Scott. Would Scott ever settle down enough to be a good father? Or a good husband?

She got up and got herself a Coke and then reread what she'd already written, finally deciding to leave the sentence in and to move on...

For Christmas William and I celebrated together in the morning, then went to Adam's parents' house for dinner. They are still keeping William a lot for me as I have enrolled in a nursing program and I need to be in school two days a week after he finishes school. Ted picks him up from kindergarten and keeps him until I pick him up from their house around six. If all goes as planned, I should finish in spring of next year.

William adores Ted and I can see how much he enjoys having a man in his life. He's one of the smartest kids in his class and makes friends easily. He played tee-ball last spring and loved it. He rarely talks about Adam, and hard as I try to tell him about his father and remind him how much his father loved him, it gets harder as the months pass.

I met a divorced father of one of the other kids on the tee-ball team. He asked me if I would consider going out sometime. I told him no, but I may re-think the idea if I see him again. Otherwise, it's just me and the five-year-old and the in-laws. Hanging in there though, so don't worry about me.

Don't forget to send me your address and news about the new baby.

I miss you!

Love,
Mandy

She heard the back door squeak as William came walking through the living room trailing dirt and dropping his windbreaker onto the floor.

"Whoa fella," she said. "Take a look at the mess you're making on the floor."

William turned his head and looked at the floor as Mandy noted the mud caked around his left sneaker.

"Sorry, Mommy. I have to go to the bathroom," he said.

"Well, go and then we have some vacuuming to do when you're through. Not to mention a jacket to pick up and hang where it belongs."

She smiled as she saw him hold himself as he rushed into the bathroom without closing the door.

Ginger: August 1974

Rachel toddled into the kitchen dragging a tiny wagon in one hand and her doll baby in the other. One of P.J.'s blankets was spread across the base of the wagon and a white cloud of dust puffed from it as she clumsily turned the corner.

"Rachel, what is in the wagon?" Ginger said, rushing over to see what was emitting into the air.

"Bay poddah," she said dropping the handle of the wagon onto the floor with a thud and hugging her doll. "Soft for Bay Bay."

Nearly a cup-full of baby powder sat in small piles across the blanket. When Ginger looked closer at Rachel, she realized it was in her hair, across her cheek and down the front of her dress.

"Oh Rachel, babies don't need this much powder. Just a tiny bit of baby powder," she said, patting Rachel's doll with one hand and grabbing a tissue from her pocket to wipe her daughter's nose and face.

Rachel was two and seemed so grown up since P.J. had been born four months earlier. Her precocious nature intensified once she became a big sister and Ginger found herself exhausted most days keeping up with her. Pete was enamored with their daughter and son and only laughed at the stories she'd tell each night when he got home.

"Let's go shake this powder outside," she said folding the corners of the blanket into itself and taking Rachel's hand and leading her toward the back door.

A rare August breeze captured the powder in the dank air and held it for a brief second before dropping white flakes all over the backyard as Ginger shook the blanket. Rachel danced and spun in the powdery shower.

"Let's go check on P.J.," she said, imagining the mess that might be in their shared room where P.J. was sleeping.

P.J. was stirring from his morning nap as they entered the room. The bottom dresser drawer had been pulled open and Ginger was easily able to imagine the scene whereby Rachel stood inside the drawer to reach the folded blankets and baby powder from the top of the small bureau. Circles of congealed powder dotted the linoleum floor. The scene was further unraveled once Ginger spotted the lid of a jar of Vaseline under P.J.'s crib and the open jar itself next to the dresser.

"Rachel!" Ginger said, grabbing Rachel's hands. They were covered in the gooey Vaseline. She spotted a glob of the thick gel setting a stain into the back of her dress.

Rachel smiled, her seven teeth taking over her face as her eyes squinched together. Pete called it Rachel's "puppet face" as movement of the mouth seemed to affect the eyes and visa versa.

"Oh gracious, Rachel," Ginger said, grateful that it would be easy to clean Vaseline from the ugly floor in the base apartment versus the shag carpet she hoped to have some day. "Let's get you cleaned up."

P.J was awake and crying. Ginger had only enough time to clean Rachel's hands and pull off her dress before P.J. reached full volume.

She picked him up and nuzzled his head and then placed him on the changing table. "Rachel, you stand right beside Mommy's legs," she said. "Don't walk through the powder. We'll all get some lunch and we will get this cleaned up as soon as we finish."

Once P.J. had a fresh diaper, she took Rachel's hand and closed the bedroom door with her foot.

Two hours until afternoon naptime. I'm going to kick my legs up and finally write the letter to Mandy I've wanted to get to.

"Lunch. Then cleanup. Then it will be naptime, my precocious one."

Rachel looked up at her mother and smiled. Her eyes closing as her tiny teeth flashed against her rosy lips.

Two hours later, Ginger rinsed the mop in the kitchen sink and carried it to the back step to dry, then pulled her lined pad of stationery paper from the drawer and snuggled into the sofa's cushions to write her letter.

Dear Mandy,

I can't believe how this year is flying by! It's already August and I am just getting you these photos of little P.J. I hope all is well for you and William. Thank you for the adorable school picture. I have it on the refrigerator and think of you both every day. He is so handsome! Does he look like Adam at that age? The light hair throws me, but he's got your eyes, for sure.

We welcomed Peter James McCarthy, Jr. on April 10. He surprised us by announcing himself while I was dropping off Rachel at the day care program she goes to twice a week. My water broke while I was standing at the front counter at the school and he was born just four hours later. Even though he was almost two weeks early, he weighed nine pounds, five ounces. He's a good baby and sleeps even more than Rachel did. He's already more than sixteen pounds and I think he's going to be tall like his dad with my green eyes.

Rachel is loving the big sister role. She turned two in June and is a handful and then some. She's talking up a storm, though most of it we can't understand. She's going to a pre-school two days a week at the church we joined here. It gives me a chance to catch up on a few errands and spend time with just the baby. Her hair is definitely going to be red. It's darker than mine, so maybe auburn. She is the apple of Pete's eye—and visa versa! They are completely in love with one another.

Texas is hot. So hot, in fact, they often put fans on the trees. We are at Fort Hood in central Texas. Not much here, but we are in between Dallas and Austin, and we've made day trips to both cities. The Army is keeping Pete in the logistics role, and he is currently managing artillery supplies for six bases. Be sure to save the return address label with our address here. Looks like we'll be here for another year at least. I hope soon we can settle somewhere and buy a house, but it won't be in Texas, I'm afraid. Who knows where we'll be sent next. I'm not complaining though. Pete is doing great and I would expect another promotion any time now.

Pete's mother came from Indiana to help out for two weeks when P.J. was born. My mom and dad just left yesterday. They are both still teaching and had to get back and ready for school. They are a big help with both kids so I'm already missing them.

We do have a nice group of wives living on base. I've made some pretty good friends but miss our fun in Columbus and miss you! I haven't heard from Millie in a while but have a photo of P.J. to send her too. Did you and William ever visit her in Columbus?

How is nursing school? I'm anxious for an update. Please take care and know that we think of you and William all the time!

Love,
Ginger

RACHEL: NOVEMBER 1998

Right on time, the receptionist buzzed the phone at Rachel's cubical, "Miss McCarthy, you have a visitor at the front desk. Roxanne McCarthy is here to see you."

Rachel laughed at the formality and imagined what Roxanne must be thinking as she waited in the plush ELG Global lobby for her to emerge from the depths of the marble-walled thirtieth-floor office. The sisters had made the plan the night before when Rachel had picked up Roxanne at the Atlanta airport: Roxanne would drive Rachel's car the next morning, drop Rachel at work, then go back to the apartment to shower and relax, come to her office for a quick tour and lunch, then she could walk around Buckhead for another hour before meeting back at Rachel's office.

"The company closes early today to give employees the chance to get started on the Thanksgiving holiday," she had explained. "So we can shop together in the late afternoon and then pick up the groceries we need for the green bean casserole."

Poppy would pick up her parents and P.J., who were arriving on separate flights in the late afternoon, and everyone would meet at Oodles and Poppy's that night for Chinese takeout before their big dinner on Thursday.

"Miss McCarthy?" Rachel teased. "Would you like to come back and see my office?"

Roxanne stood. "Sure, Miss McCarthy," she said, glancing at the receptionist with an eye roll and following Rachel down the elegant hallway.

Rachel introduced her to several co-workers and showed her the sparsely furnished cubical. "Well, I've only been here a few weeks," she said when Roxanne teased.

The sisters walked across Peachtree Street to Phipps Plaza, Atlanta's swankiest shopping mall, for a lunch of salad and soup at The Tavern restaurant.

"I'll be in San Francisco for training next month," Rachel told her. "You could stay in my hotel room for a few days and we could hang out at night. Maybe P.J. could join us too."

"Sounds like fun. It's a five-hour drive for me though and I'm not sure my car will make it."

"Why don't you look for a job in Atlanta?"

"I've thought about it. But it doesn't feel like home here any more than California does. That's the trouble with being an Army brat, I guess."

"At least Oodles and Poppy are here. And me! The only other choice would be New Mexico."

"No way to New Mexico. As soon as I did that, Mom and Dad would announce they are retiring to Florida or something."

"True," Rachel admitted. "I think they actually like uprooting every few years."

"Do you think you'll stay in Atlanta?"

"Probably. I like this new job a lot, and I like being close to Oodles and Poppy."

"No boyfriend?"

Rachel blushed and cussed to herself that her face would turn red even in front of her little sister. "Actually," she confessed. "Kind of."

"Kind of?"

"It's just that I haven't introduced him to anyone in the family yet. I'm just being cautious."

"Did you invite him to Thanksgiving?"

"No. He's with his family in St. Louis," Rachel said. "But he'll be back Saturday and Oodles said I could bring him to dinner that night. Everyone will meet him then."

They discussed Roxanne's job, her friends in California and offered more guesses toward their parents' next move when Rachel finally looked at her watch.

"Oh crap," she said. "My hour is up. Shop around here and then meet me back in the lobby at two o'clock. The office closes then."

Back at the apartment, they made the green bean casserole, covered it with foil and placed it in on the back seat of the car, along with their duffel bags filled with pajamas, a change of clothes and makeup bags.

"Why don't we just stay at your apartment tonight?" Roxanne asked.

"I just think it's more fun to all be together when we wake up on a holiday," Rachel said. "It reminds me of when we were little."

Though the opportunities were few and far between, the routine was the same as it had always been: Rachel's parents slept in her mother's childhood room, P.J. slept in Carlton's old room; and Rachel and Roxanne slept on the twin beds in the guest room. On the rare occasion that Carlton and his family were in town at the same time, Carlton and his wife went to his old room, and P.J. and their son slept in sleeping bags in the basement.

They reached Oodles and Poppy's house and found their dad in the driveway pulling bags out of the trunk of Poppy's car.

"There are my girls," Pete said walking to the car and poking his head into the passenger's side and kissing Roxanne on the cheek. "Get out of this car and give your old man a hug."

"You're looking slim, Dad!" Rachel said. "Very nice!"

"Yes, your mother has put me on a diet. And a walking routine every night after supper."

Their mother and P.J. joined the reunion on the front lawn. Her hair was blonder than the last time Rachel had seen her and she suspected she had finally had to start coloring to cover gray. "Your hair looks nice, Mom. Cute glasses."

"Isn't this wonderful we're all here together?" Ginger said, hugging them both.

P.J. looked like a wayward rocker with his hair down to his shoulders and a scruffy beard, but had a big smile and hugs for his sisters too.

Oodles and Poppy joined the crowd on the front lawn and the entire family enjoyed getting reacquainted and telling stories. After a few minutes, Oodles and Poppy's neighbor, Sarah Thompson, pulled into her driveway and jumped out of the car to greet the crowd.

"Ginger, so good to see you, honey," Sarah said.

"You too," her mother said. "Pete? You remember Sarah Thompson, right?" She pulled Rachel's father into the conversation and re-introduced Roxanne and P.J. to Sarah.

Sarah put her arm around Rachel as she spoke to the rest of the family. She nodded toward her car when a second woman closed the car door and walked toward them. "Do you all remember my niece Lorna?" she asked.

The group greeted Lorna who looked at the crowd with distant, glassy eyes.

"You know what, I need to check on something in the oven," Ginger said and scurried back into the house.

Rachel was surprised when her mother didn't come back outside. She watched the front door regularly. When the conversation eventually waned, Sarah and Lorna left to get groceries out of the car, and Rachel's family moved to the inside of the house.

Once inside, Oodles and her mother made assignments and a schedule for the cooking: P.J. and Poppy would pick up the Chinese takeout while Oodles and Ginger made pumpkin pies. After dinner, Rachel and Roxanne would make Pilgrim and Indian hats from construction paper—one for each member of the family—while Pete and P.J. gathered firewood and Oodles and Ginger started the bread dough and set it out to rise.

In the morning they would have oatmeal and hot cocoa for breakfast while they put the turkey in the oven and watched the first half of the Macy's Thanksgiving Day parade. Midway through the parade, they would start preparing the dressing and the sweet potatoes, set the table and put the green beans and other casseroles and the bread in the oven. Like every Thanksgiving at Oodles and Poppy's house, the men of the family were responsible for keeping the fire going, emptying trash and reaching the rarely used serving dishes that Oodles kept at the top of the pantry.

And like clockwork, the plan worked to perfection. Thursday's dinner was delicious and full of all the memories, jokes and family teasing that Rachel craved. She and Roxanne stayed in the guest room for a second night, and on Friday the ladies of the family shopped the Black Friday sales while Pete, P.J. and Poppy watched football.

"Mom, did Oodles mention that I'm bringing someone to dinner tomorrow night?" Rachel asked as she and her mother browsed through Macy's blouses.

"She did," Ginger said. "Sounds interesting. Must be someone special."

"I like him a lot," she said. "Oodles and Poppy haven't met him either, but I'm anxious to see what you think of him."

"Well, I'm sure we will be quite impressed if you think that much of him, Rachel. I'm looking forward to it."

By Friday night, P.J. and Roxanne were both tiring of family and plotting to find a new source of fun before they flew back to their respective homes on Sunday.

"Come on, y'all. Oodles has a spaghetti dinner planned and I want everyone to meet Liam," Rachel whined to her siblings.

"Sorry Rach," P.J. said. "There's a group playing in Macon with a bass guitar I want to see. I'm going to say 'goodbye' to everyone in the morning and then leave from there."

"Roxanne?"

"Actually, I think I've had enough of family, too. I'm going with P.J."

"I really don't understand you two," she said. "You see Oodles and Poppy once a year at best."

"But we aren't close like you are," Roxanne said.

"Because you don't spend time with them!"

"We don't live here, Rachel," P.J. said.

"Which is why you need to spend as much time as you can when you *are* here!"

Her brother and sister exchanged glances and Rachel could tell she was losing the battle.

"What about Mom and Dad?" she added. "We barely see them anymore either. It's been almost a year since our entire family has been together."

"But we were together for Thanksgiving and now we're ready to get back to our lives," P.J. said.

"Didn't you both get enough of short-term relationships growing up like we did? How can you not want to spend every minute of time you can with those few people that have been consistent in our lives?"

Rachel looked at Roxanne who just shrugged.

"You know what?" she said. "Fine, if that's the way it is, just go. I really wanted Liam to meet my family, but he'll just have to miss out on my brother and sister if you two won't stay."

"Are you that serious about this guy, Rachel?" P.J. asked.

"I don't' know yet. Maybe."

"Well when you know, we'll meet him.

"I am serious about Liam," she said quietly.

Rachel didn't even bother looking at her brother or sister to see if they had changed their minds after hearing that. She was more intrigued to realize it was true.

I am serious about Liam.

I think I love him.

MANDY: MAY 1975

"Happy Wednesday, Carla," Mandy said as she pulled out her wallet. "The usual, of course."

"How you doin' today, Miss Mandy. You're looking pretty today."

Mandy looked down at her pink uniform dress, white nurses shoes and white stockings and laughed. "Thanks Carla."

The corner table at Carla's Sandwich Shop and the lobby pay phone next to it had become Mandy's office every lunch break. Just two weeks after completing nursing school, she had been offered a full-time job with Dr. Robinson's general medical practice. The job was convenient and the hours were consistent, but her thirty-minute lunch break from the office two stories above was the only opportunity she had to handle the many calls that could only be made during weekday business hours.

Even the simple dentist appointments for William, the occasional hair appointments for her, and the calls to the school for this or that had become something that she had to list and keep organized in a pocketed spiral notebook, then check off as she completed them. Correspondence with the Army continued as she completed the details of settling Adam's estate, and phone calls could often only be made during workday hours. And now that she'd added the wedding plans, she found that calls to the caterer, photographer and dress shop were all best made then too, during the short period of time each day that her mind was on life's day-to-day management.

Carla, the restaurant's owner, manager and only employee, was an understanding single mother herself. She was happy to accommodate and kept the chair tipped onto the table at Mandy's spot in the back until she arrived every day at noon carrying the tote bag where she kept her spiral notebook, various papers and the rubbery oval squeeze coin purse where she kept dimes for her daily calls.

She didn't even mind that Mandy brought her own sandwich. Every day Mandy would buy a medium sweet tea and one of Carla's fresh baked chocolate chip cookies that she wrapped in waxed paper for Mandy to take home for William's lunch the next day.

"I'm just happy to be doing my thing, Carla," she said. "And happy to have you for a friend. William says you make the best cookies on planet Earth, by the way. They're studying the planets in first grade now."

"You tell William that if he has any ins with Jupiter or Mars, I'd be happy to ship," she laughed, handing Mandy the tea. "By the way, Dr. Robinson was in here yesterday afternoon. Mentioned he was very happy having you on staff."

"Did he really? That's nice to hear."

Carla handed Mandy the cookie and she dropped it into her tote bag and settled in at the corner table. No calls needed today; just the chance to sort through the mail from the day before.

She pulled out the spiral notebook and the stack of mail from her tote bag. The first two were bills. She reviewed each, placed the outside envelope and other trash on the edge of the table and tucked the bills in the inside cover pocket of the spiral notebook. She sorted out the next few pieces of junk mail and then stopped quickly when she realized the next envelope in the stack was her own handwriting. And it had "Return to Sender" stamped across it in black block letters; underneath, the words: Address Unknown.

This is the letter I sent to Ginger last month.

She picked it up and turned it over.

The Christmas card I sent to the Texas address wasn't returned, she thought.

And I received a card from her at Christmas from there.

She studied the address.

Maybe I transposed a number?

She slid her finger through the opening on the back of the envelope and pulled out the letter.

If Ginger didn't see this, she doesn't know about Glenn. Or the wedding. Or even my job!

"Is everything okay?" said Carla, busing the tables around Mandy.

"Yes, why? Do I look scary?"

"Just a little upset."

"Well, I guess I am a little upset," Mandy admitted. "I just realized a letter I sent to a friend has been returned. She and her family move a lot with the Army, but I'm surprised that it didn't forward. And even more surprised that I didn't know about another move for her."

A customer entered the shop and Carla scurried off with a sympathetic groan.

Mandy unfolded the letter and reread the words that Ginger had never seen:

Dear Ginger,

P.J. is so precious and so is Rachel. The McCarthy clan is growing so fast and you and Pete look great. I'm so happy for you.

I'm sorry I'm not better about staying in touch. It seems like the months pass by so quickly and I realize another one has gone by and your baby is another month older — (I'm sure he's walking by now!) and I haven't filled you in on all that's been happening here either.

Lots of news though: I'm an official R.N. I've just started work at a general practice. It's a small office and I won't be using many of the skills that I learned in school, but it's close to home and the hours are consistent, so I think it's the right fit for me. In school, I really enjoyed the trauma training we did. I think someday I would enjoy working in a hectic emergency room, but for now, I'm happy to be working at mild-mannered Dr. Robinson's office. He actually reminds me of Marcus Welby, if that gives you any idea.

The bigger news: I'm getting married. I know, crazy, right? I may or may not have ever mentioned Glenn Wilson in my previous letters. He is a divorced father of a boy that played tee-ball with William (ironically, his son is also named William). He asked me out three times before I finally said yes, but it turns out we're crazy about each other. You'd like him too. His ex-wife suffers from some psychological issues and she's given Glenn full custody. He's a great father, very good to me and to William and insanely good looking. He's from Atlanta. In fact, he has friends who grew up with Adam in Avondale. He's in sales with a chemical company and we are going to have a very small wedding over Memorial weekend. William and I will move into his house in Decatur. I've enclosed a card with our new address.

The two Williams get along just fine. My William is five months younger than his, but they will both be in the same second grade next year. Glenn wants to officially adopt my William, which I think Adam would be very happy about. We've been discussing ideas for how we deal with two William Wilsons in the same grade—and brothers, at that. We'll figure it out.

I told my parents about the wedding, but I haven't encouraged them to come. Adam's parents do want to be there though. They have been so critical to helping me through all this and I think it was William that kept them sane as they dealt with Adam's death. They want to be sure to keep strong grandparenting ties to William and I'm thrilled about that too.

William and I did take a day trip to Columbus the Sunday after I graduated. Millie's trailer was there but it looked like it had been empty for months. I could see in one of the windows and most of the furniture was gone. Any word from her? I hope it means she's found Oscar and O'Ray.

Take care and write soon. I'll send a wedding pic after we've settled.

Love and miss you,
Mandy

Mandy tucked the letter back into the envelope and dropped it into her tote bag with the rest of the mail.

I'll confirm that I have the address correct when I get home and then resend.

She looked at her watch and quickly gathered the rest of the mail in her tote. She dropped the trash in the trashcan as she called goodbye to Carla and headed back up to Dr. Robinson's general medicine practice.

GINGER: OCTOBER 1975

"Feeling any better?"

Ginger managed a slight nod with her eyelids, but even the minuscule movement of her forehead and chin sent another wave of nausea through the back of her throat, chest and stomach.

"Liar," Pete said, bending to kiss her head.

Ginger took a deep breath and managed a tiny smile and a raise of her cheeks.

"We found the last of the ginger sticks on the island, and I got you some lemon-flavored sticks and three boxes of Lemonheads," he said passing her a brown paper sack. "The woman at the candy counter suggested you try peppermint, so I threw a few of those in too."

Ginger's stomach wretched sending a jolt through her back and shoulders. She looked up at Pete with an apologetic wince.

"What? Peppermint doesn't sound good to you?"

Ginger closed her eyes and her head made a weak movement to the right and then the left.

"No problem," he said pulling the red and white hard candy sticks from the bag and handing it back to her.

Rachel appeared at the edge of the bed carrying a bouquet of red tulips. Her mouth was puffed out and a ring of goo circled her lips.

"You brought tulips!" Ginger said taking the flowers from Rachel. "Thank you sweethearts." She smiled at Pete and then at Rachel.

When Rachel saw she had both her parents' attention, she dropped a large white ball into her sticky hands and said, "P.J.'s diaper is stinky." Then she popped the candy ball back into her mouth, grabbed her nose and squeezed her nostrils tight with her sticky fingers and ran back out of the room, chanting, "Stinky, stinky, stinky" around the giant piece of candy that filled her mouth.

Pete met Ginger's eyes. "Jawbreaker," he said. "She insisted. And I'll take care of the loaded diaper. You rest awhile and maybe you can rally by late afternoon and we can catch your parents about the time they are getting back from church."

Ginger nodded and watched him close the blinds and walk out closing the bedroom door.

I hope he thinks to clean up Rachel too.

She pulled a ginger stick from the bag, put it in her mouth and closed her eyes. The darkened room offered welcome relief. The sun was bright through the top of the window and even lying in bed, she could see the tips of palm trees and the Waianae Mountains beyond.

An unexpected need had the Army shifting Pete—now Sergeant First Class Pete McCarthy—to Fort Shafter in Oahu, Hawaii, almost a year earlier than they'd expected to transfer from Fort Hood. The surprise and rushed move was challenge enough for Ginger with a three-year-old and P.J., just five months, but finding out she was pregnant just after the move, and then the worst morning sickness she'd experienced with any pregnancy, made the beauty of Hawaii superfluous since they'd arrived the month before.

Pete had covered the parenting duties all weekend and let her stay in bed, but as Sunday drew further into the afternoon, she realized she was out of time and had no choice but to rally and find a way to put the nausea out of her mind. She pulled her legs to the side of the bed and steadied her upright body. The ginger sticks had helped some, even more than lemon with this pregnancy, and she looked at what was left of the candy, bit off the point she'd formed from sucking, placed the rest on a plate on the night stand and headed for the shower.

Once out, she brushed her teeth for the first time all day, pulled on a loose-fitting t-shirt and a pair of denim overalls and her Dr. Scholl's sandals, braided her wet hair down the back, dropped a box of Lemonheads in her pocket and left the bedroom.

"Mommy!" Rachel screamed and ran to her wrapping her arms around Ginger's legs. P.J. cooed from a blanket on the floor when he saw her. The tiny living room was a mess with toys and bottles and pillows scattered about.

"I'm ready for some fresh air. Anyone else?" she asked.

Rachel spun in circles, knocking into Ginger with her arms and sending another wave of queasiness.

"Are you sure?" Pete asked.

"Couldn't we walk to the admin building to make our calls?"

"It's less than a mile from here. Rachel could ride her trike."

"Let's do that then," she said, picking up P.J. and nuzzling his neck. "It should be about noon Atlanta time when we get there and they'll be home from church by then. I think it will help to look around and walk."

The base's WATS line—short for wide-area telephone service—was permitted for personal long distance calls during certain weekend hours. They had made calls the first Sunday they arrived, but Ginger hadn't even known about the pregnancy then when they called her parents and Pete's mother.

The beach was several miles away, but the salty air, sunny skies and swaying palm trees offered a welcome change. Ginger took in the island's beauty for the first time since they'd arrived. They walked alongside Palm Circle that anchors Fort Shafter with acres of grassy lawn surrounded by palm trees while Ginger pushed P.J. in the stroller and Pete kept pace with Rachel's tricycle. She was feeling better than she had in the three weeks since they arrived.

The sparse room reserved for WATS line use had only a table, telephone and eight plastic chairs.

"It's about quarter-to in Atlanta. Why don't we call my mother first?" Pete suggested.

P.J. was asleep in the stroller and Ginger pulled Rachel up to her lap as Pete dialed. His mother answered right away.

After much talk about Hawaii and hulas and the ocean and, "Yes, Mom, you must come for a visit while we're here. You've never seen anything so beautiful." Pete finally told her, "We have some more news, Mom. Ginger is pregnant and we will be having number three in the spring."

"Oh my land," Ginger heard Bea McCarthy say.

Pete handed the phone to Ginger.

"Hi Mrs. McCarthy. Yes, I'm feeling just fine," she said, noting Pete's sharp head snap when he heard her lie. "Spring would be a perfect time for you to visit, and I'd love the help."

She handed the phone to Rachel, "Say hello to Grandma."

Ginger noted a faint line of sticky candy still ringing her mouth as she took the handset and said, "Hello, Gramma."

After her string of one-word responses, Pete took the phone from her and finished the conversation with his mother with discussion of the weather in Indiana, her bursitis and the promise to call again soon.

He scooted the telephone toward Ginger and she dialed her parents' familiar number.

"Hi Mom," Ginger said, feeling a slight wave of homesickness when she heard her mother's voice.

"I told your father I thought we'd hear from you today. How are you and Pete and those sweet little children? I just hate it that we are so far away from them."

After covering sundry subjects, Ginger asked, "Where is Dad? Can you get him on the line?"

"He's next door talking to Roy Thompson in the driveway, but I can see him from here, and he's heading inside now."

"Well put him on the other phone when he gets in because I have some news for both of you," Ginger said. "But first, I'll let you talk to Rachel."

Ginger listened as her mother chatted away and worked to encourage Rachel's responses. Rachel listened intently as her grandmother asked her about being a big sister.

Always shy on the telephone, Rachel responded with only, "P.J."

Ginger could hear both sides of the conversation as her mother described going to a pumpkin festival. "Rachel, your Pop and I saw the most beautiful pumpkins. I wish you had seen them. There were oodles and oodles of them."

And she could hear her father's voice when he picked up the second line in the bedroom. "Well howdy-hoo, Miss Rachel-roo, I'm so glad you called," she heard him say.

As Rachel's attention waned, Ginger took back the handset and filled her parents in on their move and the kids and Pete's new job.

"And we're going to have another baby," she said. "In April."

"You're what?" her mother cried, then quickly, "That's wonderful! And so close together!"

"Haven't you and Pete figured out how this keeps happening?" her father teased.

"Very funny, Dad."

"How are you feeling this time, sweetheart," her mother asked.

"Horrible."

"Oh, sweetheart, I'm so sorry to hear that."

She saw Pete turn toward her.

"Pete pretty much let me stay in bed all weekend while he took care of the kids. It's been tough since we got to Hawaii, but I feel better right now than I have in a while."

"Well, that's some good news, Ginger. We are very happy for you and Pete," her father said.

"Thanks, Dad. I'll let you tell him yourself," she said, handing the phone to Pete.

Pete stretched the phone cord across the room as he picked up Rachel from the floor on the other side of the room.

"Thank you, Van," Pete said. "We wish you were in Hawaii to celebrate too. Please plan a trip when school's out in the summer. Yes, sir, here she is."

He handed the phone back to Ginger as Rachel started squirming in his arms. "Your dad wants to talk to you again. I'll take this one out for a quick walk," he said nodding toward the toddler.

"Ginger, I meant to tell you," her dad said. "I did go to that Sycamore Street address you gave me. A woman there said Mandy Rooks had moved and she didn't have a forwarding address. In fact, she had a box full of mail, and she gave me two sealed letters that you'd sent to her."

"Oh, no! I suspected she wasn't getting my letters. I haven't heard from her in months."

"She said she was the new renter and that Mandy and her son had been gone for a month or more before she moved in. She said she'd never met her."

"I'm so disappointed. But thank you for going there and trying, Dad," she said. "Would you please send those letters here when you can so I can resend if I hear from her?"

Pete came back into the room with Rachel trailing.

"Rachel, come say goodbye," Ginger called as Rachel ran toward her mother and placed the phone's handset to her ear. "Bye Poppy," she said clearly into the phone. "Bye Oodles."

Rachel handed the phone back to her mom and marched across the room.

"Did she just call you Poppy and Oodles?" Ginger asked.

"Sounded that way to me," her father said.

RACHEL: FEBRUARY 1999

"I talked to my mom this week," Rachel said. "She keeps calling you 'Leeman,' by the way."

"I guess I really made an impression then," Liam said.

"She was just distracted and upset after scorching the spaghetti sauce," Rachel laughed. "Don't take it personally. Plus, I don't think she's ever known anyone named 'Liam.'"

The restaurant was crowded and despite Liam's Valentine's Day attempt to make reservations at a favorite restaurant, the hostess assured them the wait would be short.

It had been forty minutes since they arrived. They were sipping red wine and sharing a retro-style, circle-shaped leather chair made for one. Patrons that had arrived after Liam and Rachel were crowded in the small lobby and stood in front and around them.

"Well, what did Mom have to say?"

"She wondered if we were still seeing each other."

"Why am I feeling even more unpopular with your parents?"

Rachel stretched her neck and placed a kiss on his lips, just as a woman standing in front of them pivoted among the crowd. Her over-sized bag banged across both of their heads and pushed Liam's wine glass into his white button-down shirt. A quarter-sized stain seeped into his collar.

Liam stood and placed the wine glass on a marble ledge and pulled Rachel to her feet.

"How would you feel about a Valentine's Day pizza picnic, instead?"

"Sounds intriguing," she said batting her eyelashes flirtatiously.

"I've got some blankets in the back of the Trooper. We could pick up a pizza and take it to the park and eat it while we snuggle under the covers."

"Anchovy and Italian sausage?"

Liam nodded. He picked his wine glass up again and clinked it against her glass.

"Let's do it," he said.

Once back in the car, Liam ordered a pizza from his cell phone and pulled into a 7-11 for a six-pack of beer. They picked up the pizza and drove to Piedmont Park. A clear, chilly night, there were few people around as they pulled two quilts from the trunk and meandered toward a level spot under a tree to spread their blankets.

"So, it sounds like I have some serious work to do to impress your mom and dad." Liam said, as he held up the pizza box for Rachel to take the first piece.

"Actually, I think she's feeling bad that she didn't pay more attention the night you were there. Oodles and Poppy have been gushing over Liam stories and Mom's feeling a little left out."

"Gotta love that Oodles. She's got a big fan in me too," he said. "And Poppy's the bomb. I wonder if he whistles while he's asleep."

"And Mom and Dad were a little pissed about P.J. and Roxanne bailing on the family weekend. Now that she knows we're serious..."

Rachel stopped, wishing she could rewind her last words.

"Continue," he said.

Rachel blushed, thinking she was fortunate that the moon was behind her so he couldn't tell.

"I told her that I like you a lot."

"Like?"

"A lot," she managed, taking another bite of pizza.

"I love you, Rachel."

Rachel looked around the park, trying to understand whether she'd heard it or imagined it. She quickly chewed and swallowed the pizza.

"You do?" she said finally.

"I do. Anchovy breath and all."

Rachel covered her mouth with her fingers. "That's good," she managed. "Because I love you, too."

"I've loved you since the day I spilled beer on your lap."

"So that *was* planned, I see," she said.

"Definitely not planned, but your adorableness was never more obvious."

"Adorableness?"

"So much."

"Nice job taking so long to tell me."

"Yeah, I have been slow on that front," he said. "But it's clearer to me every day."

"That you love me?"

"That I want to love you forever."

Rachel dropped the slice of pizza she held back into the box.

"Wow. Forever," she said, her voice trailing.

A cold wind blew through the park shaking the limbs of the tree above them. Neither spoke or acknowledged the chill.

"Should I take that as non-interest?" he finally said.

Rachel looked surprised. "No! Indisputable interest."

Liam laughed. "That's a nice legal term."

"I am completely interested in forever. You just shocked me."

"I was hoping you'd say that," he said, opening two beers and handing her one. "And speaking of legal terms, I got a formal offer to join the firm today."

"You did! That's fabulous!"

"I'll go full time after graduation in May, but I'll have to pass the bar before I get my real stripes."

"Congratulations!" she said clinking her bottle against his and reaching to kiss him before they'd had a chance to drink and complete the toast.

"So here's my proposition, Red," he said, reaching into his pocket.

Rachel felt blood rush toward her chest and head. She looked around to take in the peaceful park scene. A couple walked a dog along the path. Cars moved slowly up and down Piedmont Road.

He held up a plastic ring with a red band and a pink plastic Valentine's Day candy heart on the top. Across the heart was the word, "Forever."

"Whereas, Rachel McCarthy and *Leeman* Wilson share indisputable interest toward a forever together," he began, "I decree this ring to serve as a placeholder for a permanent sign to come via a formal engagement at a later date whence Liam Wilson has had a few full-time paychecks under his belt and the couple have had more time to discuss plans for a forever, and in the interim, it is my hope that Rachel McCarthy understands that Liam Wilson is full-on nuts about her and loves her more than he ever thought was possible."

Rachel held out her hand and he slipped the ring on her finger.

"Second," she said.

"So moved," Liam announced, closing the pizza box and shoving it to the side and pulling Rachel close and under the second quilt.

Mandy: December 1978

Dr. Robinson took off his glasses and turned quickly with his back to the small crowd. Mandy saw him wipe a tear before turning back toward the reception room filled with his staff.

"Our team is like a family here," he said, his voice steadying as he spoke. "And when a member of our team moves on, it's a mighty big loss to our hearts. Mandy, you've been a constant source of sunshine for all of us here for almost four years. Your compassion for patients and your co-workers is bar none, and you've got darn good nursing skills."

He nodded to Cindy, the office receptionist, who handed him a small package wrapped in exam table paper.

"So to our beloved friend and family member, we'd like to give you this in hopes that you will always remember us. We are going to miss you and we wish you well in your new ventures."

Sounds of agreement filled the room, despite the fact that with Sue, the lab technician, and Ann, the billings clerk, the room totaled only five.

He removed the paper and turned over a framed photograph to present to Mandy. It was a photo of the office staff that Dr. Robinson's wife had taken a month or so earlier. He handed it to her and hugged her. The rest of the staff followed suit.

Every member of the staff already knew Mandy's plans: Glenn had been offered a new job in St. Louis. They were able to delay his start date until after the new year and had already found a buyer for their home and made an offer on a home in St. Louis. They would drive two cars with the older boys right after Christmas in time for them to start their new school in January. Ben, their two-year-old, would spend a week with Glenn's parents while they settled in. Then his parents would drive him to St. Louis the next weekend. Once all of that was in place, she hoped to find another position that would match the one she'd loved so much at Dr. Robinson's family practice.

"Let's have some cake!" Cindy shouted. She handed Mandy a knife and nodded toward the small sheet cake on the reception room coffee table. "Will you do the honors?"

"Of course," she said. "And thank you, everyone. I will never forget any of you, and especially to Dr. Robinson, I thank you for giving me my first nursing job. I hope I can find a new position in an office that's just as loving and caring, but I sincerely doubt it. I expect it to be impossible to replicate the family atmosphere we have here."

When she realized she was going to cry, she took another look at the photograph and set it on the table. "Time for cake," she said stifling a lump in her throat.

Driving home, she made a mental checklist of all the things she had left to do. Between packing the house, caring for three children and Christmas, the list in her head was growing rapidly. She finally pulled into a gas station to park so that she could write down the thoughts whirling through her mind.

The house was partially lit with candles in the windows when she pulled into the driveway. With the house under contract, they had opted to forgo lights lining the roof and instead had put the older boys in charge of plugging in three-tiered plastic candles for each of the front windows every night at dusk. They'd missed the dining room window, but she was pleased, just the same.

Glenn had already picked up Ben from day care so that Mandy could stay late for the cake at the office, and she found them all in the kitchen with a bucket of chicken and Styrofoam quart cups of mashed potatoes, gravy and green beans on the counter.

"Yay, Mom's home!" the boys shouted. "Can we eat now?"

"Go for it guys," Mandy said, passing out paper plates and stretching to give Glenn a kiss. "I'm all for anything we can do to simplify life between now and moving day. How did your last day go?"

"A little uneventful, but that's to be expected when you're moving to the competition," he said. "How was the cake?"

"Nice. And they gave me a framed photo of the staff to remember them all by. I think Dr. Robinson cried a little bit."

"Don't blame him a bit," Glenn said, plopping another kiss on her lips.

"We've got four full days to pack. Then there's Christmas and then two days before we head west," she said. "Let's check the list after we eat. I think we can make this work."

"I've seen your elaborate checklists, darling. We'll be just fine, and the boys and I will be at your service. Just tell us what to do next."

After dinner, they tossed the paper plates and plastic forks and Mandy pulled out her list. "Will, please plug in the light in the dining room. That's the only one that's missing. Then I'd like all three of you boys to start packing games and small, unbreakable toys. Use the boxes and tape that are in the hallway upstairs and let Ben help as much as he can. Glenn, how about you start in on the china cabinet? Use the extra thick boxes in the garage, and I'll finish up the office."

"That's my drill sergeant," Glenn said smiling. "You amaze me, my love."

"Yeah? Well back at'cha."

With everyone at work at their respective stations, Mandy relaxed with the realization she had no more outside-the-home work obligations until she found a new job in St. Louis. She was excited at the idea of a new city and was pleased that the children had seen enough on their short weekend there to be excited too.

"It's as ideal as we can expect for a big move," she and Glenn had justified. "Before high school for the older two and long before kindergarten for Ben."

She stacked the framed photos from the built-in bookshelf in the office to wrap and box. On the top shelf was the family photo of Adam, William and Mandy at Six Flags. Underneath was the decoupaged box she'd made for Adam with the same photograph centered on top and photos of William and of the couple from their early days together surrounding it.

Her arms were shaking as she guided herself to the desk chair and sat to study each image. She looked deep into each set of eyes.

Innocence.

I'll never stop loving Adam and wishing he had made it home, but it was such a different kind of love—an innocent kind of love. And I think he would be happy how things have turned out for us. He would have wanted a father in William's life. He would have wanted me to move on too.

She'd miss Atlanta. She'd miss their house in Decatur. She'd miss the school. She'd miss their neighbors. She'd miss her job. But it felt like the right thing to do for so many reasons. She and Adam had met in Atlanta. Glenn and his first wife had lived in Atlanta. St. Louis could be *their* place. It might just turn out to be an opportunity for more healing from the pain she and her son had endured.

With each passing year, Mandy felt more guilt that she hadn't been able to keep Adam's image more alive for her son. He couldn't possibly remember much about him, she realized, but it weighed on her just the same. And as life moved on and into school and sports and new friends for William, the opportunities to try became fewer and farther between as well.

She filled the box with photos and taped it shut just as the phone rang. It was Scott.

"Hi bro. Where are you calling from today?" she asked.

"I'm back in Charlotte," he said. "I'm wondering if you have my adoption papers there? Mom says she gave all that to you several years ago."

"She did. She gave me yours when she gave me mine. I've already packed the files for the move, though. Why?"

"A little issue I've got," Scott sighed. "Any chance you could get to them before you leave for St. Louis? Maybe I could pick them up over the weekend?"

"Probably if it's important. I've labeled everything pretty well."

"It's important, Mandy."

"Scott, what' so important that you need your adoption papers?"

"Nothing I really want to talk about now."

"Scott!"

"A woman I barely know had a baby and she says it's mine," he said reluctantly. "Now she has an attorney. They want child support from me, and the attorney is requesting complete medical records including information about my biological parents."

"*Is* it your baby, Scott?"

Mandy's head and chest felt like they were filling with slow-drying cement.

"Well, I had a paternity test and it looks that way."

"Scott! This is nothing like a *little* issue!"

"She's someone I was with *one* night."

Images of Ginger and Rachel flashed through her mind as Scott's insensitivity and immaturity slapped with each word. The words Ginger had written in a letter years before appeared in her mind: She is the apple of Pete's eye—and visa versa! They are completely in love with one another.

"Okay, Scott, but there's a baby. How old is this baby?"

"Two months."

"And you are the baby's father."

"It was *one night*, Mandy. I can barely even remember this woman."

"Oh my God, Scott, you're thirty-two years old. Be an adult. This is a *child* we are talking about."

"I shouldn't have told you."

"No. You shouldn't have had unprotected sex if you are too imma-ture to accept the consequences and responsibilities that come along with it."

"I'll accept it. The attorney has made that part clear. I'll accept it."

"Is she wanting you to marry her?"

"Mandy, I wouldn't even know her if she walked in my apartment right now. Of course I'm not going to marry her. I'm talking about paying the child support."

"You're damned right you will. And if she has a brain she will realize that marrying you would only make her situation worse anyway."

"Nice. Appreciate the support, sister."

"Scott, seriously. If you are this baby's father you need to man up and think of this child instead of just yourself."

"Enough with the lecturing, Mandy."

"Well don't give me reason to lecture, Scott. Be a responsible adult."

"Do you think I can pick up the papers on Sunday?"

Mandy was quiet. Finally she said, "I'll have them ready," and hung up the phone.

GINGER: JANUARY 1982

"Nothing like the smell of a sweaty church gym," said Pete as he held the door for Ginger, Rachel and Roxanne to enter.

A buzzer made a sound that seemed louder than necessary and Ginger took note of the moist, pungent air as she entered the Trinity United Methodist Church gym.

P.J.'s team was practicing foul shots in preparation for their game up next, while the youngest girls' team finished its half-court game on the other side of the gym.

Rachel spotted her team gathering at the other end of the bleachers readying for practice in the secondary gym and turned toward her parents. "I see them. Can I go?"

Ginger nodded and watched her run toward the other nine- and ten-year-old girls in matching red singlets.

"Mommy, can I go play on the playground?" Roxanne asked.

The church playground was just outside the rear door of the gym and parents often let their kids play there while they watched their other children in the church's league basketball program.

"Let's walk out there and see who's there," she said, pointing her head toward the bleachers. "Pete, go ahead and get a seat. I'll be right back."

She and five-year-old Roxanne stepped out the back door and into the gated playground. Roxanne spotted a group of kids she knew climbing the slide and ran toward it. Several mothers Ginger recognized were sitting around a wrought-iron table and waved to her from across the playground.

"Ginger! Come join us," one called.

She walked in their direction and called, "I have about fifteen minutes before P.J.'s game. Let me tell Pete where I am and I'll join you for a few minutes."

Back in the gym, Pete was deep in conversation with a guy she recognized from base, so she waved to them from the gym floor with a pantomime point toward the playground and an exaggerated, but soundless, "Be right back." They waved and nodded, so she headed back outside.

"It's like our own 'Kramer vs. Kramer' story," she heard Allison say, as she approached the table. "So unfair."

"What's up?" Ginger asked, scanning the playground until she spotted the back of Roxanne's pink coat in the crowd of kids.

"Paul Paxton's ex-wife has come back and is now fighting for custody for Bobby."

"I thought she left them a year ago to make it in Hollywood," Ginger said pulling a chair to the table.

"She did! Now she's back and wants to take Bobby to California!"

"Oh, that's not right. Paul has been such a great dad to him."

"Exactly! And from what they tell him, he doesn't have a chance of winning, even though Bobby loves living with his dad."

"It's really not fair that judges always assume the mother is the better parent," said Diane. "In this case, she left without even saying goodbye! They didn't even know where she was until she'd reached California."

The conversation continued as the women discussed the Paxtons and others.

"My brother has a friend that just found out he has an eight-year old," Allison said. "Can you imagine having a child and not knowing about it?"

Ginger swallowed hard and looked in the direction of the church's secondary gym.

Scott. Does he have children now? Has he always wanted children?

"So heartbreaking," Diane said.

Ginger looked at her watch. "Would you ladies mind if Roxanne stayed out here? It's time for P.J.'s game to start."

"Sure," said Allison. "She's fine. Go on in."

Ginger entered the gym and P.J. waved to her from a line-up of drills. The time clock indicated the game would start in less than two minutes. Pete was still in conversation, so she took a seat alone on the bleachers.

The words nagged at her temples.

Can you imagine having a child and not knowing about it?

For so many years, Ginger worried about Pete's reaction should he ever find out Rachel wasn't his biological daughter.

Below the surface though, she realized she also feared Scott's reaction should he find out he had a daughter.

What if he's never had children? What if he's always wanted children and couldn't have them? Did I betray him with my secret too?

She worked to push away scenarios that formed in her mind of Scott learning about Rachel and wanting to be a parent to her. Pete's reaction to knowing was one thing, but Pete finding out because another man wanted to be a father to Rachel was still another she couldn't bear to imagine.

The buzzer sounded again and Pete joined her on the bleachers as the game began.

"I was talking to Tom Gray," Pete said as he sat. "You won't believe what he told me about Paul Paxton."

Ginger forced a look of interest, but was grateful when Pete stood. P.J. was circled for the jump shot to start the game.

"Remind me to tell you," he muttered as he focused on the game.

I wonder if Scott knows. Did Mandy tell him? Whatever happened to Mandy?

Sketchy visions of Scott pinged through her memory.

I wonder if I'd even recognize him if he were right in front of me.

Was I right to assume he wouldn't care to know? Or did I betray two men to avoid revealing my own indiscretion?

Pete and the crowd clapped and Ginger realized the two-point basket had been P.J.'s. She shook her head to put focus back on the game.

Rachel: March 1999

The plastic "Forever" ring Liam had given Rachel had been safely tucked in her jewelry box since the day after he gave it to her. They had discussed keeping their plans between themselves until the engagement was official, though she had shared the news with Cameron.

Her job was keeping her busier than ever, and Liam had another six weeks of school before he started full time and then had to prepare for the bar exam. "We have enough to keep us busy for now," they both agreed as they shared the sofa in Liam's apartment.

"I do want you to meet my parents, though," said Liam. "And my brother, Ben, graduates from college in early May. Why don't you come to Austin with me?"

"Won't they be coming here for your law school graduation?"

"They will, but I doubt Will and Ben will come then. This way you can meet the whole family."

They made calls to airlines for airfares and found flights that would take them in the day before the graduation ceremony and back to Atlanta the day after.

"I'll call my mom and tell her."

"Does she know about me at all?" Rachel asked.

"Only that I've been seeing a girl for a while. With three boys, she's learned not to ask a lot of questions."

"Okay," she said. "I'll take my laundry next door and start a couple loads while you call."

When she returned with the empty basket, Liam was on the phone and she sat to listen to his side of the conversation, imagining the side she couldn't hear.

"Yes, of course, I'll be there," he said. "I have a ticket to arrive late Friday afternoon."

"I'd like to bring someone with me though," he said, winking at Rachel.

Her heart pounded loudly as she waited to hear what he'd say next.

"Of course a girl. A lovely young woman, in fact."

She blushed as he watched for her reaction.

"Yes, the same one. Since last fall."

"Yes, same flight. And we'll leave on Sunday afternoon."

"One time at Thanksgiving. They live in New Mexico. I've spent a good bit of time with her grandparents, though."

"Of course, they're very nice!"

"Rachel McCarthy."

"Yes, McCarthy."

"All over. She's an Army brat. Why?"

"How could you know her?"

"Yes. Ginger and Pete."

Liam was standing now and motioning Rachel to him.

"New Jersey?"

"A little bit."

"Are you sure, Mom?"

Rachel was standing next to him with confusion all over her face.

"Hold just a minute, okay Mom?"

He held the phone to his chest and said to Rachel, "She says she and your mom were good friends when we were babies. She says she and I actually visited you and your family when you lived in New Jersey."

"What?" Rachel questioned, picturing the cute young woman she had seen in Liam's photos. "How can that be true? Plus, my mom met you at Thanksgiving. Seems like..."

"I know but I do kind of remember a little girl from a trip we made when I was little. How weird if that was you?"

Liam put the phone back to his ear. "Mom, this is really crazy. Yes, New Mexico. Okay."

"She wants to talk to you," he said.

Rachel took the phone. She hesitated before speaking, "Hi, Mrs. Wilson. This is Rachel."

"Hello Rachel," she said. "This is so exciting that you and Liam have met. I was with your mom on the day you were born."

Rachel was silent, not sure whether to be excited or afraid.

"Your dad was not yet back from Vietnam and your mother asked me to come to the hospital that day. I lost touch with your parents after they moved to Texas and I've been trying to figure out how to find them again ever since."

Rachel searched for a means to verify, but her mother had never shared a lot of details with her. "That's so neat," she managed. "I'm just shocked by all this. I'll call my parents this afternoon."

She handed the phone back to Liam and collapsed into the closest chair.

"Mom, this is really freaky," she heard Liam say. "I think Rachel wants to call her parents. I'll call you later, okay?"

He hung up the phone and stood above her. They stared at one another with disbelief.

"Could this be true?" she said.

"I have to admit I feel like I kind of remember that trip to New Jersey," he said.

"Your mother's first name is Mandy, right?" she said. "I'll call and see if my mother remembers Mandy Wilson."

"Well, that would have been before she remarried that we went to New Jersey. She would have been Mandy Rooks then."

"Mandy Rooks with a son named Liam."

"Well, everyone called me William then, because when Mom married my Dad, he already had a son named William."

Rachel squinted her eyes and cocked her head. "What?" she said studying him. "All this seems like something you might have mentioned before."

"Why would I? This was all like before I was five."

"So you and Will are both named William Wilson?" she said trying to put it all together.

"Right. That's why I go by Liam and he goes by Will."

"Okay, maybe I should have made that connection before," she began. She noted her hands and arms beginning to shake. "I really want to talk to my mother. This all seems so strange."

"You act upset," he said.

"I don't mean to be. This is all just such an odd coincidence," she said. "I'd like to confirm it makes sense to my mother."

"Well let's call her then."

"I will," she said. "Let's give this a few minutes to settle. I'm going to take a quick walk and then move my clothes to the dryer. I'll give her a call when I get back."

Liam nodded.

"Do you have any wine, by the way?"

Liam gave her a thumbs-up sign and nodded.

When she returned, he handed her a glass of wine and the telephone.

She settled into the chair, put her glass on the end table and dialed her parents' number.

"Hi Mom," she said when she heard her mother's voice.

"Hi sweetheart. I saw 'William Wilson' on the caller ID and wondered if I should recognize this number. Is this Leeman's telephone?"

"Liam, Mom," she said. "It's a nickname for William. And yes, I'm calling from his apartment."

"So glad you called! How is everything? How is the job?"

"Everything is good, Mom, but I need to ask you something."

"What's that?"

"Have you ever had a friend named Mandy Rooks?"

"Of course! I have wondered about Mandy for years. Why do you ask?"

"She's Liam's mother."

Rachel's words were met with silence. "Mom?" she said.

"Mandy is Liam's mother? Liam is... William?" Ginger made an audible gasping sound.

"That's right," Rachel said.

"Oh my," her mother said after a long pause. Rachel waited, listening for more.

"Are you all right, Mom?"

"He was so young when I last saw him... I can't imagine that I didn't recognize..."

"Well like you said, he was very young," Rachel said brightly, trying to lighten her mother's languid reaction. "Do you remember Mandy and her son coming to our house in New Jersey?"

"Of course I do. William was probably four. You were just learning to walk."

"When was the last time you saw her, Mom?"

"New Jersey was the last time we actually saw one another. We exchanged letters for a while, but then my letters came back and I never heard from her again."

"This seems like such a wonderful coincidence, but so hard to believe it's true. Liam and I actually met more than twenty years ago." She glanced at Liam who was sitting quietly in a recliner on the other side of the room.

"Where is Mandy living?" her mother asked slowly.

"St. Louis. Liam and I are going to his brother's college graduation and I'll meet them then."

"William has a brother?"

"Two brothers. I'll meet the whole family when we go to the graduation."

"This is..." her mother said.

Rachel waited.

"This is what, Mom?"

"Just so hard to believe," she said.

"Seems like there's more to your voice, Mom."

"Rachel, I'm thrilled. This is great news. I'd love to see Mandy again."

"I spoke with her earlier today. I know she'd love to see you too."

"That would be so nice," Ginger said. "Rachel, I have some brownies in the oven. I'd better hang up and check on them before they burn."

"Okay, Mom. Goodbye."

"Bye, sweetie."

The line went dead.

I thought she would have at least asked for Mandy's number.

"Well it's true," she said to Liam, relaxing as he smiled at her. "We have known each other longer than we ever knew. But my mother is really shocked. In fact, I'm not sure I've ever seen her so shocked. Maybe it's menopause."

MANDY: SEPTEMBER 1980

The employee exit at Mercy General was backed up with cars for two turns of the parking lot. Mandy stretched as far as she could in the Volvo's front seat to examine the front of her scrubs.

Not bad. No visible blood, at least.

She applied a fresh coat of lipstick, ran a brush through her hair, refastened the clip on her ponytail and then followed the car in front of her almost three car lengths.

She was lucky to get the day shift in the hospital's emergency room, but it was rare that she was able to leave right on time and the later she left, the harder it was to get out of the parking lot.

She turned on the radio just to find something to take her mind off the wait.

"It's times like this I still think about cigarettes," she said to herself.

Her first job after moving with Glenn and the boys to St. Louis had been in a small general practice office, but everything about Dr. Stewart, including the staff, the office atmosphere and even the patients was polar-opposite that of Dr. Robinson. Mandy was miserable from the very first week and lasted only two more before she presented Dr. Stewart with her two-weeks' notice.

"I've realized my three sons need me too much right now," she lied. "We need to get settled in St. Louis a little longer before I get back into a full time job."

But it was only a month later that a day-shift position at Mercy

General opened and Mandy jumped at the opportunity to practice the more dramatic side of nursing that she'd always felt she'd enjoy.

And she was good. More than sixteen months into the job, she liked the unique combination of protocol and quick thinking that the emergency room required and had been praised by many of the doctors and other nurses for acclimating so quickly.

Wishing she'd brought a change of clothes, she inched her car toward the exit gate.

At least a change of shoes, she thought, stretching to peer onto the backseat floorboard.

"Bingo," she said out loud, reaching for her flip-flops. "It's warm enough still."

She kicked off her white nurses shoes, rolled off her knee-high stockings and dropped them onto the floor in front of the passenger's seat as she pushed her toes through her flip-flops and pressed her five-digit code into the gate's dial pad. The gate arm rose for her turn to exit.

The sun was still bright and she smiled at the thought of seeing Glenn and their sons as she turned toward the shopping center where they had made plans to meet. Glenn took the afternoon off and picked up the older boys from school and Ben from day care so that they could spend the afternoon riding the carnival rides that had been set up as a temporary fair not far from their home. The school bus passed the shopping center every morning and afternoon, and Liam and Will, both twelve, had been begging to go since the first day they saw it. An article in the local newspaper said that there were rides appropriate for younger kids, too, so Glenn suggested he take all three boys. Mandy would meet them there when she got off work and they could all enjoy a healthy dinner of corndogs and cotton candy.

She parked the car and spotted Ben's curly brown locks from all the way across the fair. He sat atop Glenn's shoulders and was biting into a caramel apple. They were watching a giant ship swing back and forth cresting at the top to an almost-complete rotation. Screams were coming from the Jolly Roger ride with each fall and Mandy quickly picked out Liam and Will screaming among the ship's passengers.

"Mommy!" she heard her four-year-old yell as she approached.

Glenn turned around and met her with a kiss as he lifted Ben off his shoulders. Ben wrapped his arms and his gooey caramel apple around her legs.

"Hi there, sticky face," she said, kissing Ben on the head and reaching for her purse.

She squatted, listening to Ben talk about the rides and dragon game and Ferris wheel as she fished around for the plastic bag she kept with a wet washcloth inside. She wiped his face and hands and picked him up, just as the riders from the Jolly Roger were spilling from the exit queue.

"Mom, it was the coolest," Liam said. "I almost barfed."

"Did you see us?" asked Will. "We had the row that went the highest. Dad, you need to ride this. Mom, you too, if you want."

"Let's ride the bumper cars next!" Liam screamed.

"Bumper cars!" screamed Ben.

Glenn looked at Mandy. "That's a good idea. Ben can drive you."

"Perfect," she said to no one, as all four had turned and headed toward the bumper cars.

Will, Liam and Glenn each jumped in separate cars as Mandy strapped Ben into one they shared. The electric wiring above them cracked and snapped as they zoomed across the metal floor and rammed and bounced into one another and cars carrying people they didn't know. Ben worked the steering wheel and Mandy pushed the gas pedal as they buzzed through the carnival ride trying to knock the others out of their seats.

"That was rad," Will said afterwards.

"That was rad," Ben repeated and ran to catch up with his older brothers.

Next, the family rode the Ferris wheel, and then Mandy and Ben watched as Glenn and the older boys rode the Fireball, a mini roller coaster.

"Who's hungry?" Glenn asked as they perused the food vendors.

"Hot dog!" "Corn dog!" "Ice cream!" the boys exclaimed as Mandy passed around the damp washcloth for everyone to clean their hands.

After dinner they strolled toward the fair on the other side of the food vendors.

"Dad, look!" Liam shouted. "They have a mechanical bull."

"Can we do it, Dad? Please?" begged Will. He ran ahead and stood at the metal fence that surrounded the bull as the rest of the family joined him. A young woman in short cutoff jeans and a tube top was riding the bull, moving seductively for the first few moves and then clearly holding on for dear life. She held one hand up in the air as long as she could, then after a few more bucks of the mechanical bull, she flew off the ride and landed in a pile of hay.

Glenn looked at Mandy.

"I'm not going to ride it," she said, shaking her head. "Ben and I will watch this one."

"I'm going to pass, too," Glenn said, doling off tickets for Will and Liam to ride. The boys ran toward the queue line with the tickets.

They watched a middle-aged man and then a young girl, no older than Will and Liam ride, both with little finesse or luck. Two people were still in front of the boys in line when Mandy noticed a silver trailer set behind a bed of trees on the other side of the mechanical bull ride.

The large logo painted across its side was hard to read through the foliage.

"Ben," she said to both Ben and Glenn. "Stay with your dad for a minute. I want to get a closer look at this trailer."

Glenn looked in the direction Mandy was pointing and then at her.

"Sure," he said, shrugging.

She walked around the fence and through the trees until the trailer was in full view: "Swift Carnival Productions," it said. "Good Family Fun. Rides, Food, Games" was centered underneath.

She looked back at the mechanical bull ride, but could tell neither Will or Liam were riding, and then back at the trailer. It had a set of steps leading to a closed door in the center of the trailer. Blinds or curtains covered all the windows.

She climbed the steps and knocked.

A thin, middle-aged woman with long, stringy hair came to the door and looked at Mandy. She had a stack of paperwork in one hand and a stack of cash in the other.

"Something I can do for you, ma'am?" she asked.

"Yes, please," Mandy hesitated. Then, "I was wondering if Oscar Swift was here?"

"You mean 'Junior'?"

"I don't know. I just saw Swift on the sign and wondered if it was Oscar Swift."

"O'Ray," the woman yelled and then nodded to Mandy and went back into the trailer.

Mandy stood at the door, not sure what to do, when a young man, no more than twenty, came to the door. He wore a t-shirt with the same Swift Carnival Productions logo printed on the front and a red bandana tied around his head. His hair was pulled into a greasy ponytail and his face was in need of a shave, but he was attractive and smiling.

"I'm O'Ray Swift. What can I do for you ma'am?"

A chill ran through her body as she faced him.

All these years Millie has looked for him.

She finally managed, "Hello. I'm Mandy Wilson."

He nodded, encouraging her to continue.

"I once knew your mother, I believe," she said. "When I lived in Columbus, Georgia. Millie LaMurphy was a friend of mine."

O'Ray stepped out of the trailer, onto the steps and they both stepped down to stand on the open grass.

"Well, I'm happy to know you," he said, offering his hand.

Mandy shook his hand, unsure of how to proceed.

"Have you seen your mother?" she finally asked. "Do you know where she is? I've lost touch..."

"She and my dad are working the fairs," he said. "She's telling fortunes and he's running rides like mine." He lifted his hand and swept it across to indicate the entire carnival set-up.

"Oh, that's great. She's with your dad, then," Mandy said.

"Oh, yeah. They've been back together for six or eight years," he said. "I broke off on my own. Last time I spoke to 'em, they were somewhere in Florida."

"Do you have any idea how I might reach her?" Mandy asked.

"Best I can suggest is you hit the fairs and ask around," he said. "Aint no tellin' really, other than that."

"Okay. Thank you, O'Ray," she said reaching for his hand again. "Your mother talked about you so much. It's really a pleasure to meet you."

"You too, ma'am."

Mandy turned to go and then turned back to him again.

"She'll know me as Mandy Rooks... if you happen to see her. Please send her my regards."

"Will do, ma'am," he said gesturing as if to tip an imaginary hat.

She hurried back toward the mechanical bull ride. She could see Liam's green t-shirt swaying back and forth on the bull as she stepped through the trees. She hurried around the fence watching and saying a little prayer that she hadn't already missed Will's ride when the bull tossed Liam onto the hay. She saw him get up and run toward the gate as the attendant opened it and Will sprinted toward the bull.

She saw Glenn watching her as she hurried back to their spot along the fence.

"Someone I knew from Columbus," she said hurriedly, as Liam ran to them.

"How long do you think I stayed on?" he asked excitedly.

"You did great, son," Mandy said. "You looked like a real rodeo rider."

"You were the best, Liam," Ben offered.

"Someone from the Army?" Glenn asked.

"Do you remember me telling you about Millie LaMurphy, the woman that I met through a friend named Ginger? Ginger lived on base when I did and our friend Millie was a kind of a wonderful but kooky woman? She told our fortunes with the tarot cards?"

"Maybe," Glenn said, his voice trailing.

"I just met her son," she said to Glenn.

"Will's on the bull!" Liam screamed, and they all turned their attention toward the ring.

GINGER: MARCH 1999

Three heartbeats pounded between each clipping measure of dial tone. Ginger wiped her face with a damp dishtowel.

It had been more than a week since she had spoken to Rachel, and she'd barely slept.

Her nightmare was coming true. Ironically, the secret she'd carried for twenty-seven years suddenly seemed workable: She could admit her one-time indiscretion to Pete, and for the first time ever, felt confident that they could see it through without permanent damage to their marriage.

It was the agonizing consequence of that nightmare that she could never have imagined that had kept her at the edge of breakdown since talking with Rachel. She would take the risk of telling Pete a hundred times over if she could avoid the rest—the part that would crush Rachel's happiness and future with Liam, not to mention the relationship between her and her daughter.

I've got only one hope: That their relationship isn't permanent.

Thirteen audible pounds from her chest and her mother finally picked up the telephone.

"Just calling to say hello," Ginger lied.

They chatted over sundry subjects while she cooled her neck and forehead with the dishtowel.

"Have you seen much of Rachel lately?" Ginger asked. "Do you get the impression she and Liam are getting serious?"

"Oh, I do," her mother said. "They were here on Sunday night for dinner. Poppy and I talked after they left and we both sensed that they have been discussing marriage. I think an engagement is right around the corner, Ginger."

Ginger was silent.

"He's a wonderful boy, sweetheart. And he's going to be a lawyer. It's clear they are crazy about each other."

"Oh, I know. I'm happy for them," she said.

The volume of her heartbeats intensified again and Ginger made a quick excuse to conclude the conversation.

Afterward, she rinsed the dishtowel with cold water and placed it over her face as she lay on the sofa to think.

How can I possibly unload this on my daughter? One: your father is not your father. Oh, and two: You can't marry the man you love because he's your first cousin.

For twenty-seven years she'd been afraid to tell Pete, but now she wondered if Pete was the only one that she could share this information with. Could they figure out what to do together? Or would he react so harshly to the news that he would distance himself from her?

And to think she'd even worried that Scott Everly would someday come back into the picture and want a piece of fatherhood. All of the reoccurring nightmares she'd kept to herself for almost three decades were suddenly benign in comparison. This truth could not be denied to her daughter; the consequences were much, much too great. And the blame would all befall to Ginger and one stupid drunken night.

Lorna.

If it wasn't for Lorna none of this would have ever happened, she thought. I hate her. God, I wish I knew what to do.

Of course, if it wasn't for that night, there would be no Rachel, she thought, her senses mixing between emotions.

Own this, like your father always told you. Besides, Lorna was long-gone pursuing her own sins when you got into Scott Everly's bed.

Could Mandy figure out how to deal with this? she wondered. Is she worried about the same thing?

Mandy's side of this hadn't even occurred to her until then.

Maybe she is wringing her hands with the same worry about her son?

Of course she is! Mandy will be worried about her son's happiness, too. Maybe she will have an idea what to do.

She heard Pete's car pulling past the house and the sound of the garage door rising. She jumped from the sofa and tossed the dishtowel into the laundry room as she went to greet him.

Pete was walking through the kitchen with one hand behind his back when she turned the corner. He pulled his arm around and presented her with a bouquet of red tulips.

"You seem out of sorts lately," he said. "I'm hoping your favorite flowers will cheer you up."

"Tulips!" she exclaimed. "Thank you sweetheart."

He kissed her lips and looked at her deeply. "Everything okay? You're worrying me a little."

"Oh, of course," she said, feeling her chest and forehead break out in a clammy sweat. She grabbed a clean dishtowel and wiped it across her face.

"I hope so," Pete said, looking at the dishtowel and then back at Ginger.

"Everything's fine." Ginger opened a cabinet and reached for a vase from the top shelf. "The flowers are beautiful."

The vase slipped from her hand and crashed onto the granite counter.

Pete caught her just as she nearly collapsed with the deafening sound and spray of glass across the counter and floor.

He steadied her toward a chair. "I want you to see your doctor, Ginger, and we'll make sure everything is okay. I'll clean this up and find a vase for the flowers."

Rachel: April 1999

Liam's last weeks of law school included a mock trial that he and his group had been preparing for since the fall.

He'd quit the courier job and had increased his hours at the firm to thirty hours each week. Combined with the last three weeks of classes and the mock trial, he and Rachel had barely seen one another for close to a month.

May would be crazy too. They had secured plans to attend Ben's graduation in Austin at the beginning of the month. Liam's parents would come into town for the law school graduation two weeks later. And Rachel and Liam made plans for a road trip to New Mexico over Memorial Day. "There's something I want to talk to your Dad about," he'd said with a wink.

Rachel knew her parents would be home for the holiday because her father had chaired the Memorial Day ceremonies for every base they'd lived on. She wanted to wait until later in May before telling them of their visit to avoid the inevitable questions.

Rachel had spoken with her father once in the last few weeks. Liam passed on the McCarthy's telephone number in New Mexico to his mom when she called, but Rachel had heard nothing from her mother since the phone conversation about Mandy almost three weeks before.

She and Liam had been apart for a full week when Sunday turned out to be the first beautiful spring day of the year.

"I'm going to ease up on studying today and take a little time off," he said. "How about we get together?"

"Why don't I cancel with Oodles and Poppy tonight and I'll come over in the afternoon and cook dinner for us at your place? You can study while I cook."

"How could I refuse that?"

Atlanta was bursting with azaleas, cherry blossoms, tulips and daffodils as she drove to Liam's apartment. Peachtree Street was full of pedestrians and drivers in cars with windows down and radio stations mingling. With her elbow set on the open window frame, Rachel tapped the top of her car to the beat of the Backstreet Boys as she pulled out of the grocery store parking lot headed toward Liam's with charcoal, steaks, two large potatoes, asparagus and a pre-made key lime pie.

A prism of color spun across the sky as she turned toward his apartment and saw Liam in front of the building washing his Trooper. Each time he moved the water hose back and forth across the top of the car, the sun would send a rainbow of tiny flecks of bouncing color. He turned toward her and waved as she parked and turned off the car. He was wearing the mustache shirt.

Rachel gasped. It was only the second time she'd seen him wear it. She hadn't even thought about the shirt in months.

Her mouth was still agape when she got out of the car.

"What's up? Do I have mustard all over my face or something?" he asked, walking toward her and kissing her lips.

Rachel laughed. "No, it's your shirt."

Liam looked down. "My mustache shirt? Yeah, a fraternity party shirt from way back."

"You were wearing it the day I saw you at the post office."

"I was?"

She nodded and Liam shrugged.

"Well there's actually more to that shirt that I've never told you," she said.

"Okay? Let's hear it."

Rachel wasn't sure if he sounded perturbed or perplexed.

"It's a good story, but I'll tell you over dinner." She reached in the car and handed him one of the two grocery bags. They went inside and put down the groceries and came back out into the sunshine to finish washing his car.

As Liam recited fictitious deposition details out loud, Rachel oiled and salted the potatoes and wrapped them in foil for the oven. She lit the charcoal and marinated the steaks.

His veiled attempts at studying were thwarted by his self-imposed interruptions to see what she was doing, follow her around, start new conversations and to kiss her over and over again.

"You're a complete distraction," he said with a mischievous smile. "And way more interesting than these deposition details."

"I missed you," she said, folding into his arms.

After a long hug, Liam pushed away and surprised her when he bent down and easily lifted her. Her legs were flopping over his arm and she was still wearing an oven mitt on one hand.

"Could I interest you in a little pre-dinner love making?" he asked.

Rachel pulled off the oven mitt and tossed it over his shoulder.

"Thought you'd never ask."

Thirty minutes later, they scurried out of Liam's bedroom.

"You check the charcoal, I'll make sure the potatoes aren't burned," she said, her bare feet slapping across the hardwood floor toward the kitchen.

"Bring the steaks! The charcoal is more than ready!" she heard him shout. The potatoes were fine. She grabbed the pan with the marinating steaks and headed to the back deck.

He was spreading the white lumps across the bottom of the grill when she opened the door. He dropped the rack back onto the grill, and she placed the steaks over the coals. They both laughed when they heard a faint sizzle once the meat hit the heat.

"That was a close call," she laughed. "Distracted and seduced by my sous chef!"

"It's pretty common knowledge around here that your sous chef has the serious hots for you, Chef."

"Is that so?" she said, batting her eyes.

"So much," he said bending as if he were going to pick her up again.

"No!" she said wiggling out of his grasp and laughing. "We'll ruin dinner!"

She nuzzled her face into his chest and kissed it. "How about you go put that mustache shirt back on and then open a bottle of wine. I'm going to get the asparagus. We can discuss the serious 'hots' over dinner."

"Yes, Chef," he said.

The asparagus was undercooked but the steak and potatoes were perfect.

"So, what is it about my mustache t-shirt that turns you on so?" he asked as he poured her another glass of wine.

"What makes you think the story has anything to do with being turned on?"

"Wishful thinking."

"Well, if I'm being honest, I guess it is part of the story," she smiled.

"Go on."

"It's really about a prediction that I got from a fortune teller," she began, "that a man with a mustache would come into my life."

She told him about the tarot card reading and about how the boxes he was carrying in the post office covered the front of the shirt and how she'd crouched down in the front of her car to watch him come out of the post office.

"And when you walked by with the giant mustache across your shirt, I kind of freaked. I've been too embarrassed to tell you the story, but I think Madam Sylvia kind of knew about us before we did."

"A toast to Madam Sylvia," he said, holding up his glass.

They clinked glasses and each took a sip.

"Would you excuse me for one minute?" Liam asked.

Rachel nodded and watched him round the corner of the bedroom.

She stepped into the kitchen to gather the pie and two plates and a knife. He met her at the door to the kitchen and took each item out of her hands and placed it on the counter.

"Something about your story and Madam Sylvia and this shirt is making me feel kind of invincible right now," he said, taking her hands in his. "And as it's a foregone conclusion anyway that I have no intention of living my life without you in it, I suddenly feel I need to take this exact moment to ask you the most important question I will ever ask in my life."

Rachel felt her chest heat and could hear her pulse hammering from behind both ears. The heat rose through her neck and face.

Liam knelt. His knees and bare feet straddled the doorway of the kitchen and protruded into the apartment's main living space.

He put his hand in his pocket and pulled out a shiny gold band with a large center diamond and two smaller diamonds on either side. "Rachel Jane McCarthy, will you marry this love-sick sous chef, who promises with all his heart to love and cherish you through eternity?"

He held the ring toward her and looked at her sheepishly with an adorable question mark across his face.

The words "I do, I will, I love you," all ran through her head, but she wasn't sure if she'd said any of them out loud or not as she watched him slide the ring on her finger.

"Yes!" she finally said and knew she'd said it out loud when the word echoed through the small kitchen and Liam stood and pulled her face into his.

MANDY: APRIL 1999

Mandy looked at the phone number she'd written in her address book after talking with Liam.

She knew Ginger had learned of the connection between Rachel and Liam and had been surprised she hadn't heard from her right away. She'd called Liam for Ginger's number and was disappointed and confused to learn that she hadn't even requested Mandy's.

She picked up the phone and settled into a favorite chair, determined to reconnect with her friend.

"Ginger?" she said when she heard the familiar voice. "It's Mandy!"

"Hi Mandy," Ginger whispered.

"I've been trying to call. I thought I'd hear from you by now."

"I know. I've wanted to talk to you, too. I'm just feeling a little nervous about the whole thing."

"Nervous? And why are you whispering?"

"I'm sorry. I'm hiding in my laundry room so Pete won't overhear me."

"Ginger, what's the matter? Why would you have to hide from Pete?"

"Oh, I don't. I was just nervous about talking to you. I didn't want him to hear."

"Ginger, I've been wanting to find you for almost twenty years!" her voice turned to hurt. "We are finally reunited with this amazing coincidence and I'm thrilled. I thought you would be too."

"I just don't know how to handle this. I haven't slept in weeks and I'm so upset."

"Ginger? What are you upset about? Is there something I don't know?"

"No, it's just...."

"Is it Liam? I thought you had met and it all went well."

"He's wonderful, Mandy. We met at Thanksgiving and he was so sweet. I never made the connection, of course—that Liam was William. I couldn't believe it when Rachel called me."

"We are looking forward to meeting the grown-up Rachel. Liam will be bringing her with him to Austin for our youngest son's college graduation next month."

"I heard. That's so nice," Ginger said.

"Ginger? I don't understand what's going on here. You don't sound happy at all about any of this, including my call."

"I'm sorry. You're right. I'm not myself."

"Are you okay? Is everything all right with you and Pete?"

"Yes, of course. It's fine."

"We have so many years to catch up on," Mandy said. "I kind of expected you'd be more excited and receptive, thrilled to finally find one another."

"I just don't know how to tell her."

"How to tell *who what*?"

"How to tell Rachel. About Liam."

"To tell her *what* about Liam?"

"Mandy, I'm so afraid they are going to want to get married."

"And you wouldn't like that? I really don't understand."

"Mandy, they are first cousins!" she said, quickly and sternly and a little louder than she'd intended.

Mandy went quiet.

She heard a door open and close on the other end of the line.

"Wait. Oh, you mean..."

"Of course that's what I mean," Ginger said.

"Not biologically, Ginger."

"What do you mean 'not biologically?'"

"Scott and I aren't biologically related. We were adopted separately about a year apart. I was in an orphanage in south Texas. Scott was adopted through a private agency in Georgia."

"You never told me that."

"I rarely talk about it. Or think about it, for that matter."

"So Scott is not William's biological uncle?"

"He's barely even Liam's 'sometimes' uncle. We see him about as often as we see my parents."

"Oh my," Ginger said.

"Ginger," Mandy said with hesitation. "Does Pete know about Scott?"

Zillions of thoughts whirled through Ginger's mind. Pete knew something had been bothering her all week. He'd been pushing her to talk. He'd been pushing her to make a doctor's appointment.

If Scott and Mandy weren't biologically related, then Liam and Rachel weren't either.

"Ginger? Have you told Pete?"

"No, but I was going to this weekend. I wanted to confess to him and to Rachel before she and Liam actually got engaged, to at least save her from having to break it off."

"Oh my God," Mandy said slowly. "Now I see why you were so upset."

"Frantic. Out of my mind. My God, Mandy, this changes everything."

"I had no idea..."

"So you don't think I need to tell them now?"

"No! No, I don't see any benefit or reason to open up that at this point at all."

"What about Scott?"

"What *about* Scott?"

"I've always wondered if he would somehow find out he was Rachel's father and want to be back in the picture. Even now that she's an adult... It's always worried me. Did you ever tell him?"

"Put that out of your mind too, Ginger. He has no clue and never will."

She was back to her original concern, the one she'd carried for twenty-seven years: Her betrayal to Pete.

I know now that I can tell him and I'm confident we'll survive it. The question is, should I?

"Ginger, does that set you on a different course?" Mandy asked hopefully. "My little William loves your little Rachel. How in the world did the universe line that up?"

Tears burst from Ginger's eyes. "I can't even imagine," she laughed.

"We could be co-inlaws!"

"That would be so wonderful!" she cried.

"It's been two decades since we've talked, Ginger. Tell me everything I missed."

Part II
February 2000

MANDY

Mandy had lived in Atlanta long enough to know that Februarys always include a few days of unseasonable warmth and she and Glenn took the opportunity to meet and greet the members of the wedding party as they arrived at the Friday night rehearsal on the front steps of the Peachtree Road Methodist Church under the fading day's sun and warm temperatures.

"We didn't even need our jackets on the course," Glenn remarked to Mandy as they noted some early buds on the trees surrounding the church. "Pete's so fair-skinned, he actually got bit of a sunburn on his nose today."

"We noticed a few daffodils getting ready to pop in Oodles and Poppy's backyard," Mandy said. "The tent's up and the dance floor was installed this morning. It's going to be gorgeous."

Oodles and Poppy—nicknames that had now gone way beyond their grandchildren—were hosting several members of the two families at their home for the weekend. A few more were at their next-door neighbor Sarah Thompson's house. More, a eighty-foot tent had been erected in their backyard and would be the location for the reception following the next day's ceremony. A shuttle bus had been arranged to carry guests the short six blocks between the church and the Hills' home.

Mandy and Glenn had made half-a-dozen weekend trips to Atlanta or New Mexico with Ginger and Pete over the months leading to the wedding, and Ginger and Pete and their families had come to St. Louis to celebrate Thanksgiving in the fall. The two women had made infinite lists and organized every single detail that Rachel and Liam allowed them to cover. They had a job for everyone and a timeline for every job.

As guests arrived, she and Glenn stood proudly as the pre-wedding hosts for the rehearsal and dinner reception.

Mandy and Ginger had shopped together for their rehearsal outfits and chose metallics—Mandy in a silver sheath and Ginger in gold palazzo pants and a black wrap top—before Liam announced that he'd like to have the rehearsal reception at The Beer Mug. They opted to stick with their plan anyway, and Rachel agreed, despite the ambiance of the casual bar. They'd found their dresses for the wedding while shopping in Santa Fe and were wearing the same fabric and color in different styles.

With most of the family members inside the church, Rachel and Liam came outside to join them on the front steps and greet the additional guests.

"Grampa and Gram Wilson are really enjoying Oodles and Poppy, Dad," Liam said to Glenn. "The four of them have found so much in common. They are all talking over one another in there."

Glenn chuckled. A car pulled in front of the church parking lot and they all turned their attention.

Once again, the Everly contingent is unrepresented, Mandy thought.

Her parents had phoned with a scheduling conflict, but sent an oversized Waterford vase to the bride and groom.

"That's my roommate, Cameron," Rachel said to Mandy and

Glenn as they watched Cameron wave from the passenger's seat and Dave pull into a parking spot and open the door. "And her boyfriend Dave. Liam set them up on a blind date more than a year ago."

"Don't you two look like the celebrity couple of the year," Rachel said as they walked up the stone steps. Cameron's peach-colored satin dress was a very similar shade to Dave's dress shirt.

Liam introduced them to his parents.

"We have Liam to thank for introducing us," Dave told them wrapping his arm around Cameron.

As they passed them and walked into the church, Cameron whispered loudly to get Rachel's attention. She and Mandy turned and the three women shared a laugh when Cameron mouthed an exaggerated, "Bouquet" and pantomimed the bouquet toss. Rachel offered a thumbs-up.

The next car was Jay's. He came with Melody, whom he'd been dating since Christmas. Tim-bone, who had RSVP'd for no date, was in the back seat.

Liam introduced them each to his parents and they headed inside.

Audrey poked her head through the doorway of the church. "Liam, the preacher wants to know if you have the copy of the license for him," she said, and then turning to Rachel, "Rachel, do you want the overhead lights dimmed or full brightness?"

Liam pulled the license from his jacket pocket and handed it to Audrey.

"Audrey, thank you so much for being the world's greatest wedding coordinator and bridesmaid combo," Rachel said. "I trust your judgment on all of those details."

"Audrey is a concierge at an office building," she told Mandy. "Between you and Mom and Audrey, I barely had to do anything. Thanks again for all you've done. Mom has loved this time spent with you."

"We have no intention of stopping just because our kids will be hitched by this time tomorrow," Mandy laughed. "We have lots of adventures planned."

The next car approached and Mandy and Liam both walked into the parking lot to help the older couple from their car and walk with them up the steps to the church.

"Rachel, I'd like you to meet my grandparents," Liam said.

Rachel stepped forward and Liam made the introductions.

"It's my Grandmother Rooks, whose diamonds are on either side of your ring."

"Liam told me that they were your earrings, Mrs. Rooks, and I'm so grateful for your sweet generosity to pass them to Liam. The ring is so beautiful," Rachel said holding her hand out for Mr. and Mrs. Rooks to admire.

"Absolutely our pleasure Rachel," Sandra Rooks said. "Our William is a special man and he deserves a special lady. We are so pleased that he's found her."

Glenn stepped forward. "Mr. and Mrs. Rooks, it's so nice to see you again."

"Indeed, Glenn," Ted said shaking his hand. "And we have you to thank for taking such good care of our Mandy and grandson all these years."

As the Rooks entered the church, Mandy stretched to kiss Glenn on the cheek. "They're right, you know," she said smiling, then segued. "Did you put the guest list in your pocket?"

One more car pulled up to the church as Mandy checked off the names from the list Glenn had handed her. A tall, lanky man with light hair stretched from behind the front seat and nodded to them as he approached.

Mandy prompted with the final name on the guest list and Glenn greeted him as he ascended the steps. "You must be Ginger's brother, Carlton," Glenn said extending his hand. "Welcome. We are Liam's parents, Mandy and Glenn Wilson."

The church's large wooden door swung open as the trio approached and Ben and P.J. met them at the door. Ben was carrying Mandy's clutch.

"Your phone has been ringing, Mom," Ben said, handing it to her. "P.J. and I were just thinking it might be a good idea for us to go on over to the Beer Mug since we don't really have any rehearsing to do. Get the party warmed up a little?"

Mandy and Glenn exchanged looks and shrugged. "I don't see why not," she said. "Remind them to have our bar ready by eight and that we would like them to open the buffets forty-five minutes after I give them the thumbs-up."

"Will do," the new friends said in unison as they sprinted toward the parking lot.

Glenn led her into the church and Mandy reached into her purse to check her phone.

"Everything okay?" Glenn asked as he saw a hesitant frown move across her face.

"Scott," she said. "I'll call him back later."

GINGER

"Change in plans," Ginger whispered to Pete just fifteen minutes before the ceremony was scheduled to begin.

"What's that?"

"Since the weather is so warm, Rachel and Liam would like to parade to the reception."

"Parade?"

"The shuttle buses will still run, but they would like to walk in a parade line across Peachtree and to the house and they want to invite anyone that would like to walk to join them. Can you ask Reverend Cox to announce that?"

"On it," Pete said as he headed toward the sacristy.

Ginger ran through the checklist in her mind again. Every detail was confirmed. She served as liaison for the caterer and everything else related to the reception while Roxanne handled the seating chart and band. Oodles coordinated the flowers and the cakes, while Mandy made arrangements for out-of-town guests and kept accurate notes of locations and contact phone numbers for each. Glenn and Pete ran back and forth to the airport to transport guests and Poppy coordinated pick-ups and deliveries with P.J. and Liam's two brothers. Audrey coordinated the ceremony details and Liam's friend, Sam, would be the deejay at the reception.

Ginger relaxed and smiled. The time had arrived. Rachel was glowing and happy. She and Pete were over-the-moon pleased with her choice of Liam, and she and Mandy had enjoyed every moment of co-ordinating details and rekindling their friendship.

She looked at her watch just as Mandy came around the corner. The robin's egg blue was a fabulous contrast to her dark hair and dark eyes.

"Hey, soul sister," Mandy said smiling.

The two exchanged hugs and shimmied in their same-color dresses. "We're up in five."

Ginger looked at her watch. "Go time. How are the guys?

"Groomsmen doing their job. All have their boutonnieres on the correct lapel now. The church is filling fast."

"High five, sister," Ginger said, holding up her hand.

"We are good at this!" Mandy said slapping her palm. "Maybe we should work on Roxanne and Will or Ben?"

Ginger laughed as they entered the lobby. Audrey was peeking from the back staircase and gave Ginger a thumbs-up when she saw them to indicate the rest of the bridesmaids and Rachel were not far behind her.

Hand-in-hand, Mandy and Ginger stepped into the doorway and the bridesmaids lined up behind them. The door behind them opened roughly, hit the stone wall and echoed through the back of the church just as the first notes of Debussy's "Clair De Lune" began on the piano indicating the mothers' signal to enter.

Both women turned around quickly to see Scott Everly enter the church, sheepishly apologizing to the line of bridesmaids in front of him for the commotion.

Ginger made an audible gasp as Mandy squeezed her hand and subtly pointed it toward the aisle and their queue to proceed.

Her heart raced as they walked the aisle and stepped up to the altar. With hands shaking, she removed the candle from the left side of the candelabra while Mandy removed the right one. Together, they used them to light the center candle as a symbol of the two families uniting.

Mandy caught her eye and offered a confident nod and then a hug before the two mothers took their seats on the front row.

Scott! As if I weren't nervous enough about this day!

She worked to keep her attention on Rachel throughout the ceremony, but was surprised when it felt like just a few short minutes before the couple were kissing and heading back down the aisle, and Reverend Cox was making his announcement about wedding party photos and a parade to the Hill home for the reception following.

The wedding party photos were followed by photos of the McCarthy family with the bride and groom. The photographer's assistant made a call for Wilson family photos and Ben stepped into the back of the church with his Uncle Scott.

Ginger diverted her eyes as she rushed Oodles, Poppy and Pete out the back door to make it to the house before the crowd.

The backyard reception filled quickly and Ginger was grateful to be distracted with music details and checking the bar set up between questions from the caterer and chatting with the guests that stepped in to greet her in between.

She'd almost forgotten about his presence until she turned from a conversation with the caterer to find Pete and Scott standing in front of her.

"Ginger," Pete said. "I don't know if you've ever met Mandy's brother. This is Scott Everly. He was able to make it at the last minute."

"Hello Scott," she said extending her hand. "Welcome."

She knew he recognized her. He probably even suspected they'd spent an evening together. But he didn't show it; he simply greeted her as if he was meeting her for the first time. But Ginger also sensed a distance in his eyes that reassured her that he had no clue about the rest. She'd spent twenty-seven years atoning for her sins in her prayers and inside her own head. It took an instant of looking into his face to understand that he had never been a part of the equation after a short spurt of fertilization. Some men would have wanted to know; some men would have felt a sense of responsibility; some men would have wanted to take part in the parenting of their own child. But Scott didn't, wasn't and never was.

I'm lucky.

"Nice to meet you, Ginger" he said.

"We are happy to have your nephew in the family, Scott," Pete said as he led him toward a bar.

Ginger looked through the crowd and saw that Mandy had witnessed the interchange from the other side of the dance floor. Mandy offered an assuring nod before another guest took her attention away.

After time for mingling and hors d'oeuvres passed through the crowd by the wait staff, the couple's first dance was followed by Rachel's dance with her father.

Ginger's eyes watered as she watched them. Pete's starched dress uniform offered a startling contrast to the lace and flow of Rachel's gown. His face beamed as he twirled her across the floor. She felt her knees nearly buckle as she felt a hand on her shoulder and turned to find Poppy smiling and steadying her, his eyes also wet with tears.

Sam-I-Am, Liam's deejay friend who wore a Dr. Seuss hat and spoke in rhymes for many of his song announcements, then took over with line dances and games to get guests on the dance floor as others made their way through buffet lines and found their seats at the round tables that surrounded the dance floor.

Ginger and Oodles took a break from their reception orchestration to join Liam and Rachel as they led a dance floor full of guests with the Macarena.

When it was over, Sam-I-Am announced, "Now it's time to see what lucky gentleman will win a dance with the bride. I need all men to form a circle around the bride while we play a game I like to call, 'Between the Top Hats.'"

The circle extended three sides of the dance floor and spilled into the grass on the fourth side as men moved to participate in the dance.

As the music began with a Frank Sinatra song, Sam explained the game. "I'm going to put the first top hat on Pete McCarthy, the father of the bride."

The crowd cheered as Sam placed a shiny black top hat on Pete's head and handed him a second white one.

"When the music starts, Pete will pass the white hat behind him and each of you will put it on your head before passing it to the gentleman behind you," he said. "Then he will start the black hat moving in the clockwise direction and each man will place it on his head before passing to the man in front of him. When I stop the music, only those gentlemen that are 'between the top hats'—moving counter-clockwise from the white hat—will continue with the game. We will play until there is only the one man standing—the winner of a dance with our bride, Mrs. Rachel McCarthy Wilson."

The crowd roared and clapped as the hat moved from head to head and Sinatra crooned.

When the music stopped, nearly a third of the men found themselves behind the second hat and were sent away from the dance floor. After three rounds, the music stopped and there was only man left standing between the white and black top hats.

Scott.

A cold sweat flew through Ginger's body when she saw what was happening and she steadied herself against two chairs.

"And we have a winner!" Sam announced as he brought a microphone to the dance floor to introduce him.

Sam chatted briefly with Scott and then announced to the crowd, "Rachel... Ladies and gentlemen, please congratulate our winner. This is Liam's uncle, Scott Everly, who has won a dance with the bride. Please give them a hand while they dance to another Sinatra favorite."

Guests clapped and cheered as Ginger watched them greet one another, their smiles spreading identically as they talked. When the music began, she watched him expertly spin her daughter across the dance floor. Mandy stepped behind her and offered a quick hug.

Ginger smiled back and nodded an affirmation and confidence she hadn't expected to feel.

This could have been so much more complicated. This could have weighed heads and hearts outside of my own.

Scott's cluelessness—and the realization that for all her years of worry, struggle and concern, he'd had none—somehow vanquished her insecurity.

Suddenly, he was no different than any other guest. While his lack of responsibility set her free from the years of worry she'd carried, it repulsed her at the same time.

How does one go through life skating right over all consequences for their actions?

What if everything were different, and I had wanted to be with Scott and raise our baby together? I'm certain I'd never have seen or heard from him again once he knew about the baby.

And, yes, Pete and Rachel do have the right to know, but what would be the benefit for either knowing at this point?

The repulsion—mixed with the scurry of people to greet and dozens of details to check—provided Ginger with an opportunity to be bigger than the problem she'd struggled with for more than half of her life.

Once the dance was over, Scott bowed quickly to Rachel.

"Please find your seats, everyone," Sam-I-Am said. "It's time for toasts."

Mandy and Ginger nodded to each another and moved toward their seats at the front table.

Rachel

The bridesmaids wore lavender. Rachel followed Audrey and Cameron up the stone steps of the church's back staircase from the bride's room as Roxanne carried the train of her dress. Her father, in his Army green dress uniform full of ribbons, medals and patches, was waiting for her when she got to the top of the steps.

"Dad, you look so handsome," she said.

"You, Rachel, are breathtaking." His voice cracked with the last word.

He hugged her gently, careful not to mess her hair or makeup, and turned quickly. She saw him pull a handkerchief from his pocket.

She felt beautiful in her dress and was pleased with the updo Cameron had created with her hair.

They watched from the shadows at the back of the church as the mothers—both dressed in identical robin's egg blue—completed their hand-in-hand walk up the aisle and lit the center candle from the two previously lit candles from a three-tier candelabra. They turned, embraced with a vocal bear hug that had the congregation chuckling and took their seats on the front row—Ginger on the left, Mandy on the right next to Glenn.

"We found our dresses," the moms had telephoned months before from one of their many weekends together since reuniting. "The styles are different, but we are wearing the exact same fabric and color."

Ginger's dress with tiny cap sleeves and a sequined skirt had a sheer jacket over the bodice that closed with sequined buttons across the front. Mandy's dress had long sleeves and a slim skirt and a low back with sequins across the waist and neckline.

The two had spoken every day on the telephone and organized every detail of the February wedding. The two dads had become fast friends too and enjoyed the couple trips between New Mexico and Atlanta and St. Louis as much as their wives did.

Audrey and then Cameron moved slowly up the aisle and took their places at the left of the altar. As Roxanne began her ascent up the aisle, Rachel and her dad moved in close enough to focus on the groomsmen waiting at the front—Will, Jay and Tim-bone were standing stiffly on the right. Then she dared to look at the center of the altar and saw Liam standing tall in his black tuxedo and bow tie smiling at Roxanne as he watched her approach and turn toward her spot in the wedding party line.

The music changed and she heard her father say, "This is your moment Rachel. Are you ready?"

She looked into the face of her handsome father, Colonel Peter J. McCarthy. Her eyes squinched shut as she worked to hold back a rush of emotions and her mouth moved into an exaggerated half moon.

She heard her father laugh and she opened her eyes. He had taken off his glasses and was wiping tears from his eyes.

"Sorry," he said. "I just had a flashback of your puppet face."

She looked at him with feigned confusion, though she'd heard him tell the story many times before.

"When you were little, your eyes and your mouth seemed to work as one. When one opened..." He choked the familiar words of explanation and turned his head to gather himself.

After a deep breath, he put his glasses back on and looked into her eyes. "You have made me a very proud father, Rachel."

She took his arm and squeezed it. They turned toward the blur of faces of the crowd, now on their feet and facing her, as she entered through the vestibule and floated through the crowd toward the altar.

She was mesmerized by the lights of the heavy chandeliers and the music and the faces for the first portion of their walk, but caught Liam's eye halfway down the aisle and the enormity of the moment filled her head and chest. Suddenly conscious of her posture, she straightened her back and finished the walk proudly toward him.

After the rush of preacher's words, the exchange of vows, a kiss to cheers from the congregation and photos, she and Liam led a parade of family and guests across Peachtree Street. Drivers ignored the traffic lights and stayed still as the wedding party traversed with dances and waves across the main city street and into the Garden Hills neighborhood on the other side of the church to the sounds of well-wishers and congratulatory horns.

Once they'd arrived at Oodles and Poppy's backyard, they were greeted with one rushed conversation after the next, dances, games, more photos and finally the chance to sit and watch the crowd from the front table.

When they were seated, waiters brought around trays filled with champagne flutes.

As best man, Will stood and took the microphone to offer the first toast. The crowd laughed at his story of the two brothers that shared the same name, and Rachel was touched by his sweet comments about always wanting a sister.

"I see a lot of lovely ladies here tonight," he teased. "And since I have your attention, I'd like to remind everyone before we toast to the bride and groom, that this William Wilson is still single!"

The guests laughed and raised their glasses as Will announced, "To Liam and Rachel, I'd like to offer a bit of advice to my brother Liam. These words are not originally mine, but rather those of the poet Ogden Nash."

As he postured for his toast, Rachel beamed at his composure. He was handsome and poised like Glenn.

Will and Roxanne? she wondered. Maybe even Ben?

The room was quiet as Will began. 'To keep your marriage brimming with love in the cup, whenever you're wrong admit it; whenever you're right, shut up.'"

Once the cheers quieted, her father stood and took the microphone. His daunting presence was intensified by his stately uniform, clear and calm but powerful voice, and softened by his sweet words about his love for his daughter and the welcoming arms the McCarthy family would have for Liam and his family.

"Rachel you have always made your mother and me the proudest parents in the world," he said. "Today, we welcome Liam into our family. I am proud to call you my son-in-law, and we wish tremendous happiness for the two of you. We look forward to the many exciting adventures we hope to share with you both."

Rachel stood and hugged her father when he had finished and the crowd clapped and cheered.

Cameron surprised her by standing and offering the next toast. Rachel watched Dave as she delivered her well-prepared speech and made a mental note to tell her about his adoring, puppy dog face.

With each toast, the crowd cheered and sipped champagne. The waiters rushed around with bottles filling those glasses that had already been emptied.

The final toast was presented by Mandy who dramatically described to the crowd her friendship with Rachel's mother, the joy of being with her on the day that Rachel was born, the trip she and William took to New Jersey where the two children played, and the heartache of losing touch with her special friend for more than twenty years.

"And then God stepped in with a wink that would enhance so many of us individually and as a family," she said, "and aligned William— Liam, that is—with Rachel, and they fell in love, completely unaware of the connection that her mother and I had shared so long ago."

"A wonderful woman that Ginger and I once knew told our fortunes with a set of tarot cards," she continued. "Among the many messages she had for us on that day, I remember one particular card—the Three of Cups—that had a lovely drawing of three women wearing gowns and floral headbands standing in the moonlight. Their arms were intertwined as they held their glasses in the air to demonstrate their strong connection. Our friend offered many scenarios for the possible relationships between the women, all of which expressed the power of femininity and kinship between women. That image has been filling my mind many times as we prepared for this incredible day."

Mandy picked up her glass of champagne.

"So to conclude my toast, I would like to ask my lovely daughter-in-law Rachel and my best friend Ginger to join me."

Rachel and Ginger stood and with Mandy's direction, the three huddled together and raised their glasses, their arms intertwined above their heads.

"To friendships, to the deep and eternal love and the amazing coincidences that grow from them, and to fabulous women," Mandy said.

The crowd cheered and Rachel heard Cameron's voice and familiar pulse of lyrics above the crowd, "The-Cup-Of-Life!"

"Al-lay, al-lay, al-lay," the crowd chanted back.

Epilogue: April 2000

Mandy drove the rental car as Ginger provided directions from a worn map that was losing its structure along the seams. She carefully unfolded and refolded it as she studied the options from Tallahassee to the small Florida town near the Alabama line.

"Look for junction signs for 71 North," she said. "That should take us into Marianna and from there, I think we'll just have to follow our noses."

"Got it," Mandy said, flipping her turn signal to change lanes.

The website offered little more than a few pictures and two sets of locations and dates for the spring of 2000 schedule. There wasn't even a telephone number for Mandy and Ginger to be certain if they were at the right location, though they figured they had a fifty-fifty shot.

The SwiftCarnivals.com website had photos of rides and midway games and Mandy recognized O'Ray standing next to his trailer in one shot and a distant photo of what appeared to be Millie and a man they guessed to be Oscar in another.

Two lists of upcoming festival dates were on the home page, and they assumed that one represented O'Ray's travel schedule and the other his father's.

"If this isn't the right one, we're only a four-hour drive to Daytona for the other one," Mandy said. "We'll just road trip until we find her."

The trees were blooming in pinks and whites as they meandered the country roads of the Florida panhandle toward the state line.

"Maybe we should stop at a gas station to see if anyone knows of a carnival in town," Ginger said.

"Not a bad idea, if we ever run across a gas station on this road," Mandy answered.

Around the next bend, the arch of a Ferris wheel came into view atop the trees.

"Bingo," Mandy said. "Looks like we've found us a carnival."

As they turned down the next road, a full set of carnival rides came into view. Suddenly, signage for parking and brightly colored banners leading to Swift Carnival Productions were everywhere.

They parked the car and walked toward the entrance. A silver trailer sat behind a ticket booth. "That's just like the trailer I saw in St. Louis," Mandy said. "Let's go see who's inside."

They stepped around a small fence on their way to the trailer when Ginger stopped. "Wait, look," she said.

Mandy followed her eyes to a small purple tent set up a short distance away. A large painted sign was leaning against a tree in front of it. "Fortune Teller," it read. "Crystal Ball. Tarot Cards. Palm Reading."

They looked at one another, nodded and headed for the tent.

A rope stanchion was connected to a tree to form a queue line that was empty. A beaded curtain with the image of a sun and moon covered the tent's entrance. No one was around as they approached and leaned toward the beaded door.

"Hello?" Ginger called.

"Toodle ooh," answered a voice from inside. "Welcome. The fortune teller is in."

Ginger and Mandy exchanged an excited look just as Millie's familiar face—adorned with a purple headdress and large hoop earrings—popped around the corner.

Acknowledgments

I truly love and cherish my female friendships. Though I can't pinpoint the genesis of *Three of Cups*, I do know that many of the elements that came together and compelled me to complete this story happened at a lovely writer's retreat on St. George Island, Florida, in weather so frigid that I never even ventured to the beach. For that, I thank Gina Hogan Edwards and her January 2018 "Around the Writer's Table" retreat where I met eleven fabulous women, learned a ton about making prose dance, and sucked energy, good vibes and a passion for this craft from each one of them.

More, I thank my beta readers: Monica McGurk, Karen Elliott, Tom Florence, LaCreta Wilson, Wayne South Smith, Ellen Lange and Carol Niemi who identified the strengths and the weaknesses in my story and helped me pave a path for Ginger, Mandy and Rachel. And my intuitive and fabulous book club that read an early draft and provided an evening full of answers to my zillions of questions. Their direction was spot-on and their ideas can be found throughout: Shelbe Zimmerman, Lindy Moir, Chris Martinek, Julie Rickey, Debby Dolinsky and Eleanor Pippin.

And I thank my uber-talented bestie Sharon Moore who is always on the ready when I need her.

I'm always impressed with the thoughtfulness of my content editor, Wayne South Smith, who is able to cut to the gut of a story with hands-down excellence for areas to rewrite, reconsider and redefine.

I'm touched—and encouraged—by the support from my late-to-the-party husband Tom Florence who fought this passion of mine for a while and is suddenly, and surprisingly, full-on supportive. While he refuses to read, he will oddly allow me to read my chapters to him, and his talent for listening and offering feedback has fueled me, inspired me and saved me. Tom Florence, you're my everything.

I thank my *Jaybird's Song* readers. Many, many of you—more than I ever imagined—*got* my story and shared your love with me. Please know the power of your support. I hope my sophomore venture into fiction will also interest and excite you. I've whittled what once took ten years to complete into a ten-month project, and an outline for novel No. 3, *Reunion of Saints*—a fictionalized story inspired by the three Wilson Family reunions that have highlighted my millennium thus far, and also happened to include a horrific experience on the Chattooga River that really needs to be told—has me inspired, excited and convinced.

And finally, I thank fate and weird coincidence. Unless I write this as fact, I doubt many will believe me when I say that Ricky Martin's "La Copa de la Vida" wasn't planned from the beginning. I simply googled "popular song in summer 1998" to come up with a tune that Rachel and Cameron might love and want to sing loudly in their car when they encounter Liam, another pop music fan, on Peachtreee Street. It was days later that I realized that the English version of that song was titled, "The Cup of Life." I'd already titled my book, *Three of Cups*. Maybe I'm stretching, but it felt prophetic to me.

Please stay tuned and please, stay a part of this process.

I am indie, hear me roar.

Indie? It means I'm publishing my novel, *Three of Cups* independently.

I published my first two books, *Jaybird's Song* and *You've Got a Wedgie Cha Cha Cha* through CreateSpace, Amazon's publishing arm, and loved the process. As an independent publisher, I take all the same critical steps a traditional publisher would: Professional content editing, line-by-line editing, cover design, focus group research and page design; but I'm my own contractor for each step.

Indie publishing is huge for many reasons. One, it's outrageously tough to secure the interests of an agent and publisher when you're just starting out as an author. Indie publishing closes that gap and gives authors the chance to tell their stories. Two, it's simpler than ever to distribute author's works via electronic e-book files and printed books created via on-demand printing. And three, the artist can present his or her story as truly his or her work. I like that part. A lot.

So, I'm presenting my words, my characters, my title, my cover design and my marketing efforts on my own with the hope that *Three of Cups* will find its audience.

Getting a story into the mainstream requires serious groundswell, however. Indie authors need readers and fans to help catapult their stories. Your support is huge, and there are so many ways you can help:

Be a reader. Indie published book libraries are loaded with talented authors and fabulous stories. Look beyond the top ten lists and spend time reading reviews. You'll be surprised at what you can uncover.

*Share posts. Help good work go viral by sharing your opinion with your own spheres. One sphere becomes two, becomes four, becomes sixteen, and ultimately becomes viral.

Leave a review. Reviews are gold to authors. There are plenty of places to review books, Amazon and Goodreads being the most obvious. Leave a few words if you wish, but even a handful (or close) of stars means so much.

Tell your friends. Invite your book club. Write your own posts. Share stories you love with people you know.

That's my hope for *Three of Cups*. If you liked my story, please tell your friends, post your thoughts via your own social media outlets, and post a review. Be a part of the groundswell! I'd be most grateful.

KWF

*My Instagram account is loaded with fabulous pictures of readers with *Jaybird's Song*. Please do the same with *Three of Cups*—post a photo of yourself with the book —or your ebook — to #jaybirdssong

Book Club Discussion Questions

With which of the three main characters did you most identify?

The story has three protaganists, yet its antagonists rarely take human form. What do you think they are?

Was Ginger justified in keeping her secret from Pete and Rachel? Was she justified in keeping it from Scott?

How did her secret affect her life? Mandy's?

How did Millie, Oodles and Poppy, and Liam advance the story in your mind?

How many references to *cups* can you recall from this story?

Jaybird's Song **readers:** There are two minor characters from *Jaybird's Song* that reappear as minor characters in *Three of Cups.* Can you identify?